Sherlock Holmes and
The Case of
The Green Dragon

By: Miguel R. Rivera, Sr.

Paperback ISBN 978-1-80424-125-7
ePub ISBN 978-1-80424-126-4
PDF ISBN 978-1-80424-127-1

Published by MX Publishing
335 Princess Park Manor, Royal Drive,
London, N11 3GX
www.mxpublishing.com

Cover design by Brian Belanger

For Barbara, my late father, and my students.

Prologue

He could hear the wind raging against the rocks and waves like a banshee. Even through the fog of drink he could hear it. The waves crashing hard against the jut of land and rock he called home for half the year. Thunder and lightning ripped the sky, revealing the boiling ocean as it raged against the power of the wind.

"Damn weather and that bleeding wind! It will be the death of me," he mumbled to himself. He stretched his fingers painfully and rubbed at his knees. "Bloody rheumatism!" He took another drink of rum straight from the bottle with craggy, wrinkled hands made steel hard by physical labor. An old pewter wedding ring on the left ring finger, the only adornment. Unshaved, now for the last five days, and sweaty, grimy, and drunk.

"Bastards!" he yelled to no one because no one was there. Not in this God forsaken lighthouse on the edge of the British northeast facing the North Sea. A tall craggy finger pointed at the heavens. Greyed and green from years of moss and lichen growth, the lighthouse stood sentinel to the ships that dared to ply the stormy northern waters of England in the dead of winter. Occupied for half the year by George Dodd, the lighthouse keeper – village drunk and bully. Husband to Dwylla and father to none.

"God damn the wind! Blow me to hell!" screamed George, and he took another drink. He sat at a small wobbly wooden table set against the cold stone of the lighthouse. The room had no corners, only the incessant circle of the lighthouse – endlessly ending where it began. One lamp lit the room from the table where he sat. Its feeble yellow light losing the battle against the grime to vainly shine through its chimney glass.

This circle of stone housed a small chest that contained his clothes, the cabinet that held his meager food and drink, the table and chair where he sat, a dirty cot where he slept, and the miscellaneous items necessary to keep a light house – rope, tools, oil kegs, rags, etc. The room smelled of candle wax, rotting seaweed, dank mold and dust. The smell of burning oil from the light drifted down to mix with the other smells in this circle of stone where he lived. One weather-beaten thick wooden door to the outside, barely five feet tall, with huge iron hinges that creaked when it was opened and closed, was the only entrance.

The wind was evidence of the winter storm that had blown up the day before. Typical of winter storms and commonplace in this late January of 1891. Rain like daggers and wind that whipped up the sea and tossed it against the rock, long pier, and lighthouse. The night was dark and terribly cold. George looked about the circle of light made by the lantern and coughed, hoarse and loud, spitting on the floor.

"Damn ye," he mumbled after he spit. He attempted to stand, using the table for balance, and almost knocked over the bottle and the lamp. "Sod it," he said falling back down to the chair and laying his head on his folded arms, pipe falling from his mouth onto the table, long ago having gone cold,

"Sod it," he whispered again, and with that, he began to loudly snore.

He screamed with unending pain. His eyes were red and swollen. His face, lips and nose were blistered and red. His hands looked burned and raw as if the skin were melting away. It was a pain that would make any rational thought impossible. His eyes and face were frozen in a mask of terror, as if his very soul was dead or dying. His breath came in rapid staccato inhalations. He was covered in cold sweat. He was running as if away from some terrible monster. He was surrounded by darkness.

He continued to run and stumble until he finally ran literally into an angled wall of stone. The force of the impact nearly knocked him unconscious. He lay on the angled stone in agony. He felt around with his burning hands and began to climb on hands and knees up the angled stone until his swollen, burned head struck flat, hard stone.

He appeared mad as he began to push the stone to escape the darkness. He laid his back against the stone and pushed, and the stone raised up enough for him to climb out. He never stopped to wonder why. There was a terrible storm raging. The wind blew a gale, and the rain outside fell in sheets of solid water. He crouched and looked all around him. He saw a light. A light that pierced the darkness of the night.

Running, he arrived at a column of stone. With shaking, swollen hands he felt blindly for an entrance and found a wooden door. He wailed against the wind and rain and scratched against the door with all his might. The sun began to rise in the east and the blood red, orange and yellow light made him squint in pain as he yelled and struck the wooden door. And then, the door opened.

Chapter 1

Holmes sat in his favorite heavily cushioned wicker chair in front of the fire at 221B Baker Street. His clay pipe between his teeth, the smoke making a small cloud around his head; he absentmindedly plucked at his violin strings and stared into the fire. He was surrounded by the detritus of several newspapers, read over the past three days, and the leftover ash and flakes of tobacco from several smoked pipes. He was dressed in his usual mouse-grey dressing gown. The coal fire burned brightly and crackled and snapped as it burned. Holmes was in a black mood. He was between cases. Between problems. Between the work his mind and body craved. Imprisoned in his rooms, as it were, by lack of work and the bitter cold January day.

Watson, visiting while his wife was away on the Continent, was busy finishing the last few bites of his breakfast. In a brown glen plaid suit he took a bite of toasted bread while he read the folded paper that lay on the table to his right. Not taking his eyes away from the newspaper, he lifted a cup of tea to his lips and drank the now tepid liquid, frowning at the lack of heat in the beverage. Dipping a piece of toast in the remains of the soft-boiled egg that sat in front of him, he cleared his throat, the only other sound in the room besides Holmes's incessant plucking at the strings of his violin.

Watson knew better than to engage Holmes in conversation when he was in one of his black moods. Better to leave the room silent and uncomfortable than try to engage Holmes in idle chatter. Something that Watson had learned from many years of living with Holmes and learning his eccentricities. He was accustomed too to Holmes's habit of randomly plucking at his violin, something that hardly bothered him after years of familiarity. "Hardly," being the operative word. He could take the discordant sound for only so long before even his near-endless patience began to wear thin. As he finished his tea, he looked over at Holmes, plucking his violin, and let out an exasperated huff.

It was Holmes who broke the silence, "Watson, London has become a commonplace and uninteresting city," he said with a deep sigh while simultaneously rising from his chair and throwing his violin down where he had been sitting. He paced back and forth in front of the fire, his unused energy like some coil of rope twisted tightly, straining to release its stored energy. "At the risk of repeating myself, I must have work. Give me problems! I recoil at this stagnation. Like some terrible machine running hard against itself about to burst the confines of its metal skin, my mind torments me when I am not at my work!" He continued his pacing.

"But Holmes, before coming round to visit, I read in the papers that you were engaged by the French Government in some matter of extreme importance to them. What has happened with that case?" asked Watson.

"I am stalemated at present and can do nothing on the matter until the early spring. I have things in the works, but nothing *now* that requires my attention or action. Wheels must turn and grind their grist before I can act again in the French matter. No Watson, I am becalmed!"

"Holmes, is there nothing in this great city to interest you? The museums? The symphony? The many fine restaurants? Why I was just reading in the paper that the British Museum has an exhibition of statuary and artifacts from Egypt. Why not go and spend a pleasant afternoon looking at the exhibits?"

Holmes stopped his pacing long enough to look at Watson with annoyance and disbelief. He scoffed dramatically and started his pacing again. Hands in his pockets, legs moving in a rapid jerky fashion. "Watson! I mean really! How would that possibly help?"

"Well, it would give you something to occupy your mind. Get you out of these rooms, amongst the people, enjoy the discoveries of a mysterious and fascinating civilization. I will accompany you," Watson said as he dropped his napkin on the table and rose from his seat. "Holmes, you must do something to occupy yourself during these stagnant periods. You will suffer from nervous exhaustion, not to mention tobacco poisoning, if you continue like this." As he turned to his right Watson looked carefully over at the drawer in the writing desk against the wall between the two windows. The drawer where Holmes kept his syringe and vial of cocaine was closed. "Come now, let's ask Mrs. Hudson to call a hansom, and we'll go to the museum."

As Watson pleaded, Holmes moved from pacing in front of the fire, kicking loose newspaper pages as he went, and walked quickly to the window, passing Watson on the way, appearing annoyed by his very presence. Holmes peered out the window down on a snow-covered Baker Street. Though the sky was clear, and it was sunny, the air was a dingy grey from the smoke of a hundred coal fires in the apartments and businesses that lined Baker Street. The snow had a black crusty coating that matched Holmes's mood, here and there interrupted by a steaming pile of horse dung. The denizens of London bundled in coats moved quickly in the cold, adding to the dingy color of the air with the mist of their breath. Even the cold could not keep the great city and its teeming masses from the daily grind and furious movement of business.

Holmes looked for something of interest. There were the three chimney sweeps moving along the street in a familiarly lazy fashion. The two bankers walking briskly to some urgent appointment. The ubiquitous street urchins running and sliding in the icy street gutters. The horse-drawn van being unloaded by two large, ill-dressed men. The hansoms moving through the snow toward their destinations. The newspaper sellers with their papers wrapped around their arms calling out the headlines. Two street beggars, men, smoking and stamping their feet in the cold, one hand on their cigarettes the other on their tin cups. Nothing out of the ordinary. Holmes took his pipe from his mouth and knocked the cold ashes to the floor in front of him, repeatedly striking the bowl against the palm of his left hand.

"What could possibly interest me about mummies and stone statues from Egypt? Why for the world would I want to be amongst London's people walking through a cavernous museum? Watson, I appreciate your concern and suggestion, but what I need is work! Nothing else will do."

Holmes shoved his pipe into the right pocket of his robe and placed his left arm against the window frame, the very picture of frustration and disgust, leaning and peering out the window as if to find some solace in the scenes that played out below.

Watson had moved over in front of the fire, taking a cigar, lighting it, and sitting in his usual chair across from the one normally occupied by his friend. "Well, incessantly dwelling upon your condition certainly is not helping. My good man, sit down. Read a book. Engage in some chemical experiment. Play your violin. Eat something!"

As Watson said this Mrs. Hudson lightly knocked twice on the door and opened it, carrying a tray to clean-up the breakfast plates and uneaten food she had set out for Holmes. "Well, at least one of you has an appetite. I do not know why I even try any more. Mr. Holmes, you must eat something. You are wasting away cooped up in these rooms smoking and pouting. Yes, pouting," she said as Holmes turned from the window and gave her a glare.

"Thank you, Mrs. Hudson. That will be all!" Holmes said in a dismissive and frustrated tone.

As she turned to leave, her tray now full and the table cleared, Mrs. Hudson turned to Watson and in a near whisper, said, "Can you do nothing with him?" Watson just shrugged his shoulders and Mrs. Hudson let out an exasperated sigh and left the room, closing the door quietly behind her.

"She has a point, Holmes. You must eat something. You must take care of yourself, old man."

Holmes turned from the window again, arm moving from the window frame and pointing derisively at Watson, "The two of you are conspiring to get me to eat and to get me out of these rooms. Do not think it has escaped my notice. The two of you have planned it."

Watson laughed. "Well, if you must know, we are both a bit worried about you. We know how bad things can get when you are between cases. I do not want my work of these many years weaning you off that abhorrent habit of taking artificial stimulants in the form of cocaine, and who knows what else, to be ruined by a few days of ennui."

"Ahh, well, things haven't come to that yet, my dear Watson. Not yet," Holmes said turning once again to the window and returning to his inspection of Baker Street. "Though the stimulating embrace of a seven percent solution of cocaine has saved me from many a day or night of blinding boredom."

"Really Holmes! How could you even contemplate such a thing? A man of your prodigious gifts and talents wasting the powers of his mind and threatening the ruin of his abilities by using such dangerous and artificial stimulants." Watson had never understood how Holmes could risk damaging one of the best minds in Europe by so loathsome a habit. It was something about Holmes he both abhorred and could never fathom.

"Not to worry. Not to worry Watson. I think some relief from my dark mood comes in the form of two charwomen now walking along Baker Street. Yes, they stop across the street looking at our address. Come here, Watson. What do you make of them?"

Watson rose from his chair frustration etched on his face, and with resignation walked to the window to stand beside Holmes. As he looked out on Baker Street, he saw two charwomen standing across the street in the cold and snow looking at their door. But two more different women would be hard to find. The one to the left was rail thin, almost cadaverous, and the one to the right was a rather large, plump woman. Each seemed to be wearing every piece of clothing that she owned.

The woman to the left seemed to be consoling the one to the right. Her left arm as far around her large shoulders as it would reach and her right arm soothingly rubbing the larger women's right arm as the large woman held a man's red and white patterned handkerchief as her left hand gesticulated. Presently the larger woman wiped her nose and eyes with the large handkerchief and turned as if to get out of the grip of the emaciated woman and walk away, shaking her head back and forth dramatically, but the smaller of the two stopped her, putting both hands on each of the larger woman's shoulders and looking her straight in the face and seeming to plead with her.

While this scene played out Holmes let out a little chuckle, "An affair of the heart, Watson. I have seen those signs before. Mark my words, the matter will be about her husband. The thinner one has recommended that she come consult with me, but the larger woman isn't yet convinced."

"That much seems clear, Holmes. But the matter could be just about a lost bracelet or family heirloom as anything."

"No Watson, it's an affair of the heart involving her husband. The larger woman is distraught and at her wit's end and has come to see her friend who has, for some reason, recommended she come see me. That tells me it is an affair of the heart. The matter most likely has to do with her husband and not some *par amour* given the lady's age and size, so I deduce husband. From how she is acting, it is not an affair with another woman. Such women suffer in silence and practiced dignity at the knowledge of their husband's infidelities. No, something has happened to the husband. Something that she is desperately worried about – either her husband's imprisonment or impending death is behind her distress. Perhaps both."

As Holmes finished his deductions the two women crossed the street. "Well, we will likely know soon enough Holmes. It appears the ladies have decided to pay us a visit," said Watson moving away from the window back toward the fire.

From below, the bell rang. After the passage of only two-or-three-seconds Mrs. Hudson's muffled voice could be heard from below and the raised voice of one of the two women as they appeared to argue. Holmes moved from the window and almost ran toward the door, practically leaping over the settee as he went. He opened the door enough to send his voice downward, and as he did Holmes and Watson heard one of the charwomen saying, "...every right to be here. I know Mr. Holmes and I want to see him. Dear Dwylla, Lord knows, is desperate for his help! Let us see him!"

"Mrs. Hudson, please let the two ladies up. Thank you," Holmes yelled toward the stairs through the half open door.

"See, I told you. Now let us in," said one of the ladies from below. Holmes moved from the door leaving it ajar, and he could hear one of the women, likely the skinny one saying to the other, "Now, now, Dwylla, we are here. All will be better, you will see, Mr. Holmes is a fine gentleman. There, there, come along."

Holmes had by now moved in front of the fire as he and Watson stood waiting for the two women to enter. Watson holding his cigar and Holmes with his hands clasped behind his back. The skinny woman entered first leading the larger woman behind her still dabbing at her nose and face with the handkerchief. Once through the door both women stopped, the skinny one let go of the other's hand and began to press her clothes flat and make over herself quickly in a nervous but deliberate fashion and then turned her attention to doing the same with the larger woman. "There now, all is well."

"Welcome ladies. To what do I owe the pleasure of your visit this cold January morning?" Holmes asked with a quizzical look upon his face and a friendly smile on his lips as his keen eyes took them both in.

The skinny woman clasped her hands before her in an act of supplication, took one step forward and said, "Oh, Mr. Holmes, ya may remember me. A few years back ya helped me with a little matter when I came to ya for help, at me wit's end. Ya were so kind and smart and such a gentleman that I never forgot what ya did for me nor how kind that ya were. Do ya remember me Mr. Holmes?"

"I must confess that at present I do not. But you are so wrapped up in clothing and scarves that my failure to recognize you is hardly surprising. Please the both of you come round and have a seat on the settee, take off some of those wrappings, warm up before the fire, and tell me why you are here."

The two women did as Holmes asked; the skinny one leading the sniffling larger one and both sat on the settee as they removed various scarves, shawls, and mufflers. The skinny one doting over the larger one and helping her through the process.

By this time, Mrs. Hudson had arrived at the door to the sitting room and with a worrying look upon her face began to close the door. "Mrs. Hudson, how about some tea for these dear ladies? Something to bring some warmth back into them," said Holmes as he sat in his wicker chair and Watson, cigar in hand, did the same in his chair before the fire.

"Yes, Mr. Holmes. I will be back presently with tea for four," grumbled Mrs. Hudson as she closed the door and mumbled something to herself as she went down the stairs.

"I think I might need something stronger than tea, sir," said the larger woman as she settled into the settee and blew her nose loudly. "Just a little something to calm me nerves a bit, if ye don't mind."

"Dwylla! We don't want to impose on Mr. Holmes any more than we must to help your poor George. Don't bother 'bout us Mr. Holmes. We can get along just fine wif out it," said the skinny one.

"No, no, it's fine. Watson, can you pour this nice lady some brandy?"

"Certainly, Holmes." Watson arose, walked the few steps to the tantalus and poured a goodly amount of brandy from the decanter in a glass and handed it to the large woman.

"Well, since you've already opened the decanter, I don't mind warming me bones too, Mr. Holmes. Ifing ya don't mind and it's not a bother, sir?" the skinny one said with rather begging eyes and a quick lick of her lips. Watson complied, repeating the process, and handing the skinny one a glass of brandy as well. Both women held their glasses in both hands, bringing their glasses to their mouths as if the brandy were the wine at Holy Communion. Both took two, then three sips and settled back into the settee with sighs and relaxed shoulders.

"Thank ye…both," said the larger of the two women.

"Now, let us get down to business ladies. What brings you to see me today? You have had a rather long trip. You traveled in a dog cart and one or two trains to get here, Ma'am. I suppose it is about your husband George and I can only imagine that you are rather anxious to tell me your story. A trip from the northeast of England in such weather could hardly have been a comfortable one," Holmes directed his comments to the larger of the two women.

She was evidently startled and almost spilled her brandy moving from her relaxed posture to as erect a posture as her large frame could manage. Her eyes went from wide and shocked to beady and squinted, her whole face one of distrust and curiosity. "Now how in blazes do ye know that sir? Are ye the devil his self?"

"Now, Dwylla, I told you 'bout Mr. Holmes. He has wizardly ways, he does. He knows things. Things no man in his right mind oughten to know, if he doesn't mind me saying," explained the skinny one with a slight laugh and an alarmed, quick glance at Holmes.

Holmes laughed, settled back into his chair and said, "Yes, wizardly ways. I rather like that apt description. It would seem like magic to two such as yourselves." As Holmes said this the skinny one nodded her head knowingly and looked first at the larger one and then back at Holmes. "Now, Dwylla, perhaps we should start with introductions. As you know I am Sherlock Holmes and this is my friend and colleague, Dr. Watson. And you ladies are?"

This seemed more than the larger lady could take. She jumped from the settee, standing as if in full alarm, drank the rest of her brandy with both hands, and said, "No Mary! Not going to do it! This man is the devil his self! Ye, stay away from me, sir," she hissed while making the devil's horns with her free hand and aiming it at Holmes in a jerking motion. "Ye, stay away from Dwylla and Mary now, hear ye!"

"Dwylla! Remember yer manners lady. The guvnor 's not from the devil, I tell ya. He's just wizardly in his ways. Knows things. Things that can help ya!" yelled the skinny one as she pulled at the larger woman's ample skirts. "Now sit down!" And with that the larger woman fell resignedly to her former seat on the settee, looking threateningly at Holmes and back to Watson. "I'll take a bit more brandy, if ye don't mind, Capt'n," she said to Watson.

Watson rose from his chair and complied with the larger woman's request pouring more brandy into her outstretched glass and then sitting back down keeping the decanter at his side. The larger woman again raised her glass with both hands to her lips sipping loudly.

"Dwylla and Mary, now don't be excited. I know your names only because you have called each other by name once or twice while seated here. I know your husband is called George because Mary said as much when coming in. As for you, Dwylla, being from the northeast of England, one could never be from anywhere else with that accent.

"That you traveled on a train, likely more than one, is clear from the stubs of two train tickets showing out of your apron pocket, and the fact that you come from the northeast means it is either by boat or train that you arrived in London. From the tickets, I deduce train. You have spattered drops of mud on the outside of your dress, three or four spatters, where only a dog cart can splash mud when moving rather quickly through muddy, dirt roads.

"Together these items make it clear that you traveled here from afar to meet your friend who brought you round, rather reluctantly, to consult with me about your problems with your husband, George. There is no wizard's magic here, ladies, just observation and deduction combined with long experience," explained Holmes in his most conciliatory tone. "Now please, sit back, ladies, relax, enjoy your brandy and tell me why you are here."

Holmes turned to face Watson and in a lowered voice said, "It's probably for the best that I was born in the age of reason, Watson, or these two ladies would turn me over to the town constable to be burned as a witch."

Watson laughed in the back of his throat and continued smoking his cigar, saying, "Ladies, I assure you that you could not be in better hands. Now tell Mr. Holmes why you are here," Watson spoke in the soothing tone that made him so agreeable to women.

Before the two could begin their story, Mrs. Hudson knocked twice quietly on the door, opened it, and brought in a setting of tea and biscuits. She stared mistrustingly at the two charwomen as she carried the tray and dishes to the table, put the tray down, and stood straight up, turning toward

Holmes. "The tea as requested Mr. Holmes," both hands in front of her, palms down, on her apron. "I will be downstairs if you need anything else." And with that Mrs. Hudson marched across the room and closed the door behind her.

Watson put his cigar in his mouth and taking a pad and pencil from his jacket pocket, settled into his chair to listen to the story these two ladies had to tell.

Chapter 2

"Now suppose you tell me why you are here, Dwylla? What is your last name?" asked Holmes settling back in his chair and taking his pipe from his dressing gown pocket and reaching over to the mantle and the Persian slipper to draw out some tobacco.

"Me name is Dwylla Dodd, and I come from Tynemouth, sir."

"Good, thank you Mrs. Dodd. Now what has happened to your husband?" asked Holmes as he lit his pipe. "Go on, the best way to tell a story is to start at the beginning. So, start there and try not leave out any details, no matter how inconsequential they may seem."

"Oh, Mr. Holmes, sir, my George has been arrested. Arrested for murder! They have 'em at the gaol and won't let me see 'em neither," and then Mrs. Dodd began to cry.

"It all happened quite suddenly, Mr. Holmes," added Mary. "Why she just came to my place this Sunday past, sir. Very late like. My man and I were near shocked to see her. But there she was all the same. Standing at the door just a crying and a shaking. It was nye near four in the morning, sir. My man and I were awake as I was getting him ready for werk, sir. And there she was in the doorway. Why I just said, 'What in the devil is this?' That's what I said, sir. And she couldn't even talk. Why, it was almost an hour before she could say a word, it was. Exhausted as much as anything.

Just exhausted and broken, sir. My poor Dwylla a suffering so," and after saying this Mary began to cry as well.

Holmes looked over at Watson disconsolately and said in a voice just above a whisper, "Watson, get these ladies some tea and biscuits."

Watson stood up and walked over to the table and poured two cups of tea and placed some biscuits on a plate and brought first the two cups of tea and then the plate of biscuits to the two crying ladies.

"Now, now ladies. Here's some tea and a little something to eat. You are here now. Here with Mr. Holmes and me. We cannot help you if you don't tell us the full story, as well as you can," Watson said with compassion in his voice.

"God bless ya, sir. It's just so hard with everything that my poor Dwylla has gone through. Just plain hard, sir." Mary took both cups of tea and handed one to Mrs. Dodd who now had a half glass of brandy resting on her ample stomach between her breasts and the cup of tea in her hand. The other hand busy with her handkerchief and her nose. Mary, now with one hand free, took the plate of biscuits offered by Watson and laid it in her lap and began rapidly eating biscuits between sips of the hot tea, looking back and forth between Holmes, Watson, and Mrs. Dodd. Mrs. Dodd took a long drink of tea and then poured the rest of her brandy in her cup and drank that too. Watson, standing there, simply bent over and took the empty cup and glass from Mrs. Dodd and walked back to the table.

"Mrs. Dodd. As Watson says, I cannot help if I do not know what happened. I understand that you are upset and have travelled a great distance to be here. So please tell me what you know. And, Mary, please let her tell her story as she knows it." Holmes was near frustration and his patience was at its end. Watson walked back to his chair and once again took up his pencil and pad and looked over at the two ladies with a mix of anticipation and compassion.

"Well, sir, there's not much to tell as I weren't there when it happened. But what I heard was there a man stabbed in the Tynemouth Pier Lighthouse and the only other person there was my George. My George has been one of the two lighthouse 'ttendants these past ten-year, sir. He's one month on and one month off, see, and this was his month to be on. Oh, I wish to God that it hadn't o' been his month on, sir. Then I wouldn't a be here a-toll."

"Ladies, I am much pressed at the moment and there are great demands on my time. I am sorry that Mr. Dodd has been arrested for murder, but I am afraid that I cannot take your case. Watson would you be kind enough to show these ladies out?" Holmes rose from his chair, placing his pipe on the mantel, and walked over to the table and poured himself a cup of tea and with his back turned to the ladies, walked over to the window, and began to look out again.

"No, Mr. Holmes. No. We cannot leave like this. Ya helped me once and I know ya can help dear Dwylla. We'll get to the point and tell ya what we know, sir. Now, Dwylla, tell Mr. Holmes what ya told me. Go ahead." With that Mary placed her hands on her lap and held herself firm as if to declare to all the world that she could not be moved.

"But sir, it's like I told ye, I don't know the details. I only know that sometime in the wee hours of the morning this Saturday past a hue and cry went through the town that a man had been murdered at the lighthouse. I was a sleeping in me bed and had just gotten up and was making me tea when there was loud knocks on me door, and I was told the news. I nearly dropped dead there 'cause I was thinking it was my man George who was dead. It was the undertaker, sir, and he was kind enough to drive me in his cart over to the pier. It was bitter cold, sir. Bitter cold. And raining too. The storm had blown itself out, but it was still a raining a bit on and off and bitter cold. Even more so on the pier as we ran to the lighthouse.

"As we got near to the lighthouse, the constables had my George, sir. One in front and one on each side of 'em. They had his hands chained behind his back and he was a cursing and a fighting as they shoved him along. When he saw me, my George stopped, and his head just went down to his chest, sir. I stopped dead in me tracks. My George looked up at me and said, 'It's the rope for me now, Dwylla. Nothing anybody can do 'bout it. I'm a dead man.' Well, I screamed, sir, and I would have dropped right there, but the undertaker held me fast where I was. And they took him away, sir. Took my George away." And Mrs. Dodd began to cry again.

"Holmes, perhaps we should give Mrs. Dodd a bit of a break. She is very exhausted," said Watson standing and placing his hand on Mrs. Dodd's shoulder.

"Watson, they don't come to me for pity, and I don't have time for banalities. Mrs. Dodd, is that all that you can tell me? Who was this man that was stabbed at the lighthouse? Do you at least know his name?" asked Holmes his patience having ended and with indifference to the crying lady.

"I don't know him, sir. But the talk in the town was that the undertaker took the German man who had been about the village for the last ten days. It was said he was a studying the ruins of the old abbey and fort and was very interested in the graveyard," answered Mrs. Dodd between sniffs, coughs and blowing her nose in her handkerchief. "I don't know the man, but the undertaker told me before I left to come here that the German man's name was...I have trouble saying the name, sir. It's foreign."

"Now Dwylla ya told me his name and I haven't forgotten it. Mr. Holmes his name was Oberstein. Gustav Oberstein, I think she told me," offered Mary as she took Mrs. Dodd's hand.

The change that came over Holmes was immediate. He turned suddenly away from the window, put his cup of tea down, and placed his two hands together with steepled fingers and said, "Are you sure about the name? Are you absolutely certain?"

Mrs. Dodd turned and looked over her shoulder at Holmes and said, "Yes, sir. That's the name that the undertaker said. A German fellow named Goosetab Oblersteam. Yes, sir, that's the name he said."

Holmes's eyes lit with energy and excitement. He walked quickly back to his chair and sat down leaning forward towards the two ladies. "It is absolutely critical that you are confident in what you say. You are quite sure that the dead man's name was Oberstein? Gustav Oberstein?"

Both women said in unison, "Yes, Mr. Holmes, sir."

Watson sat staring at Holmes with bewilderment. "Do you know this man Oberstein, Holmes?"

"I don't know him, but I do know of him, Watson. Ladies, Mrs. Dodd, I will take your case. Where did you say Mr. Dodd was being held?" asked Holmes with barely hidden glee.

"My George is being held at the gaol in Tynemouth, sir. Can you help me, sir?" asked Mrs. Dodd.

"I don't know if I can help you, madam, but I will certainly look into your case. Will you be staying with, Mary?"

"Yes, Mr. Holmes. After all she is my sister, all be it from a different father. But she's kin and that's that. She's staying with me sure enough," Mary said decisively as though the thought of where Mrs. Dodd would stay had just occurred to her and had been decided. Mary looked at Mrs. Dodd and the two women hugged each other and wept the more. "Mr. Holmes my last name is Willard. Mary Willard and Dwylla is staying with me at number 17A Bethnal Green, East End, sir. You can reach us there."

Holmes motioned for Watson to record the address in his note pad. "Very well then. Mrs. Dodd and Mrs. Willard, thank you for coming to see me. I will be in contact once there is something to tell. Watson, can you show the ladies out?"

The two ladies began the laborious task of covering themselves with shawls, scarves, mufflers and whatever else they came in with and slowly began to walk toward the door. "God bless ye, Mr. Holmes. God bless ye and everyone that lives in this place!" cried Mrs. Dodd.

"One moment, Mrs. Willard. What case did I help you with and when was it?" asked Holmes.

"Why it was some ten years ago and ya helped me learn the whereabouts of my lost tea pot and tea set that me mum passed down to me. If it weren't for you, Mr. Holmes, I'd have never known it was nicked for gin money by my neighbor. I'll never forget how ya paid to retrieve it from the pawn broker's shop and laid it before me. You're a wizard, Mr. Holmes. A wizard."

The two women left, going loudly down the stairs and out the front door in a continuous stream of, "By heavens!" and "The Lord be praised!" As Watson closed the door and turned to Holmes, both men looked at each other and began to laugh heartily.

"A tea pot, Holmes? A pawned tea pot?" laughed Watson.

"It is indeed a small world, is it not Watson? My career has come full circle. I must have helped this lady just as I was beginning. When we first moved into these very rooms. And now, she brings her sister and perhaps a very significant case indeed," Holmes said walking back to the fire and retrieving his pipe.

"But Holmes, there's nothing to it. She told you nothing of significance and yet you told her you were taking her case." Watson was in utter disbelief.

"Watson, did you not hear the name? The name of the German man who was evidently stabbed by George Dodd at the lighthouse?"

"Yes, Gustav Oberstein," answered Watson, "What of it? Obviously, you put more significance on the name than I do."

"Watson, a significant aspect of my art is having a prodigious memory and having that memory loaded with facts of the criminal world. There is little new under the sun, and if you are familiar with the details, the very facts, of thousands of criminal cases from around the world, any new set of facts is likely to be found to be quite similar to some other crime from the past. So, names are of particular interest in this art. The names of certain living characters and their eccentricities. So, it is with the name Oberstein. Do you not remember?"

"I confess Holmes that the name means nothing to me. I can't remember it ever coming up in any of our cases."

"Do you not remember the case of the unfortunate letter written by the foreign potentate that we were asked to find after it went missing from the dispatch box of the Honorable Trelawney Hope, Foreign Secretary to Her Majesty?"

"Yes, of course I remember the case. A very interesting matter and one that you so brilliantly resolved. Recovering the letter as I remember and protecting the Foreign Secretary's wife in the process. It was a brilliant piece of work. But what does that have to do with the case before us?"

"Watson, I recall mentioning that there were only three men in England who could have stolen the letter and made off with it to the Continent. Those names were, Oberstein, La Rothiere, and the unfortunate and late Edwardo Lucas. Gustav Oberstein is a German spy. He operates in England and London is his base. His father, Hugo Oberstein, is also a spy, but his sphere of operation is primarily the Continent. They are the only father and son European spies of which I am aware. Why Gustav Oberstein was in Tynemouth and why he is dead are questions of much greater import than the fate of poor George Dodd. That's why I have agreed to take the case. To get to the bottom of what Oberstein was doing in Tynemouth."

Watson's jaw was agape, and his eyes were wide. "Why Holmes, you have stumbled upon a mystery that may have international consequences. This case is of the utmost importance."

"Very possibly Watson. Very possibly. But we have no facts, and it is a grievous error to conjecture without facts. We need to go to Tynemouth to see things for ourselves and speak with this George Dodd and hope that he is more helpful than these two charwomen were."

"But your case for the government of France, Holmes. What of that?"

"Watson, as I said, it is January 20th and I am free for at least a few weeks and very likely until early spring when matters will develop sufficiently to allow me to take up the case again. Until then, we have this potentially interesting little problem to fill our time. Now where's my railway schedule?" Holmes began rummaging through a stack of newspapers on the writing desk. "Ahh, here it is. It will be a long trip, Watson. We will have to take at least two different trains to get there. Are you up for it, old man?"

"Of course, Holmes. Delighted. Should I go home and pick up some clothes and my other needs and meet you at the railway station this afternoon?"

"Let me see, it's a little past 11:00 now, and we wouldn't get there until very late tonight if we leave this afternoon. No, Watson. I think we leave first thing in the morning. There is a train leaving on the first leg of our journey tomorrow morning at 7:20. In the meantime, I think I should take your advice and go to the museum. Are you coming?"

"Holmes, you are an enigma! Yes, I will join you presently."

Chapter 3

The trip by train from London to Tynemouth was a long and arduous one. Holmes and Watson arrived in Tynemouth in midafternoon. The bad weather reported by Mrs. Dodd had apparently passed. Holmes and Watson, after having ridden in a rickety carriage driven by a local whom Holmes had paid, arrived at a modest inn in the middle of the small town. On the bottom floor of the three-story brick building was a pub, and the first and second floors contained the guest rooms.

During one of their stops, Holmes had sent a telegram to the inspector in charge in Tynemouth, alerting the inspector of their pending arrival and asking to meet with him that afternoon. By mid-day Watson was hungry, and he and Holmes shared the picnic lunch that Mrs. Hudson had prepared for them. Watson eating the lion's share of the food.

Upon arriving at the inn, Holmes and Watson registered with the landlord and left their bags with him, asking for directions to the constable's offices in town where Holmes anticipated the inspector to be. It was only a short walk, and the jail and offices were in the same smallish, square, stone building.

As Holmes and Watson walked through the front door, they were almost immediately greeted by an amusing looking short, plump man with red hair, heavy side whiskers, dressed in a rather worn tweed suit that did not fit properly, being a bit too small for his weight. "Mr. Holmes and Dr. Watson, I presume?" said the inspector looking back and forth at Holmes and Watson as if not knowing who Holmes was, and who was Watson. "I am Inspector Hamish MacDonald, and I am pleased to meet ye."

"I am Sherlock Holmes, Inspector MacDonald, and I am pleased to meet you. This is my friend and colleague, Dr. Watson," said Holmes by way of introduction.

Inspector MacDonald shook Holmes's hand heartily and with a beaming smile on his face. "It is indeed a great pleasure to meet ye, Mr. Holmes! A great pleasure indeed. We don't have much opportunity to meet folks from London in this part of England and certainly not one whose reputation precedes him. When I received ye telegram I had half a mind to take it as a bad joke, but one never knows when they will be visited by Providence, so I decided to meet ye here as the telegram requested. I must confess that I didn't expect that ye would actually show, but here ye are, in body and soul!" Inspector MacDonald looked from Holmes to Watson as if believing they might disappear at any moment. "Where are me manners? Please come in and sit. Sit and make ye selves comfortable."

Holmes and Watson were led into a windowless office containing a small desk, long narrow table, a filing cabinet, and two guest chairs. Holmes and Watson sat down in the two chairs offered them, and the inspector moved to sit behind his desk, all smiles and nervous energy. "Ye will have to excuse me office. We cannot afford to hire a cleaning woman. I do not have a secretary. All the things I need I have around me for quick reference. No, I don't throw anything away. It's when it's thrown away that sure enough ye need it. That is how we work out here in the hinterlands, gentlemen. We must be self-sufficient ye know. Can't be calling on Scotland Yard for everything. Well, what can I do for ye, Mr. Holmes? What brings ye to Tynemouth?"

"Thank you for agreeing to meet with me, Inspector. I have been retained in the matter of George Dodd, by his wife Dwylla Dodd," explained Holmes.

The inspector's faced immediately changed from eager smiles to confusion and disbelief. Shaking his head, he said, "What, the Oberstein murder, Mr. Holmes? There be no great mystery in that matter! George Dodd has confessed to the murder of the German fellow, and the evidence against him is solid sir. I could have saved ye a long trip if ye had asked about the case via letter or telegram. Believe me, sir, there is nothing here that would warrant a man of your talents and reputation. Dodd stabbed Oberstein in the lighthouse. That's that."

"I appreciate that, Inspector" said Holmes, "but I would like to make my inquiries just the same, with your help and cooperation of course."

"What kind of inquiries, Mr. Holmes?" asked the inspector now with a look of suspicion and distrust.

"You will find, Inspector, there is no reason to be fearful that I have come to rob you and your office of the credit for the arrest and eventual conviction of Mr. Dodd, if that is indeed what eventually happens. My name does not have to appear in the matter at all. If you have doubts, you can contact Inspector Lestrade of Scotland Yard and he will confirm what I say. I would simply like to spend two days here, speaking first with Mr. Dodd, then I would very much like to see the body of the deceased, visit the scene at the lighthouse, and finally speak with some of the locals about the case. You are free to accompany me if you wish. In fact, I would be honored if you would associate your investigation with mine," Holmes finished, looking directly and confidently at the inspector as if to say that this was all perfectly routine in London.

"Why Mr. Holmes this is a bit irregular. With no intention of offending ye, ye are not a part of the official police force and sharing our investigation with ye would be irregular, very irregular indeed." The inspector paused and seemed to be engaged in an internal debate about how to proceed. He nervously turned in his chair, picking one of his pipes and began to fill it with tobacco.

Watson started to raise a hand and appeared about to speak, when Holmes quickly placed his left hand on Watson's right arm, in a signal to remain still and quiet. Both Holmes and Watson sat in silence as the inspector filled his pipe and lit it, looking first at Holmes and then down at his desk, puffing nervously in quick short puffs, creating the illusion of a train just starting up and ejecting quick little clouds of steam. Given his appearance, the puffing smoke, the inspector's red face and side whiskers, Watson looked as if he was about to break out in laughter. He avoided looking at Holmes while they sat waiting for the inspector's answer, staring instead at the front of the inspector's old wooden desk.

Finally, the inspector spoke, "Ye say, Mr. Holmes, that ye just want to spend two days here and that I can associate my investigation with ye during this time, using all the facts and evidence that ye may come upon in support of our case against Mr. Dodd?"

"Yes. If that will be quite satisfactory, Inspector," agreed Holmes.

"Well, I can't say that it is routine by any means, but I can't say it would do any harm either." The smile returned to the inspector's face, "I would be honored to work alongside ye, Mr. Holmes, honored indeed." With that the inspector reached across his desk and energetically shook Holmes's hand, with a large toothy smile spread across his red face.

Inspector MacDonald rose from his chair, "I suppose ye will want to speak with George Dodd. He is just down the hall in his cell. Follow me, gentlemen."

The inspector led Holmes and Watson out of his office and walked down a short hallway that ended in a large, dark green, iron door. The inspector knocked on the door and waited. There was no response. He knocked again, "It is Inspector MacDonald, William, open the door." Holmes, Watson, and the inspector waited.

"It seems that no one is home," Holmes said with a wry smile on his face.

The inspector knocked again, this time harder and longer. The slide on a rectangular port in the door at eye level shot open and the bleary eyes of a constable looked out.

"Sorry, sir, didn't hear ye," said the obviously sleepy constable.

"I've got Sherlock Holmes and his colleague here to speak with George Dodd. Kindly let us in," the inspector was not amused. "Have ye been neglecting ye duties, William?"

"No, sir. Sorry, sir. I'll let ye right in."

With that the slide was closed and the sound of keys and a lock turning could be heard through the door. The inspector led the way into the small anteroom that formed the constable's small sitting area. Holmes and Watson signed the logbook and moved forward to a locked door made of iron bars, the last door between them and the cell area. There were six cells, three on each side, facing each other on either side of a wide hallway.

"George Dodd is in the last cell on the left," Inspector MacDonald pointed as he led Holmes and Watson down the hall and to the last cell on the left. The remaining cells were empty. "It's a busy place on Friday nights, I tell ye. What with drunks and fist fights, we can have three to a cell in here. But today it's calm. Just Mr. Dodd," explained the inspector.

The inspector pulled the slide back and looked inside the cell. It was gloomy and dark save for the light coming from a small steel-grated rectangular window high up the farthest eight-foot stone wall. "It's the Inspector, George. I have brought some visitors to see ye," he announced. There was a grunt from inside the cell. The inspector pushed his key into the door, unlocked it and opened it enough for Holmes to step in.

The room smelled bad. Not only were the filthy smells normally associated with jail cells present, but also the stink of human sweat. The elimination bucket sat in one corner and was emitting its own foul stench. Holmes recoiled at the stench, and Watson took out his handkerchief and covered his nose and mouth.

Sitting on the floor with his back against the stone wall in a pile of hay was George Dodd. He was the worse for wear. Smelly, dirty, sweaty and for all the world he bore the look of a man who has been totally defeated. He shuffled his feet and stood up slowly. "Now who might ye gents be?"

"I am Sherlock Holmes, and this is my colleague, Dr. Watson. We have been retained by Mrs. Dodd to investigate your case. I have a few questions I would like to ask you."

"Sherlock Holmes? I don't need no doctor, guvnor. I am for the hangman. It's the rope for me, sir. Nothing ye nor anyone else can do about that," mumbled Mr. Dodd.

"We will see about that Mr. Dodd. Now, let us get down to what happened in the early morning hours of January 17th at the Tynemouth Pier Lighthouse." Holmes stepped forward and handed Mr. Dodd a cigarette from his case and lit it as George Dodd looked at him with a mix of astonishment and suspicion.

He took a long drag from the cigarette and said, "I've got nothing else to do so, if it's what ye want, I'll tell ye what I know. Does the Peeler have to be here?"

"I am afraid the inspector must be present for this interview," said Holmes, "Now, shall we get started. Suppose you tell me what happened that evening at the lighthouse." George Dodd took another long drag from the cigarette and exhaled the blue smoke into the air. He stood a little straighter and looked at Holmes, then Watson, and then the inspector with a sneer.

"Ye say me Dwylla asked ye to look into me case?" he asked.

"Yes," said Holmes now beginning to show some impatience.

"How's that?" asked Dodd.

"She came to see me in London, with her sister, Mary, and asked me to look into your case," explained Holmes.

"We ain't got no money for this kind of thing. How she say she would pay ye?"

"We didn't discuss payment, Mr. Dodd. Do not worry about that, I believe my expenses and fee may eventually be covered by another person or persons. Now, can we please talk about what happened in the early morning of January 17th?" Holmes's patience was at an end.

"All right, I'll tell ye. Not much to tell, but I'll tell ye what I know," and with that Dodd took another long drag from his cigarette.

Chapter 4

George Dodd stared down at the floor and smoked. Holmes stood with his arms crossed waiting for Mr. Dodd to start telling his story. Watson folded his handkerchief and put it back in his inner coat pocket. The inspector stood to the side, smoking his pipe, leaning against the wall, and waited to hear what Dodd was going to say. Finally, Dodd spoke.

"There ain't much to tell ye, really. It was me month on, so I had been at the lighthouse for about half the month, I think. It gets lonely there. Nothing to do but care for the light and drink really. Sometimes some maintenance, but otherwise nothing to do. It was bad – especially when it stormed. That's the worst of it. Sitting there in that circle of stone with nothing to do while the sea tries to tear down the lighthouse with wind and water with me in it. It's loud. Sometimes the whole lighthouse shakes something fearful.

"Well, that night I started drinking early. Right after me dinner. I was blazing drunk by about 10 o'clock and passed out at the table. That should have been the end of it, but it wasn't!" George Dodd stopped talking and finished the cigarette, dropping it to the stone floor and stepping on it with his shoe. "If'n you got something stronger than that fag, I'd be happy to tell ye the rest."

Holmes looked over at Watson and nodded. Watson took his flask from his coat pocket and handed it to Dodd. The inspector started to protest but stopped himself and continued to smoke his pipe, leaning against the cold stone wall. Dodd took a long drink from the flask, wiped his mouth with the back of his hand, looked over at Watson and nodded his head in thanks, and continued with his story.

"Like I said, I had been three sheets to the wind and a sleeping it off there at the table. The lamp had gone out and it was dark in the lighthouse except for what light came down the steps from the big light itself. I don't know how long I had been asleep, but when it was all over, and it didn't take long, the sun was coming up, so it must have been near 5:30 or so when it all happened."

In the dim light of the cell, Dodd's story began to take on a life of its own. Holmes closed his eyes listening intently. Watson took out his notepad and pencil in anticipation of fresh details. The inspector tamped down his pipe with an old nail and lit another match to relight it. Everyone waited for Dodd to continue.

"I woke up because I heard yelling and something hitting the lighthouse door with great force," Dodd explained and stopped to take another drink from the flask. "At first I didn't know what was happening. The drink had worn off, but I was still only half awake. I wasn't sure that I was even hearing someone and not just the wind and the storm. I had been sleeping and I had been drunk. I was confused. But the screaming and the banging didn't stop. I lit a match and looked around me. I finally realized the sound was coming from the door and that it wasn't the storm. The storm had mostly blown itself out. I could still hear the rain and a little wind, but it was the screaming and the banging that was the loudest."

Holmes opened his eyes and looked at Dodd, "Could you understand what was being said? What the person was yelling?"

"No, it wasn't in English. I'd taken the King's shilling and served in the Royal Navy for five years. The yelling sounded like German, but I am not sure. It was loud and didn't make any sense to me."

"Go on then," said Holmes.

"I walked over to the door and yelled out asking who it was, but the banging and the yelling continued. I lit another match and looked around me. I found a large spanner that we use to make repairs on the light. I picked it up to use it to defend meself. I didn't know what else to do. Would you have done anything different?" The three, looking on with increasing interest did not respond, each simply watched Dodd and listened to his story. "No one comes to the lighthouse at night. No one. Especially not anyone in a storm. I began to think maybe it was the spirit of some long dead sailor or fisherman. I started shaking all over with fear. I didn't know what was on the other side of the door. But whoever it was, he wasn't going away."

"You said, 'he'?" asked Holmes, "How did you know it was a man?"

"I could tell by the sound of his voice. The voice was that of a man. I was sure of that. And then I thought I understood something that he said."

"What was it?" asked Holmes.

"I thought I heard him say, 'The gruel. Drank it!' It made no sense and I thought that he must have said something else and that I didn't hear him right, but he kept saying it over and over, 'The gruel. Drank it!'"

"That makes no sense Holmes," said Watson. "No sense whatsoever. Surely you must have heard him say something else, or, because of drink and being awakened so quickly, you misunderstood."

"No! I may not be sure of a lot of things that happened to me that night, but I am sure that he kept yelling, 'The gruel. Drank it!'"

"Come now, Dodd. Ye know that no man in his right mind would be a yelling that blasted thing outside a lighthouse in the rain and cold in the wee hours. Mr. Holmes, surely, you're not going to take what this man says seriously? Sounds like a wild tale brought on by drink or a man desperate to save his neck!" exclaimed the inspector.

"I don't know what to make of it, Inspector. Please, let Mr. Dodd finish his account. Mr. Dodd, you are sure that the man outside the door was yelling, 'The gruel. Drank it?'"

"As God is my witness, that's what I heard him say, sir. Everything happened very fast after that. It's all like a dream to me now. I walked to the door and slid the lock over and almost at once the door was violently pushed open knocking me to the ground. A man came in forcibly and stood over me. He was soaked to the bone and his shoes were covered in mud. His pants were torn, and his knees were bloody. I could see that much from the pale light of the rising sun, and I imagine because of the fear that made me eyes see like cat's eyes in the dim light."

The inspector scoffed and started knocking the spent tobacco from his pipe against the stone wall. "Lord have mercy, the man is spinning a tale as sure as anything, Mr. Holmes. It's a bunch of lies, it is."

"I'm a telling ye the God's honest truth I am! I've got nuthin to lose, have I? I'm going to hang as sure as the sun's going to rise tomorrow. I just want me Dwylla to know what happened." Dodd stood straight with his left hand balled in a fist at his side, his legs spread out wide, and still holding the flask. He looked determined and sure. He took another drink from the flask and again wiped his mouth with the back of his hand.

Holmes looked at him closely, looked over every inch of his face, and his stance. "If he is lying, Inspector, he is doing a very good job of it. He at least believes what he is saying. Of that, I am sure. I have no reason to doubt him and the evidence at the lighthouse will either confirm or contradict what he is saying. Go on, Mr. Dodd."

Dodd relaxed his body posture, leaning against the stone wall again. "Thank ye, sir. But it's nuthin' more than I deserve. I tell ye the truth."

The inspector laughed, "Yeah, and I suppose that makes me the pope, doesn't it now?"

"Inspector let him finish!" Holmes ordered.

"Aye, he can finish his load of malarkey!" answered the inspector bitterly. "Go on Dodd, spin ye tale ye lying bloody ratbag!"

"I ain't spinning no tales! And I ain't no ratbag neither! Damn Peeler! Anyway, I looked up at his face and it was as red as fire and covered over in large blisters. His hands were likewise covered. He had a crazed look in his eyes, like he had seen the devil he self. He was mad! As sure as hell, he was mad! The sight of him made me cold with fear, Mr. Holmes. Cold and desperate with fear. I struggled to stand, but before I could the man reached around his back and when his hand came back, he was holding a long-bladed knife. A dagger I think they call it. He just kept yelling, 'The gruel! Drank it!' I swung the spanner at 'em, and I think I hit his left arm 'cause he let out a scream and looked at me with those crazed eyes and went down on me as if to stab me with the knife. I grabbed both of his arms with me hands and we rolled around a bit on the stone floor. Me trying to keep from dying and he trying to kill me."

"I suppose he sang you a song while he was at it too, didn't he?" mocked the inspector.

"Quiet!" demanded Holmes. "Go on, Dodd."

"Well, in all the rolling around and pushing and shoving, I got the best of 'em and I gots on top of 'em. He was holding the knife in his hand, but I was controlling his hand. I turned his wrist until the knife was pointing at this heart, and I pushed for all I was worth until the blade went in deep. As far as I could shove it." Dodd took another long drink from the flask and handed it, empty, back to Watson.

The room fell silent as each man took in Dodd's story. The silence was broken by the inspector. "Have ye heard enough, Mr. Holmes?" he asked scoffing and standing straight again.

"What happened then, Mr. Dodd?" asked Holmes, ignoring the inspector.

"Well, he grew quiet, and his eyes grew large, and his face was contorted and twisted. He breathed in short gasps and next thing, he just stopped breathing. Staring at me with cold dead eyes and a contorted face! I'll see that face every time I close me eyes for the rest of me days and dream about it when I sleep, I swear it. I laid there on top of him still holding his wrist and pressing the knife into his chest and in comes me mate, Bill, the other lighthouse keeper. 'What the bloody hell!' he says, 'You've gone and done it now, George! Ye killed a man!'

"I didn't know what to do or say. It started to dawn on me mind what I had done. I got off the man, leaving the knife in his chest, I stood and me hands were covered in blood. I stared down at the man. I couldn't take me eyes off 'em. Bill grabbed me by the arm and twisted me around to face 'em. 'We gots to get the Peelers! Ye killed a man! Ye stay here. Don't ye go anywhere and I'll go get the Peelers!' he said. I was dazed. I was like a man walking in his sleep. I just did what I was told. I picked up the chair from off the floor where it had fallen after we kicked it in the struggle and just sat there a staring down at the man dead on the floor and the knife sticking out of his chest!"

"Why was Bill there?" asked Holmes.

"I found out afterward he had come out to check on me after the storm. To see as I was okay and to check if I needed any help with fixing any damage to the lighthouse. I don't know what I would have done with the dead man and me self if he hadn't have come by!"

Holmes was silent. Thinking. His hands in front of his face with steepled fingers. "You are sure that the dead man was yelling, 'The gruel! Drank it!'?"

"Yes, sir. I am sure of that." Dodd slapped the palms of his hands on both his legs. "That's it then gentlemen. That's what happened. I swear on me mother's bones. It's all the truth!" Dodd sank back down to the stone floor, sitting in the straw, and put his head in his hands and began to sob. "They'll hang me for sure! I killed 'em, as God is my witness! I killed 'em!"

Holmes turned to the inspector, "I think I am done here for the time being, Inspector. Thank you, Mr. Dodd. Do not lose faith! You are not hanged yet!"

With that Holmes walked out of the cell and down the hall at a rapid pace. Watson and the inspector came out of the cell much more slowly. Watson leaned into the inspector and said, "Inspector, I implore you, send one of your constables to his house, get him a change of clothes. Let him wash-up and shave. And, please have someone empty the elimination bucket. He's a man after all." The inspector looked at Watson and nodded his head, closing the cell door behind them and locking it.

The constable had unlocked the door for Holmes, and he was standing in the anteroom waiting for Watson and the inspector. "There's a considerable amount of important information in Dodd's story, Inspector. I advise you to take what he says seriously." Holmes and Watson signed out on the constable's log and waited for him to unlock the large green door.

"William, send one of the other fellows over to Dodd's place and fetch him a change of clothes and whatever else he may need to get cleaned up and go down and empty the elimination bucket. Thank ye," the inspector said to the constable. "And don't sleep on duty. If I catch ye doing it again, you'll be up queer street. Understand?"

"Yes, sir." With that the constable unlocked the door and let them out. Closing and locking the door again behind them, with him on the other side of the locked door. The inspector stopped and knocked on the door, "How ye gonna carry out me instructions if your locked in the bloody gaol, William? Dodd ain't going nowhere!"

The constable unlocked the large green door and came out shamefaced. "Yes, sir. I'll get on it right away."

Chapter 5

"Mr. Holmes, ye can't be believe'n this load of malarkey from the likes of George Dodd. He's got a reputation in the town as a drunk and a bully. When the drink is in him and he's in a foul mood, he'll punch ye in the face as look at ye. He's a spinnin' a yarn, Mr. Holmes. That's all."

"I understand that is your position, Inspector. But let me ask you, how do you explain Oberstein's appearance at the lighthouse in the middle of a storm if his story is not true?" asked Holmes.

"Well, it's a simple matter, Mr. Holmes. Here in Tynemouth all our little crimes are simple, sir. Not like your big mysteries in London where the rich and powerful can afford to do things in a complicated way. No sir, it's a simple thing. My theory is that the German fellow was drunk, as pissed as he could get, and wandered out to the lighthouse in the rain for reasons only a drunk man can understand. He started a banging on the door, probably thought it was the door to his own room at the inn, as drunk as he was. Dodd was drunk too. Much drunker than he be letting on. He was in a foul mood and as I told ye already, when Dodd is drunk and in a foul mood, he is not a man to be bothered with. He opened the lighthouse door, in came the German fellow; there was an argument, a scuffle, and Dodd stabbed the German fellow in the heart with his own dagger. That's how it happened, Mr. Holmes, simple."

Holmes thought about the inspector's theory, looked at Watson as if exasperated and asked, "Then how do you account for Dodd's description of Oberstein's face and hands, not to mention the screaming and yelling and the words, 'The gruel! Drank it!'?"

"Well, the words are the easiest part man, if he said them at all. To what would a drunk man refer when talking but of drink. He drank his liquor that's what he is referring to. As to 'gruel,' that maybe some German slang for a beer or a swig of whiskey for all I know. It's not important to the case at all, Mr. Holmes. You're one of those fellows what gets lost in some tangent, some unimportant detail. Take it from me Mr. Holmes, those trifles never matter. As for the face and hands, between the pub and the light house maybe the man burned himself when he was lighting his torch or something else. Again, just a trifle Mr. Holmes. Not important. Simple. Simple is the way to go in these parts." The inspector sat down appearing quite satisfied with himself and his theory of the case.

"Inspector, it is the trifles as you put it that in my experience are the most important aspects of a case. It is usually where the solution lies. I advise you to pay attention to the details. To the trifles." Holmes looked frustrated with the inspector, but then that was his usual feeling towards them. Holmes sighed, looking again at Watson who simply shrugged his shoulders and looked down at his feet. "*Et tu brute*?" Holmes asked.

"You have to admit, Holmes, the inspector's theory has some merit, and it is the simpler explanation. I am inclined to agree that Dodd's memory and *what* Oberstein said are both flawed and make no sense. They hardly help us solve the case." Watson looked guilty for agreeing more with the inspector than he did with Holmes, but he had always given Holmes his true opinion and now was no different.

"On the contrary, Watson. The case becomes clearer when one takes what Dodd said seriously and deduces from those facts." Holmes gave Watson a quick glance, but it was clear that Holmes was hurt by Watson's siding with the inspector. "But we linger. Inspector, there are maybe forty-five minutes of good light left to us," said Holmes as he took out his pocket watch and looked at the time. "I would like to go out to the lighthouse before it is dark and see what we can learn there. Do you have three lanterns that we can take with us as we start to lose the light?"

Holmes did not make eye contact with Watson as the two followed the inspector out of his office and watched him retrieve three dark lanterns shaking them to test that they each were filled with oil. He next checked his pockets for matches and satisfied that he had them, handed Holmes and Watson each a dark lantern.

"Follow me then will ye?" he said to Holmes and the three of them left the jail and walked down the road toward the lighthouse.

Watson and the inspector were chatting amiably about the rugged beauty of the British northeast and Tynemouth in particular. As they approached the general area of the lighthouse, the inspector was describing the ruins of the old abbey and fort that were to the left and before the lighthouse. There was a small graveyard between the abbey and the sea. The abbey and the fort were now no more than ruined walls with little to no roofs – the framework of what used to be.

The sun was setting to the west and they had about 30 minutes of useful light left. Holmes hurried forward leaving Watson and the inspector behind. As he approached within five yards of the lighthouse, Holmes slowed his pace and looked intently down at the stone pier for any signs or evidence. Too many people had walked over this area to make any evidence discernable. As he approached the lighthouse, Holmes looked over the walls and the circular path around the lighthouse formed by its foundation and followed it around. Holmes stepped carefully while he looked closely at the walls and footpath around the lighthouse. There were signs and evidence of recent scratching and scuffing, as though someone had shuffled along the walking path unsteadily and had made scratch marks on the stone wall, removing some of the mold and lichen. Holmes terminated his circuit of the lighthouse at the door, just as Watson and the inspector arrived.

"Have you noticed the scratch marks and smudges on the sides of the lighthouse and on the walking path around the foundation, inspector?" asked Holmes now turning his attentions to the large wooden door.

"Mr. Holmes, those markings could have come from anyone and at any time. They are of no importance to the case. I tell ye, focus on facts, Holmes, and not the trifles," the inspector scolded.

"Humm," was all that Holmes said as he began to examine the door and its frame. "Here, here, and again here. Fresh scratches in a pattern consistent with a human hand. More precisely, human fingers digging into the wood. Ah, and here, a broken fingernail embedded in the wood and a small stain of red, probably blood. All consistent with someone scratching violently at the door."

As he finished saying this, the door to the lighthouse opened very suddenly and there stood a large and threatening man raising a spanner as if to strike. "And who might ye be?" he yelled threateningly.

"Ahh, Bill the lighthouse keeper, I presume. I am Sherlock Holmes, and this is my friend and colleague Dr. Watson. The inspector I believe you know."

"Put the damn spanner down, Bill, before ye gets ye self in trouble like ye friend George! Put it down! Be a good lad!" the inspector said moving forward in between Holmes, who had taken a step back, and the man standing at the door.

The man slowly lowered the spanner turning to walk further into the lighthouse. "That's a good lad. Mr. Holmes just wants a wee look around and we will be gone," said the inspector. The man grunted and sat himself down at a chair by a small wooden table against the wall of the lighthouse.

Holmes walked into the lighthouse with Watson and immediately began to look around the room and floor. "Too many people in this small space, Inspector. I ask that you and Watson step just outside while I look around."

"If that's what ye want. Come Dr. Watson," and with that Watson and the inspector stepped just outside the door. "I've got me eye on ye, Bill!"

"I ain't a going to make any trouble for ye, Inspector," Bill said with a mixture of resignation and disdain.

"I do not expect to be here long, Bill. Are you in the mood to answer some questions?" asked Holmes.

"What do ye want to know?" Bill asked.

"What you saw and heard when you came into this very room during the morning of January 17th, this Saturday past?" Holmes asked.

"I've done told all that to the Inspector. Ask him."

"Well, yes, but I would appreciate it if you could tell me," said Holmes applying pressure with his voice.

"I saw me mate, George, on top of a man and pushing a bloody knife into his chest! That's what I saw! No more, no less. I then went 'round for the coppers. Stopped for a second at the inn to tell me friend, the landlord, and get a quick nip to help me, what with what I had just saw. That's the whole of it. Like I said, I done told the inspector everything."

Holmes looked at the man with disdain and frustration, "Did you hear anything that the dead man said or yelled before seeing George on top of him?"

"I heard some scuffling and cursing, and I heard a man a screaming like, but nothing I could make any sense of," grunted the keeper. "I was just coming down to check on me mate after the storm and to see if the lighthouse was damaged and if he needed any help. Now I got meself stuck in the middle between the coppers and me mate and have to man this bloody lighthouse outside me month. Me woman is pissed, she is. Probably leave me over this mess. Suits me for trying to be a good mate and not looking after meself, first."

"Yes, I am sure that is exactly how you see it," said Holmes walking out the door of the lighthouse. "Things have been cleaned up and put back in order, Inspector. Nothing I can glean inside the lighthouse. Outside is another story and what I have seen so far collaborates Mr. Dodd's account of what happened and is perfectly consistent with it."

"Yes, consistent all right. Consistently points to murder!" replied the inspector.

"Points to a bit more than that I should say, Inspector. Considerably more than that," answered Holmes. "The light is beginning to fail us. Let's light our dark lanterns and see what we can find in the yard in front of the abbey. Have you checked there already Inspector?"

"Why in blazes would I do that? The scene of the crime is inside the lighthouse Mr. Holmes. Ye are getting a bit afield here aren't ye?" laughed the inspector incredulously.

Watson looked at the inspector and explained, "Holmes is meticulous in his methods, and I recommend letting him continue his routine. I have seen him do great things, Inspector. Great things indeed. He knows what he needs to do."

The inspector shrugged as if to say, "If that's what the madman wants, that's what the madman can do!" and began to light the dark lanterns.

"Do you know what kind of boots Oberstein was wearing, Inspector?" asked Holmes.

"His boots?" The inspector looked at Holmes with disbelief and confusion.

"Yes, his boots," said Holmes.

"No, I don't know what kind of boots the man was wearing, Mr. Holmes. Why in blazes would I care about that and why would ye?"

"Well, we shall have to look for boot marks and confirm whether they belong to Oberstein afterward," said Holmes leading the way down the pier and toward the yard in front of the abbey. "Please stay behind me at least five feet and shine your lanterns around me, one on the left and the other on the right. I will shine mine in front."

As the three arrived at the yard, Holmes began to move deliberately back and forth in parallel lines, focusing intently on the ground. "Ahh, here and here!" he said pointing. "Round-toed boots." Once Holmes found the boot marks, he began to follow them back from where they appeared to have started. "It looks as though he was running."

The inspector looked at Watson and asked, "How the bloody hell does he know that?"

"The boot marks are deeper and heavier at the toes and lighter toward the heels," said Watson. "That's a sure sign that he was running."

"It looks like he fell several times as he ran. Look here, there are knee marks and palm marks where he fell!" exclaimed Holmes. "The boot marks lead into the ruins of the old abbey. So much for your theory, Inspector, that he came from a pub in the town."

The inspector had nothing to say. He looked completely out of his depth and amazed at what Holmes was finding. They followed the boot marks, stopping several times to look at places where Oberstein had fallen. Once inside the ruins of the abbey it was much harder to find a trace as the stone pavers were still intact in places where the grass and earth had not reclaimed them. The trail was lost several times but quickly found again until it reached the area of the abbey previously used as the altar. There a large capstone that both acted as the foundation for the altar and sealed in the holy relics below, marked the location of the old altar.

"The trail has gone cold, Watson. It looks as though the dust and dirt around the capstone have been disturbed, but I cannot see well enough with these dark lanterns to make a closer inspection. I will need to return when it is light." Holmes stopped, a bit out of breath, and looked around. He had followed the trail of boot marks as far as they could take him. "Well, Inspector, I would very much appreciate it if you could take us to see Oberstein's body."

"Holmes, it is dark, and I would like to have dinner soon," Watson pleaded.

"In time, Watson. Very soon. Inspector, can you take us to where Oberstein's body is being kept?"

"Well, yes of course. The body is being kept at the undertaker's. That's where Dr. Philby conducted the autopsy. I asked him to be there at 6:30, on the chance that ye might want to see the body after speaking to Dodd and seeing the lighthouse. We may be a little early, but we can wait for him to arrive. The undertaker is always there as the house doubles as his home."

"You are invaluable, Inspector," praised Holmes. "Please lead the way. Watson, come along."

The inspector looked tired from the afternoon's work, but with bent shoulders and a slower gait, led Holmes and Watson on a twenty-minute walk through the east side of the town and to an area occupied by homes and poorly lit by only a few gas street lamps. Watson stopped under one of the gas lamps and took out his watch. He breathed out a long sigh and rejoined Holmes and the inspector.

The house was a large wood structure of three stories with a covered porch that extended the entire width of the front of the house and several wooden steps that led up to it. The windows were well lit from the gas lights inside the house. Watson stopped at the foot of the steps leading to the front door and took several breaths. Holmes had bounded up the steps and was standing by the front door waiting. "Come along, Watson," he said. The inspector knocked on the door and it was quickly opened by a man who could have been nothing other than an undertaker.

"Ahh, Inspector. I wasn't sure that you were going to come. So glad to see you. And this must be Mr. Holmes, what?" The undertaker was a tall, very thin man dressed in a black suit. His voice was deep and hushed. His movements were slow and languid. "I am Franklin Macmaster, and I am the funeral director here in Tynemouth. Welcome to my home, gentlemen. Welcome. Come in please."

"Mr. Macmaster, I am pleased to meet you. I am Sherlock Holmes and just now arriving is my friend and colleague, Dr. Watson. I am sorry to arrive at this late hour, but our investigation has taken up our entire afternoon. I am afraid we got a rather late start having only arrived in mid-afternoon."

"Good to meet you as well, Dr. Watson. May I offer you gentlemen some refreshment?" asked Mr. Macmaster with a sweep of his hand toward the dining room where through the open French doors one could see that the table was laid out with cheese, breads, meats, and wine.

"Oh, that would be very…" Watson began to say before Holmes interrupted him.

"We appreciate the offer, very kind of you, but I would prefer to examine the body of the deceased if you don't mind. Has Dr. Philby arrived?"

"Well, Mr. Holmes, ye are free to conduct ye inspection of the body, but I am going to help me self to Mr.

Macmaster's hospitality. Would you care to join me Dr. Watson?" The inspector took off his coat and hat, threw them onto the nearest chair in the large sitting room, and walked towards the table with an eager expression and rubbing his hands together.

"I am afraid that I will be needed at the inspection of the body," said Watson looking forlornly as the inspector arrived at the table and began to sample the cheese.

"To answer your question Mr. Holmes, yes, Dr. Philby is in the cellar where I keep the bodies before burial. Please, allow me to lead the way." Mr. Macmaster pointed toward the back of the house. Holmes and Watson followed the undertaker through the dining room, passing the spread that was laid out before them, through a short hallway and to some steps that led down to the cellar. "Please join Dr. Philby below. I will stay here and entertain the inspector. Thank you, gentlemen."

Holmes and Watson went down the steps to the cellar to examine Oberstein's body. The cellar was large and had been converted to an area for the preparation of bodies for burial. It was roughly L-shaped. The longer part of the "L" contained four porcelain tables on metal frames, in the middle of the room, arranged side by side. At present, there were no bodies on the tables.

The shorter part of the L-shaped room was divided from the rest of the area by several French doors. One pair of these doors was open, and there stood a man waiting in the next room. As they approached, the man looked up, smiled, and took a step towards them as they walked through the French doors.

"Gentlemen, I am Dr. Philby, Dr. Alistair Philby," he said.

"Dr. Philby, it is good to meet you. I am Dr. John Watson, and this is Sherlock Holmes," said Watson by way of introduction.

Dr. Philby shook Watson's hand and then Holmes's hand and said, "It is truly an honor to meet you both. Dr. Watson, I must confess to being a devoted reader of the stories that you publish in the *Strand Magazine*. And to be able to meet you and Mr. Holmes and to collaborate with you is the honor of a lifetime."

The smaller room had wooden tables along the walls. One of the tables had a large block of ice and lying on the ice was a body covered in a sheet. On another of the tables were neatly folded clothes, a pair of boots, and several personal items, all carefully arranged.

"It is a pleasure to meet you as well," said Holmes. "I would imagine that you two doctors probably have some matters to discuss of a medical nature. May I see the body, Dr. Philby?"

Dr. Philby was a smallish man, not more than five foot, five inches tall, of middle build. He was balding on the top of his head with gray hair on the sides and back of his head. He was clean shaven. He had the appearance of a quiet, shy, and amiable man. His light grey eyes twinkled and positively shined with intelligence and hidden energy. He was meticulous in his appearance and spoke with a soft, gentle, even voice.

"Yes, yes, of course, Mr. Holmes. Mr. Oberstein is lying just over here under that sheet. I am afraid that I have already completed the autopsy, have placed the organs back in the body, and have closed the "Y" shaped incision. I have also had the body washed in preparation for embalming, but we stopped when we learned that you were coming. Dr. Watson, I have taken copious notes of my procedure and findings, and I would be happy to share the same with you and discuss it with you if you wish," explained Dr. Philby.

Holmes looked frustrated. Dr. Philby's washing of the body meant that there would be almost no evidence that Holmes would be able to extract from the body. "I understand," he said. Holmes walked over to the body and removed the sheet. "Is there no better lighting in this room, Dr. Philby?"

"I am afraid not. This room is not used for examinations, but to store the bodies pending burial. I am sorry. Had you arrived just thirty-hours earlier, you could have been with me as I conducted the autopsy. But, alas, all has been completed." Dr. Philby seemed genuinely distressed to have missed the opportunity to collaborate with Holmes and Watson. "You can understand, Dr. Watson, that I get very few opportunities to consult with another professional, such as yourself, and I am truly sorry that we missed that opportunity."

"Thank you, Dr. Philby," said Watson. "Holmes, I can go upstairs and retrieve one or two of our dark lanterns if you wish?"

"That is a good idea, Watson. Thank you," said Holmes.

Watson hurried upstairs, retrieved two of the dark lanterns, and quickly returned to Dr. Philby and Holmes. Holmes was examining Oberstein's clothing and Dr. Philby was standing off to the side patiently watching. Dr. Philby looked intimidated by the presence of the great detective and seemed to almost shrink in his presence.

"I see that the clothes were cut off the body with sharp scissors. The trouser knees are interesting. They bear marks of mud, grass, and a curious white, chalky powder. I notice that the same white, chalky powder is on the bottom of the shoes, round-toed boots matching the boot marks we found in the yard, along with caked mud and little pieces of gravel. What do you make of the chalky powder, Dr. Philby?" Holmes was scraping some crystalline substance off the sleeves of Oberstein's coat into a small square of brown paper folding the paper carefully and putting it in his own coat pocket. He turned to look at Dr. Philby, who addressed his comments to Watson, rather than Holmes.

"Yes, I made detailed notes of what was on the clothing, the shoes, and between the fingernails. Dr. Watson, you will find my handwritten notes in the lab book I placed beside the body." Dr. Philby seemed both happy to be there and almost afraid at the same time.

"Watson, a man after our own hearts! Excellent Dr. Philby! And did you draw any conclusions from the presence of the white, chalky material?" Holmes looked genuinely impressed with Dr. Philby.

"Well, yes. If you dig more than say three feet anywhere underground in this area, you will strike veins of chalk. None is at the surface. It seems likely to me that Mr. Oberstein had spent some time in a mine or underground shaft in the hours before his death." As Dr. Philby said this he walked over to the table with the body and picked up his lab book and handed the same to Watson.

"Excellent. Excellent. That piece of information is very telling. Did you make any other findings from your examination of the clothing?" asked Holmes as he moved from the shoes and clothes to the body itself. He lit both dark lanterns placing one facing the head, holding the other as he examined the body.

"No, no other findings from the clothing," said Dr. Philby.

"Well, you have been very professional and detailed in your work, doctor. Very impressive indeed," Holmes said with some genuine feeling as he examined the body.

"Yes, thank you, Mr. Holmes. Dr. Watson, the immediate cause of death was from a sharp bladed object of approximately eight inches in length that entered the body at a slight angle between the third and fourth ribs about an inch and a half to the left of the sternum. As it penetrated the body, the blade nicked the fourth costal cartilage. The blade then penetrated the heart muscle bisecting the left atrium and coming to rest just inside the pulmonary trunk. Death would have been almost instantaneous." Dr. Philby's description was professional and precise.

"When you examined the lungs, I am assuming with such a wound, the lungs and chest cavity were filled with blood. Am I correct Dr. Philby?" asked Watson.

"Yes, quite so. But that was not the peculiar aspect of the lungs. The lungs were each red, swelled with edema, and copiously blistered along all the lobes. Many of the bronchioles were ruptured and the general condition of the lung tissue was quite bad. Very damaged, as if the tissue had been exposed to some strong acidic substance. The trachea was in the same general condition, as was the throat, the mouth, the tongue, and all the mucus membranes of the mouth and nose. I have never in my almost thirty years of medicine seen anything like it."

"Very strange indeed," agreed Watson.

"Doctors, what do you make of the blisters and redness of the skin on the face, neck, and hands?" asked Holmes as he was lifting the right arm of the body and closely examining it.

"Holmes, I haven't had the opportunity to examine the hands and face yet," Watson said as he moved over to the hand that Holmes was holding up. "May I?"

Watson examined the skin of the right hand and Oberstein's face, lips, and the inside of his mouth and nose.

"It is all very red, swollen, and blistered. I have only seen this condition associated with burns by either fire or strong acids. What is your opinion, Dr. Philby?"

"Oh, I concur. The condition of the epidermis of the face and hands seems consistent with chemical burns. But I have no idea what kind of chemical or from what source," answered Dr. Philby.

"You said earlier, Dr. Philby, that the immediate cause of death was the stab wound through the heart. In your professional opinion, was there a secondary cause of death?" asked Holmes.

"Yes, I believe that there was." Dr. Philby looked thoughtful and decisive as he softly said, "From the condition of the lung tissue and the mucosa, Mr. Oberstein would have died of suffocation brought on by severe lung failure, leading to acute cardiac arrest. His death, I estimate, would have occurred within fifteen to at most twenty minutes, had he not been stabbed through the heart by Mr. Dodd. He was, gentlemen, essentially a walking dead man. There is no treatment that I am aware of that could have arrested the chain of physical events that would have led to his death."

"And I presume that this is the dagger that was used to stab Mr. Oberstein?" asked Holmes as he unwrapped an ornate dagger that had been folded inside a plain, white towel. "The dagger has a blade of about eight inches, sharp on both sides and comes to a very sharp point. One side of the blade has ornate, gold etching starting about halfway up the side of the blade proceeding to just under the hilt. Both the hilt and pommel are gold and the handle itself is composed of an alternating blue and silver metal strip. It is a beautiful German dagger in the French style."

"Yes, that is the murder weapon. In this bag you will find the rather intricate leather vest like apparatus that was used to carry the dagger behind the back. The sheath is attached to these leather straps and the dagger would have rested in the small of the back with the handle facing downward. It would have been easy to conceal under a jacket or coat." Dr. Philby displayed the intricate leather straps and sheath to both Holmes and Dr. Watson. "Both the dagger and the leather apparatus for holding it look to be custom made and expensive. The clothing and shoes were finely made and of good materials as well. Apparently, Mr. Oberstein was a man of expensive taste and could afford to indulge those tastes."

"Dr. Philby, I am impressed!" exclaimed Holmes. "You have really done this right. May we borrow your autopsy notes and return them to you tomorrow before we leave for London?"

"Well, I will need those notes for my records and to reference at the inquest, but so long as you return them to me tomorrow before you leave, I see no harm in letting you borrow my notes overnight." Dr. Philby looked worried and glanced quickly at Watson as if to plead for his assistance, not able to deny the great detective his request.

"I give you my word, Dr. Philby, as a fellow physician. I will ensure that your lab book is returned to you before we leave tomorrow," promised Watson.

Dr. Philby seemed both satisfied and relieved that Watson had given his word and said, "Oh that will be very satisfactory. Thank you, Dr. Watson."

Holmes and Watson, having shaken Dr. Philby's hand, thanked him again and left him in the room with the body and proceeded upstairs to where the inspector and Mr. Macmaster awaited their return. The inspector was in lively conversation with the undertaker and finishing a glass of wine when Holmes, having entered the dining room with Watson behind, said, "We are all finished here, Inspector. Did Mr. Oberstein stay at the inn during his brief but eventful visit to Tynemouth?"

"Yes, Mr. Holmes. He stayed in the same inn that I believe ye are staying tonight. I am sure that Seamus, the landlord, will be happy to let you examine his rooms, if I say it's alright. You won't find anything there. I've searched it already. But I suppose ye can make another search of it just the same." The inspector put down his glass and began to walk to retrieve his coat and hat in the sitting room. Both Holmes and Watson thanked the undertaker and the three walked back to the inn in silence.

As they arrived at the inn, the inspector went to speak to the landlord and Holmes and Watson waited by the stairs that led up to their rooms. "Holmes, I am famished, and I must eat. If you do not need me further, I am going to sit in here, order a meal, and have a nice pint of the local ale." Watson looked tired, hungry, and almost desperate to eat.

The inspector walked up and said, "I have arranged it with Seamus; he'll unlock the German's room presently. Well, gentlemen, I must go home to me wife. Will you be needing me tomorrow morning Mr. Holmes?"

"Thank you, Inspector. If you will be so kind as to round-up the handful of locals that may have seen Mr. Oberstein about, I would appreciate speaking with them in the morning, say 9:30?" asked Holmes.

"Certainly, there will only be three or four, but I'll have them here tomorrow morning as ye request, Mr. Holmes. Good night gentlemen!" and with that the inspector left.

Holmes started up the steps as the landlord came over with the key. As he followed the landlord up the steps, Holmes looked quickly around the pub. Two men were sitting at a table in the corner of the pub who did not seem to fit. Both men's dress marked them as criminal members of the London underground, dressed in the fashion of the London thief trying to make an impression. Holmes quickly looked away from the men and continued upstairs.

Watson took a table and as soon as he got the attention of the landlord's wife, ordered a pint, a shepherd's pie, and some of the local bread. He looked tired and it was almost eight o'clock and he had not eaten for many hours. He sat back in his chair as the landlord's wife poured his beer from the hand pump at the bar. Watson watched the fine pale-yellow ale pour into the earthenware mug. He rubbed his hands together in anticipation of a good ale and a nice meal.

The two young men in the corner of the pub leaned into each other as they spoke. Both had drunk several ales and were working on the ones in front of them. They spoke quietly and cautiously.

"We've had an accident, we have. Lost the lot of 'em, the scientist and the potential buyer," said the one facing the pub.

"He won't like that one bit," answered the one with his back to the pub.

"Couldn't be helped. These things are bound to happen with this kind of work. It's bloody dangerous."

"When can we get back down and start working again?"

"Not for a few days. Not safe. At least a week to be safe. As soon as we get another scientist, it shouldn't take much time to work up another batch and test it. We were so close to being finished. I would say another four weeks, given what's happened."

"I'm leaving for London by train tomorrow. He doesn't like bad news and doesn't like setbacks. He usually doesn't react well to this. I'd be careful if I was you. You say we lost the potential buyer as well?"

"Yeah, he was caught up in it. Damn shame really. We will have to find another."

"Nope, he won't like that at all. Hope he doesn't kill the messenger!"

Watson was drinking his ale when his food arrived. Oblivious to the conversation of the two men sharing the room with him, he focused on his meal and his pint of local ale.

Watson finished his meal and two pints, thanked the landlord and walked tiredly up the steps to the first floor and toward his room. He stopped at the door to Holmes's room and knocked. There was no answer, and there was no movement. He knocked again, but it was apparent that Holmes was not there. He showed no concern. Watson knew Holmes's habits were not routine. It was likely that some small detail had eluded Holmes and he was out clearing it up before going to bed. Watson had experienced this very thing too many times to be surprised by Holmes's absence.

Chapter 6

Watson came down for breakfast just after 8:00 o'clock. As he walked down the stairs, he looked out the window of the inn. The sky was blue, the sun was brightly shining, and it was a beautiful January morning in Tynemouth. Watson looked refreshed. He carried Dr. Philby's lab notebook. As he sat down at one of the tables in the pub, the landlord came over and handed him a note from Holmes. The note read:

> Watson,
>
> I went out just after sunrise to look over the yard, the area in and around the abbey, and the old fort. The light of day may reveal more than we could discern last night in the failing light. I will return at 8:30.
>
> SH

Watson ordered a hardy breakfast of kippers and eggs, coffee, and toast. While he waited, he looked over Dr. Philby's notes. He was drinking his coffee and had just started on his breakfast when Holmes arrived. Holmes was full of energy. He was on the scent, and nothing could stop him when he was in such a mood.

"Ahh, Holmes. Good morning. I received your note. Any new developments?" asked Watson.

"An interesting night and an even more interesting morning. Yes, Watson, the case is developing nicely. Can you spare some coffee?" Holmes answered with barely concealed excitement.

"Of course, Holmes. Landlord, could we get another cup please?"

The landlord brought over another cup and handed Holmes a telegram. "This came for ye this morning, Mr. Holmes. I hear ye woke up the man in the telegraph office last night. He was not too happy about that this morning," said the landlord.

"Thank you, Seamus. It could not be helped." Holmes opened the telegram, read it, and handed it to Watson. "Did you notice the two men sitting in the corner of the pub last night, Watson?"

"Last night? No, Holmes. What about them?"

"Their bearing and how they were dressed. They were not locals, and they had the fog of London about them. I deduced they were two of the London criminal element trying to appear otherwise huddled together in the corner with a conspiratorial air about them. One of them is staying in this very inn." Holmes took a drink of his coffee. "The other has leased rooms in a local house not far from the undertaker's residence. I followed him there last night. The telegram you placed on the table beside you as you eat your breakfast is from Scotland Yard. I wired them last night, having awakened the sleepy telegraph officer, to inquire into their names and backgrounds. Seamus was kind enough to tell me the one staying here is named William Saacks. The other's name was provided by Scotland Yard using my description and because of his known association with Saacks. His name is Bob Whitaker. Both are known to Scotland Yard and have a record as confidence men, petty thieves, and blackmailers."

"Beyond serving your curiosity, what does this have to do with our case, Holmes?"

"I have said before, I don't put a lot of faith in coincidence. A known German spy is in town for ten days. He shows an interest in the old abbey and the fort. His boot prints put him in the abbey the night of the storm. During a terribly stormy night he is stabbed by Dodd when he runs to a lighthouse five hundred feet down a pier in the wind, pouring rain, and freezing cold. And it is just a coincidence that two of London's finest are here, enjoying a pint? No, Watson! That won't do. There is a connection, of that, I am sure. But what it is still eludes me." Holmes finished his coffee.

"My search of Oberstein's rooms turned up nothing of real interest. Some letters, receipts, and his travel papers. Nothing else. It helped confirm that he is indeed Gustav Oberstein, but of that there was little doubt. What was more interesting about his room was what wasn't there. He had no personal effects to speak of. A change of suit, a fresh collar, an extra pair of boots, his toilet, and nothing else. The room was clean and bare. I dare say that you caused more disarray in your room after only one night than Oberstein did during his ten-day stay. Seamus confirmed that Oberstein refused any maid service and denied entry into his room by anyone. That is telling. It means he meant to leave no trace and wanted no one to know his business. I see that you have Dr. Philby's lab notebook. Anything of interest in it?"

Watson swallowed the last bite of his eggs and handed the notebook to Holmes. "No, nothing of significance that we don't already know. It does reveal a very intelligent and organized mind. His methods are foolproof, and his notes are copious. He missed nothing." Watson continued to eat his bread and what remained of his kippers.

"Good man, Dr. Philby." Holmes quickly looked through the notebook at the pages referencing Dr. Philby's autopsy. He put the notebook down on the table. "I will ask Seamus to return the notebook to the doctor. We have a 12:10 p.m. train leaving from the station, and I still want to speak with the three or four people the inspector promised us. It's almost a quarter past nine and he hasn't yet arrived." Holmes glanced around him with a frustrated look. He and Watson continued in silence as Watson finished his breakfast and the landlord came to clear the table.

"Will you eat nothing for breakfast, Holmes?"

"No, the coffee is all I needed. I will likely order a sandwich of cold meat and bread before leaving for the train station." Holmes began to tap his fingers on the table in front of him. Holmes was not a patient man, and he did not like waiting. His mind was too quick and when on the scent, his penchant for action rather than loitering made any wait almost impossible for him to endure.

"Holmes, the inspector isn't due until half past the hour. He will come." Watson tried to soothe his friend's nervous temperament. But Holmes kept drumming his fingers on the table and nervously fidgeting. After just a few more minutes of waiting, and early, in walked the inspector himself...alone.

"Good morning, Inspector," greeted Holmes. "I see you come *sans* the locals I wished to interview. Is there difficulty?"

"Ye can say that Mr. Holmes. They refused to speak with ye. Not a one of them would join me here this morning. They claim they have nothing to add to what they already told me and are a bit confused about why it was necessary for them to speak with an unofficial detective not formally associated with me office or the investigation. Sorry, Mr. Holmes, but ye can't blame 'em." The inspector looked shame-faced and embarrassed.

"Well Inspector, did you tell them the man who wanted to speak with them was Sherlock Holmes?" asked Watson with incredulity.

"Yes, sir. I did. That only made the matter worse. It's a small town, Mr. Holmes. People stick to themselves, mind their own business, and protect their own. Even one such as George Dodd. People don't want to get involved and are likely as not afraid of being shunned by their own neighbors. You leave for London today, Mr. Holmes, but they have to live with each other after you leave." The inspector seemed at a loss for what else to say or do.

"Well, thank you all the same, Inspector. I understand. It is not the first time, and it will certainly not be the last. Can you summarize for me what they told you?" Holmes smiled and put the inspector at ease.

"Yes, Mr. Holmes. The German fellow had been in Tynemouth for about ten days. He stayed to himself during the first seven days or so. He spent most of his time in his room during the day and wasn't seen much except when he came down to the pub to eat and drink. He was seen at night, however, walking through the streets of the town at various places. He was also seen by Mr. Macmaster's apprentice one evening as he left the funeral parlor. He was seen walking away from town toward the homes further down the street from the parlor."

"That is important, Inspector. Was he ever seen in the yard of the abbey or in and around the grounds of the abbey and fort?" asked Holmes.

"Yes, but only in the last three days before his death. He was seen walking in the yard toward the abbey. He was also spotted walking in the yard away from the abbey. Two of our witnesses saw these two separate instances at different times and days."

"In addition to the events that you have described, were there any other instances where witnesses saw Oberstein?" Holmes was sitting back in his chair, his hands clasped in front of his face, with his eyes closed listening intently.

"No, Mr. Holmes. Not that I am aware of."

"He wasn't seen on the grounds of the old fort? On the other side of the old abbey?" asked Holmes.

"No. Why do ye ask?" The inspector leaned forward with both arms on the table.

"Because I found boot marks matching those of Oberstein around the old fort and behind it leading toward a small inlet along the beach. I could not get any further as there is a significant drop off leading to rocks and the powerful surf. Are there any caves cut out by the waves in that area?" Holmes had opened his eyes and crossed his arms.

"That be the old smuggler's inlet. There are caves there Mr. Holmes. The folklore of the area says that smugglers used that inlet and the caves to hide themselves and their booty years ago. No one goes there now. It's believed to be haunted, sir. Don't know why the German fellow would have been walking around there."

"Thank you, Inspector. Anything else to add?"

"No sir. Except that the German leased a small fishing boat, went out briefly in the North Sea, and was dropped off at the inlet. It was said he just wanted to see the abbey and fort from the sea. That be it. Is that Dr. Philby's lab notebook?" The inspector picked up the notebook and began to open it.

"Yes, but it was provided to us in confidence, Inspector. We need to return it to Dr. Philby," Watson quickly took the notebook from the inspector.

"I see, Dr. Watson. Anything in there that might be of interest to me investigation?" The inspector looked suspicious.

"Nothing that Dr. Philby will not testify to at the inquest, Inspector." Holmes interjected with a disarming smile. "And nothing that I am sure you are not already aware of."

"Humm, I suppose so. Well, Mr. Holmes what are ye plans?"

"What do you make of Oberstein's trip out to the sea and more importantly, being dropped off at the inlet?" Holmes's face was alive with energy.

"I don't make anything of it. He was here, he said, to study the abbey. It's only natural to want to view the same from the sea. Has nothing to do with the case, Mr. Holmes." The inspector appeared annoyed by Holmes. For his part, Holmes looked at the inspector with barely veiled contempt.

"We have completed what I came here to do. We will be returning to London by the noon train. Ahh, Watson, we need to settle our bill and get ready to leave for the station. Thank you, Inspector. I appreciate your assistance in this matter. May I telegram you if I need anything further?" Holmes was done with the inspector and wanted to avoid any more questions from him about his investigation.

"Surely, Mr. Holmes. I'll do what I can for ye." All three stood from their chairs, shook hands, and exchanged goodbyes. The inspector hesitated, looking intently at

Holmes and then down at the lab notebook. He appeared ready to say something more but appeared to think better of it and then walked out of the inn, returning to the jail and his offices.

As the inspector walked out the door, Holmes turned to Watson as they both sat back down and said, "I never cease to be amazed, Watson, at the absolute incompetence of the professional police. The inspector has a great deal of evidence from his witnesses that points to there being more to this mystery than a simple stabbing at a lighthouse, and yet he dismisses that information as either unimportant or unrelated. He, like many in his profession, is content to focus on the obvious with a singular drive toward the easy conviction rather than the full solution to the case."

"Well, we can't say the same for Dr. Philby. His work on this case is exemplary, and I cannot say that he left a stone unturned," said Watson patting the doctor's lab notebook.

"I sense some professional pride in your praise, Watson. Yes, Dr. Philby did a masterful job, even if he did miss the potential importance of the crystalline substance on Oberstein's jacket and pants. It is likely that the same substance was present on the body and hair, but that evidence was obliterated by the washing of the body in preparation for embalming. No, Watson, I am afraid that the inspector and Dr. Philby cannot be proud of their parts in the eventual solution to this crime.

"Everything the doctor told us was obvious from even a cursory examination of the body. It was helpful only because the autopsy had been completed before our arrival; the information he provided was necessary to the case but nothing out of the ordinary for an autopsy. Our good Dr. Philby suffers from a lack of the same thing as does the inspector. Imagination, Watson. That is what is lacking in the field of criminal detection. A complete lack of imagination."

"Well, you have no lack of imagination, Holmes. Of that I am certain."

"Shall we settle our bill and get to the train station early? I will want to stop at the telegraph office to send a telegram to the Foreign Office as well."

When they arrived at the telegraph office, which was attached to the post office, Holmes and Watson went inside and found a sleepy telegraph officer. "I need to send a telegram to the foreign office. Can you oblige?" asked Holmes.

"Mr. Holmes, another telegram, is it? I am still recovering from ye last request." The telegraph officer did not look happy to see Holmes. "Please complete this form and I'll send ye telegram immediately."

Holmes stood in thought for several minutes and then composed the following telegram:

START: IMPORTANT. READ IMMEDIATELY. GUSTAV OBERSTEIN DEAD. BODY AT TYNEMOUTH. DEATH SUSPICIOUS. INFORM MINISTER. NO

*REPLY REQUIRED. SHERLOCK HOLMES.
END*

Holmes and Watson returned to the carriage and were driven to the train station. Holmes was quiet during the short drive.

Because Holmes and Watson had arrived at the station early, they gave their bags to the porter and sat and smoked. There were not many passengers waiting and Holmes spent the time studying the people in only the way that he could. He amused himself like this for some thirty minutes, when his eyes fell on the figure of a man, smoking while standing by the tracks. The man was William Saacks. He seemed troubled and preoccupied. But Holmes noticed that Saacks saw him as well and there seemed to be a moment of recognition. Saacks knew who Holmes was. He was too professional to be obvious, but to Holmes's trained eye, it was clear. Saacks finished his cigarette, picked up a newspaper someone had left on a bench, and opened it as if to read it. As he did this, he walked slowly and casually back into the station.

Holmes made his own excuse to stand acting as though he were looking down the tracks for the train. As he turned around facing the station again, he saw that Saacks was at the small telegraph office at the station. Holmes sat back down beside Watson.

Holmes leaned into Watson and said, "It appears we have been recognized and our presence is being reported. To whom is the question? Do not turn around Watson, take my word for it. It is Saacks, the man who was staying at our inn and whom I spotted in the pub."

"Is he following us, Holmes?"

"No, I think not. He was surprised to see me. He did not expect that I would be here. My presence has troubled him enough that he felt it necessary to send a telegram reporting it to a superior no doubt. That is important, Watson. Docket it away in your mind. If I am not very much mistaken, I believe I hear the train now."

Chapter 7

The building was an unremarkable brick warehouse, down a long street of warehouses, along Shad on Thames, just short of the bridge on London's East End. It was a three-story brick warehouse with some windows on the first and second floors. No one had any reason to suspect it was anything other than one of the common warehouses along this long street. Except, that this particular warehouse, number 32, seemed to have more loiterers around it and across the street. Loiterers who seemed unusually vigilant to anyone and any activity.

The ground floor of Warehouse 32 revealed nothing unusual. It was a typical warehouse where products and other items were brought from the dockyard at Butler's Wharf and stored before being sent out to the streets of London. Except that the steps to the first floor were guarded by heavily armed men in suits nicer than they deserved to wear. And, if any of the large boxes had been opened, the items inside were not the typical items in a normal warehouse.

On the first floor of the warehouse, the large, open storage space had been converted to offices and at least three telegraph stations. The side of the warehouse facing the Thames, one third of the entire space, was occupied by a single large office. It contained its own conference room, formal working office, sitting room, and small library. It was furnished ornately with statuary, and works of fine art. In the conference room were five men. Four were "generals" who served the leader, and of course the leader himself. They were attending one of two daily meetings keeping the leader informed, engaged, and in control.

The leader sat at the head of a large wood conference table. A man of good birth and excellent education, he was endowed by nature with a phenomenal mathematical mind and was an abstract thinker of the first order. He was tall and thin with a forehead that domed out from his head in a wide curve. His head was balding, but not bald, with straight hair, black mixed with grey. His two eyes, empty, dark, soulless, evil, and unemotional, were deeply sunken in his head. He was clean-shaven, pale, and retained the air of a professor.

He was known, to those who are allowed to know him, as "the Professor," head of the Moriarty crime syndicate. The most powerful criminal in England and Europe. He was the organizer and financer of more than half of what is evil in England and Europe. The author of almost all that is undetected and clandestine in the dark world of crime in England and the Continent. A formidable criminal mind and a very dangerous man.

His generals, four of whom sit at the table before him, had sworn their lives and allegiance to him. They were paid handsomely for their loyalty and their work, but their lives could be ended in an instant, if the thought crossed Moriarty's mind. They knew it, and they acted accordingly.

This afternoon, Moriarty was being briefed on some of the many affairs, plans, plots, and actions he had planned or financed. He listened, asked questions, and made decisions. His "work" included prostitution, kidnapping, murder, assault, child sex trafficking, gambling, opium, cocaine, robbery, theft, blackmail, boxing, horse racing, bribery, political influence, international politics, the courts, the police, protection, and intelligence. He was a government unto himself.

Moriarty knew that his fifth general, Bill Saacks, was in northeast England looking after one of his most important projects. He would be back tonight, and Moriarty would get a briefing despite the lateness of the hour. The last briefing indicated that all was going well and on schedule. They had an interested buyer, and he knew that after one bought what he was selling, others would follow and at a higher price. It was a whole new area of business that he was entering. A new frontier for him and his syndicate to dominate. It was satisfying.

As he was being briefed on another project, there was a light knock on the door. One of his generals got up and went to the door, took a piece of paper that was laying on a silver serving tray, looked it over, looked up at Moriarty, walked to him and almost reverently handed him the paper. It was a telegram from Saacks. Moriarty read it and immediately his eyes went dark with anger. But you would hardly have been able to tell by looking at him. He calmly placed the telegram on the table, smoothed it out, put both hands on the table in front of him on top of the telegram, and began to think – his movements slow and deliberate. His head oscillating from side to side, like a deadly lizard, he cleared his throat and all talking around the table ceased. His generals fell silent and looked only at him.

"It appears that our old nemesis has returned to his habit of getting in the way of our plans and making things more complicated," he said with immense control, but his eyes burned with inner anger.

"What, Holmes again?" asked one of his generals.

"Yes, Mr. Holmes was in Tynemouth with the Doctor. Bill Saacks sent me this telegram from the train station in Tynemouth to report his presence. He should be back this evening and will report further when he arrives." The temperature of the room seemed to change and each of his generals simply looked down at the table, not wanting to look Moriarty in the eye. "I suppose we should have anticipated his presence and made our plans accordingly. He is vexing. Still, he is an intelligent man. He has lost many more of our little chess matches than he has won, being unaware that he has lost. But he is a worthy adversary."

"I can take care of him and the Doctor, Professor. Just give the word." The anger and aggression in the general's voice betrayed both his hatred for the dreaded detective and his confidence that he would succeed if so ordered.

"No, not at this time. That would complicate matters further. The loss of so public a figure, one whose reach extends to the highest levels here in England and on the Continent, would be both noticed and cause a severe and unfortunate reaction. No, removing Holmes from the board would simply bring more..." Moriarty paused as if looking for the right word, "impediments, not fewer. We must think this through and there is nothing yet to think about until

Saacks reports. To do so would-be mere speculation. No, we must be informed, we must understand, and then we must think. He has not made any aggressive moves against us, and this may be mere coincidence, though I sincerely doubt it. We have time to decide what to do. Now is not the proper time to reap, but to sow. Do we have anyone watching Holmes?"

"No sir. I don't believe so. At least not regularly. Only when his efforts bring him close to one of our projects."

"Well, then perhaps it is time to change that practice. We need a very good and trustworthy man. Whomever you choose must be discreet and invisible. I want Holmes watched around the clock, seven days a week. I want to know who comes to see him. I want copies of the telegrams he receives. I want to know everything that he does from the time he awakens until he sleeps at night. If possible, gentlemen, I want to know what he dreams. Can we make that happen?" All four generals almost simultaneously said, "Yes, Professor."

"Good, good. Thank you, gentlemen. That will be all for this afternoon," Moriarty said with a sardonic smile. He sat in silence, head oscillating, as his generals departed. He could not draw any conclusions without information and at present he had none. "What is your game, Holmes?" he said to himself. He stood and walked around the conference table and to the small but beautiful library. There was a small bar in one corner, and it was to this that he walked. He poured himself a tumbler of Scottish whisky, poured just a bit of water in it to awaken the aromas, and sat on the leather sofa in front of the fire to think. He thought for some time, looking into the fire and slowly drinking his Scotch. Moriarty occasionally turned the glass watching the light from the fire dance against the many facets cut into the glass. "What is your game?" he said to himself.

He sighed and finished his Scotch. Moriarty got up and walked toward one of the bookshelves along the wall, took out a key, and slid aside the cover of a hidden keyhole, unlocked the "door," for that is what it was, opening it and revealing a metal, winding set of stairs that wound around itself very tightly and led to the second floor. He closed and locked the "door" behind him and ascended the tight winding stairs to where a small landing and another locked door presented themselves. He unlocked this door, entering the sitting room of his apartment.

"Lilith?" he called. He only called once. She immediately appeared from the area where the kitchen was located, gliding into the room in a glossy pearl grey silk dress that went to just above the knees. Her hair was in an intricate bun with a cascade of hair down her back. The silk dress was revealing, plunging in the back almost to the hips and low cut in front to reveal just a hint of young, fresh cleavage. Her body was lithe but shapely. Her hips were firm, tear drop shaped, revealing their curves as the silk dress clung to her body. The girl was perfumed, clean, with tasteful makeup. Her olive-shaped green eyes were framed by her light brown hair, small ears, dainty nose, and well-formed lips. She was well-fed and cared for, but subject to Moriarty's brutality and volatile whims.

"Yes, Professor. What can I get for you?" she asked in a silky, attractive, feminine voice. She could not have been more than twenty years old. Young, fresh, beautiful, and his.

"I want to have dinner at the Savoy this evening. Please get my usual table and buy out the several tables around it so that I can have my privacy. I will have dinner at 8:00 o'clock. I will need a suitable escort from our stable, and she should be cleaned up and dressed appropriately. You know my taste, please see to it. While we are at dinner, please prepare my pleasure room with my usual instruments. I will want to use it after dinner. Is all that clear, Lilith?" He looked at her with a mixture of lust and dominance.

"Yes, Sir. This will require my absence for the next two hours. Is that satisfactory, Sir?" She was dainty, feminine, alluring, and so under his control. It was intoxicating to him to be in control and to feel her fear and obedience.

"Yes, that will be fine. Understood," he looked at her body under the silk dress and the way she moved as she glided up to him.

"Anything else, Professor?" she asked.

"No. Please carry out my instructions," he said pleased with the effect his words had on her. "Oh, before you go, please lay out my evening wear in my bedroom." Though Moriarty was furious inside he appeared cold and controlled on the outside. There was nothing he could do but await Saacks' report and then decide how to act. He sat on the settee and rested. It was still three hours before dinner, and he slowly fell asleep.

Lilith awakened Moriarty just after 7:00 and walked with him to his bedroom so that he could freshen up and change into his evening attire. "Your private carriage will be waiting for you just outside your back exit promptly at 7:40, and the escort I have selected will be at the Savoy when you arrive." Lilith helped him with his cummerbund and straightened his black bow tie. "Given your earlier instructions about your pleasure room, I selected a suitable escort who will be a willing participant and recipient of your attentions, Sir. I hope that you are pleased."

"Very thoughtful, Lilith. Thank you. Please help me with my cape. Where is my top hat and walking stick?" Moriarty stood in front of a large mirror admiring how he looked and enjoying Lilith's attentions.

"I will bring those presently, Sir. I have prepared a little refreshment before you leave for the evening in anticipation of your desire for a peaceful and restful dinner. A glass of sherry and a cigar await you in the sitting room." She stood back now and looked at Moriarty to ensure that everything was perfect. She walked over and retrieved his top hat and walking stick, quietly awaiting his leaving for the sitting room.

Moriarty walked to the sitting room and lit the cigar, took a long drag, and then took a sip of sherry. The bell in his apartment rang, signifying that someone had pulled the bell rope on the other side of the door.

Lilith glided to the door, slid open the small rectangular door at eye level, and confirmed that it was one of Moriarty's generals. She unlocked the door and ushered the "general" into the room.

"I see that you are going out, Professor. Enjoy your evening. I am sorry to interrupt but wanted to let you know that Saacks's train arrives in London around 8:00 o'clock this evening. Would you like for him to brief you this evening, or in the morning, Sir?" The "general" stood almost at attention and chose his words carefully looking at Moriarty as he smoked his cigar and drank his sherry.

"I will be otherwise engaged after dinner. If he comes around after midnight, I should be able to grant him an interview for a half hour before I retire for the evening. Thank you, that will be all." The "general" made a little bow and left the room. Lilith closed the door and locked it.

Moriarty took out his pocket watch and looked at the time. It was 7:40 and time to leave. He took his top hat and walking stick from Lilith, walked toward the back of his apartment, just before Lilith's bedroom, and unlocked the door that would lead him down two flights and outside the warehouse, where his private carriage waited. Lilith stood just behind him.

"Have a pleasant evening, Sir," she said with a smile as Moriarty walked out the door and began to walk down the steps.

When he arrived at the Savoy, he alighted from the carriage and was almost immediately joined by his escort who had obviously been instructed by Lilith. "Professor," was all she said as she slid her arm in his. They walked gracefully into the Savoy and were greeted by the maître d'.

The dinner was delicious. There was little conversation between Moriarty and his escort. A violin trio played Mozart and the candles burned warmly. He appeared relaxed and well-fed. He finished his after-dinner drink and signaled that he was ready to depart. The maître d' helped them each out of their chairs and escorted them to the exit. One of his guards, who had been waiting outside, opened the door to the carriage as Moriarty and his escort settled in. The guard took care of the bill – as he always did.

"Thank you for a wonderful dinner, Professor." His escort seemed content and a bit tipsy. "I'm not used to such fine food and wine, Sir."

"Yes, don't thank me yet, my dear. The evening's frivolity has yet to reach its crescendo," said Moriarty with a lustful look in his eyes.

His escort giggled. "Oh, yes. I am so looking forward that." She cooed the words and her left hand rubbed seductively up and down his thigh. His blood quickened and he felt aroused.

He reached over and forcefully kissed her, tasting the leftover wine upon her lips. He breathed in her perfumed hair and then, having decided what he would do, he pushed her roughly away. Moriarty instructed his driver to pull into an alley, he couldn't wait until he returned to his apartment to release his anger, his violence.

"In a bit of a saucy mood I see," giggled the escort. "We going to do our dance in the alley in the cold are we?"

"Yes, something like that." Moriarty opened the door to the carriage before it came to a complete stop and pushed the escort out as he followed. She went willingly with him into the dark alley, giggling and playful. Moriarty embraced her with force and fury, moving her against the brick wall of the alley. She laughed. Moriarty placed a gloved hand over her mouth in a vice-like grip before she could react.

All she saw was the sharp glimmer of reflected light as the blade of the knife sliced her throat. As she crumbled to the ground, Moriarty over her body, her world went black. Moriarty exorcised his demons as he tore at her flesh with the surgical knife. He looked lost in a dream state of fury, dominance, and evil. He breathed heavily and lustfully. Afterward, she lay on the ground her life spilling out of her body – dead. Moriarty stood with a long deep sigh. As he turned to walk back to the carriage a shard of light caught his face for just a second. A mask of hatred and evil, pale against the darkness of the alley.

"Why should Jack have all the fun?" he said aloud, laughing as he walked back to the carriage. Just another dead prostitute in a London alley. Just another mystery for the police to ponder. His arms and hands were covered in blood and his formal dress was splattered here and there with blood. The carriage would be cleaned. His clothes laundered. The electric blue dress removed from his victim by the guards who followed. No evidence left behind but a ripped and shattered corpse.

He opened the door to his apartment back at the warehouse and standing dutifully inside was Lilith. She walked him to his bedroom, helped him remove his bloody cloths, helped him into the hot tub she had prepared, and began to wash his body in the warm water. After the bath she helped Moriarty into his dressing gown and slippers.

"I presume you will not have need of the pleasure room this evening. Anything else, sir?" she asked.

"No, Lilith." She left the bedroom with a bow and Moriarty let out a sigh, and stood fully erect, smoothing his dressing gown, the very image of a gentleman. Moriarty walked to his sitting room. He sat at a chair and began to read a mathematical treatise from one of the professors on the Continent. His glass was full, and his cigar lit and laying in a silver tray.

The bell rang again. It was 12:45 and Moriarty motioned for Lilith to get the door. She repeated her practice of earlier at the door and let in Bill Saacks. "What do you have to report?" asked Moriarty taking a drink of his Scotch.

Bill Saacks was obviously nervous. He held his hat in his hands in front of him and hesitated to speak. "Get Bill a drink, Lilith," Moriarty ordered. Bill stood silent as his drink was prepared and given to him. He nodded to Lilith and took a great gulp from his glass. "Sit, sit Saacks, and tell me how our efforts are progressing and about Holmes," he said.

Saacks sat down in a chair next to Moriarty. He took another drink, emptying the glass as Lilith came over carrying the decanter and refilled his drink. "It's not good news,

Professor, I am sorry to say." His voice quivered as he spoke, and his hands shook as he lifted his glass back up to his mouth.

"I expected as much from the tone of your telegram." Moriarty was calm and his voice was low and steady. "Go on. Tell me what you have to report."

"Well sir, there was an accident. We lost a batch, and we lost both the scientist and the buyer's representative. It is dangerous work and despite our best efforts the scientist is dead. The buyer's representative, Gustav Oberstein, is also dead. No one suspects anything as Oberstein was able to escape through the old abbey and was stabbed to death by a lighthouse keeper in a lighthouse several hundred yards from the abbey. A George Dodd has been arrested for the murder, Sir. The local inspector has little energy and no imagination and has no clue about our efforts. The local doctor has determined that the cause of death is murder because of the stabbing. None of the locals suspect anything, Professor.

"All our efforts appear contained and confidential, except for the presence of Holmes at the train station, I was satisfied that our efforts remained secret, Sir." Saacks made his report deliberately and interrupted only by his continued attention to his glass of whiskey. "Bob thinks that the accident and the loss of the scientists has set our schedule back some four weeks. Though I think it may likely be more like three months since we must find and recruit another scientist. As for the buyer, I am hopeful that they will still be interested and not scared away by this incident. I'll leave that to you, Professor. That's the report, Sir.

"As for Holmes I have a man watching him now. I arranged that before coming to see you, sir. I don't know what he knows or why he was there, Professor. But I will know soon enough and be able to tell you shortly." Saacks finished his report and emptied his glass. He waved away Lilith's attempt to refill it. He sat awaiting the Professor's reaction.

Moriarty sat silent and stone-faced. He stared down at this lap, his head oscillating from side to side. "Has the accident made our labs unusable?" he asked.

"No, the sea air coming in from the caves will likely clear it out, Sir. I told Bob to leave it alone for a week or so, and then go in and check the area. The walls and floors will need to be cleaned and all the materials, tables, and lab equipment burned. We will have to replace those, but we should be able to use the lab itself and the raw materials stored there. We have enough of the raw materials left to make a new batch."

Moriarty was silent. He needed to know why Holmes was there. That was the missing piece to his equation. The equation in his mind that calculated the risk and whether it was too great to proceed. Only information about Holmes would supply the missing variable. "Do the others know that you have Holmes under surveillance?" he asked.

"No Sir, I will inform them in the morning. Why, Sir?"

"Because I have already ordered the surveillance of Holmes, and it is likely that has already begun. No need for two on Holmes at the same time. They will only get in each other's way and double the chances of being discovered. Take care of that in the morning."

"Yes, Sir. First thing." Saacks looked eager to leave.

"That will be all, Saacks," said Moriarty with another of his sardonic smiles. Saacks got up and bowed to Moriarty and was led to the door by Lilith. "Oh, and Saacks, I think that Bob Whitaker has outlived his usefulness, don't you?" Moriarty stared at Saacks with cold, dead eyes.

"Yes, Sir. I'll take care of it myself." Saacks walked out the door and jumped as it closed behind him. Another trip to Tynemouth would be required after he found a replacement for Bob.

Chapter 8

Holmes arrived back in Baker Street a little past 8:30 in the evening. Watson had decided to return to his home after the two-day trip, and Holmes was alone. As Holmes put his key in the lock of the front door a look of satisfaction came upon his face. Holmes was home, here, in the streets of London. Where he belonged. He paused for a moment and looked down Baker Street. The familiar sights and sounds surrounded him. As he opened the door, he was met by Mrs. Hudson.

"I thought that might be you," she said. "How was your trip, Mr. Holmes?"

"It was satisfactory, thank you Mrs. Hudson."

"Is the Doctor not with you?" she asked.

"No, he chose to return home for the evening and should be here late tomorrow morning. Do you, by chance, have something to eat? All I have had all day is half a cold meat sandwich. I shared the rest with Watson, and I find that after my long trip, I am hungry." Holmes looked at Mrs. Hudson with pleading eyes.

"Oh, Mr. Holmes. I am used to your ways. Yes, I can bring up dinner in about an hour. Is that sufficient?" Mrs. Hudson looked happy that Holmes wanted to eat.

"Yes, that will be perfect, Mrs. Hudson. Thank you." Holmes climbed the stairs to his room. As he entered, he let out a long sigh. The fire was burning, the gas lights were on, and he recognized the comfortable and familiar place he called home. He went immediately to his bedroom, dropped his two carpet bags, took off his coat, gloves, and hat. He took the folded piece of brown paper containing the clear crystalline substance he had scraped off Oberstein's clothes and laid it on the table by his small chemistry lab. He removed his jacket and put on his favorite mouse grey dressing gown. He walked over to the fire, picked a pipe, filled it with shag tobacco from the Persian slipper, and sat in his chair to enjoy a good smoke.

It had been a long two days, and he looked tired. He reached down between the chair and the fireplace to lift his bow and violin. He began to play a slow, dramatic piece composed by Mozart and lost himself in the music.

As he played, Mrs. Hudson came in with the plates and silverware. She paused and listened as Holmes played the piece. Pipe in mouth, eyes closed, lost in the music, Holmes was much better than he admitted, having taken lessons since the age of five. She remained, standing there for several minutes enjoying the piece, and then moved toward the door to check on dinner.

Holmes closed his eyes, and dreamily struck his fingers on the arm of his chair, making little sounds as he did so. His nervous energy was dissipating, and his shoulders began to relax. His head swayed to some imagined music and his lips twitched, smiled, and moved as if his mind had conjured the flow and rhythm of some imagined piece of music.

"It's not much, mind you," said Mrs. Hudson interrupting his reverie as she carried in a serving tray. "I have what's left of a roasted chicken, some peas, a bit of gravy, boiled potatoes, some bread and butter, and some good hot tea."

"Thank you, Mrs. Hudson. This will do nicely," said Holmes as he stood up and walked over to the table. "Perhaps some sherry to go with the chicken?" he asked.

Mrs. Hudson walked over to the small cabinet where Holmes stored the sherry and brought it to the table with a glass. "Here you go, Mr. Holmes. Glad to have you home. I wish you would play like that more often, instead of that incessant scraping that you usually do when you are thinking or aggravated. It is so nice to hear." Holmes looked up at her and just smiled as he took a bite of potato dipped in the gravy. "I'll leave you to your meal." She smiled at Holmes, turned, and left the room. Holmes could hear her muttering to herself as she walked down the stairs.

Holmes finished his dinner, he stood up and walked to one of the windows to look out. It was getting late. The night was clear, but cold. The snow was still present, but some had melted during his trip to the northeast. Few people walked down the street and those who did were dressed in evening wear, clearly returning from dinner, a play, or a concert. Two or three hansoms moved up and down the street.

Holmes finished his sherry and was about to turn and walk back to his chair by the fire when he suddenly stopped and looked down the street. There was a poorly dressed, blind beggar, with his white cane in front of him, leaning against a building a bit down the street, smoking. Holmes looked at the beggar in the dim light studying him. He watched the man for a minute or so and then the beggar simply receded into the shadows and Holmes could see him no more.

Holmes returned to his chair by the fire. Despite being tired, Holmes could not sleep until he had thought through the problem of Oberstein, the lighthouse, and the events of the past few days. As he had said to Watson many times before, this affair was indeed a three-pipe problem. He picked his long-stemmed cherry wood pipe, filled it with tobacco, lit it with a flaming piece of coal he had retrieved from the fire with the long tongs, and sat down to think it out. Hours passed as he sat and smoked and thought through the problem.

The fire crackled and popped. Its yellow, white, orange, and red flames danced in the air as the smoke rose lazily up the chimney. The fire was dazzling to a sleepy mind and in his tiredness Holmes's head began to nod, but suddenly, as if some thought had occurred to him, his eyes opened wide. He sat erect in his chair, and he said allowed, "Dragon!" He had it.

Chapter 9

Bill Saacks was back at the warehouse first thing in the morning. He looked tired from his long trip back to London and his late-night report to the Professor. Two or three other "generals" had arrived at the warehouse early and were milling about.

"Bill, how's the Tynemouth project coming along?" asked Harry Pennyworth, a short, stout, and ruthless man whose left eye continuously twitched, thus his nickname, "Twitch."

"We've had a bit of bad luck. Lost the scientist, the buyer's representative, and a batch." Saacks looked hesitant to give this report to the likes of Twitch, who he knew would sell his mother to the devil himself to move up in the organization or gain favor with the Professor. But there was a code amongst them that called for openness and truth, even when reporting failure – perhaps especially when reporting failure.

"I'll be damned. Dangerous work. How'd the Professor react to that news?" Pennyworth's feigned concern was transparent from the light in his eyes, even from the eye that twitched.

"Well, I'm still here aren't I, Twitch? That's the good news. I must replace Bob and you know what that means. Going to be thinking about that this morning. I need someone who can move in without causing suspicion, who is ruthless enough to get this done on an accelerated schedule, and who can recruit and motivate a new scientist." Saacks's head was hanging, as he talked about disposing of Bob.

Pennyworth grunted and went on about his business, displaying no signs of concern. Saacks, having got some tea, went to his office and began to thumb through his file of three-by-five manila cards with short biographies and the talents of independent contractors the syndicate used from time-to-time to carry out special assignments. The list included good prospects to rough someone up, to apply torture, to kidnap and to murder someone if you wanted a fall guy and did not want the organization implicated in any way. There were also the names of professional assassins who would do the job neatly, quietly, and without raising suspicion. This latter list was short – it had three names. These people were generally intelligent, very well-organized, and perfectionists. They could be counted on to get the job done right.

Saacks stopped his search and lit a cigarette. From his past experience the syndicate needed someone who would be ignored or accepted by the community in Tynemouth without a second look. Someone whose presence would not draw any attention, or if it did draw attention, no one would ever suspect the person of any criminal conduct. "I need a woman who will blend in. Be inconspicuous, effective, organized, intelligent, and ruthless," he aloud to himself.

He started looking at the three cards in front of him again. There was only one woman in the deck. He stopped to read the summary provided on the card. The card read:

Name: Saint John, Rebecca. Prefers "Becca."

Educated: Royal Holloway Academy.

Description: Intelligent. Beautiful. Cunning. Ruthless.

Skills: Contract killer. Prefers to kill men. Five-year career. Three kills.

Style: Ice pick to base of skull. Seductress.

Working: Smythe's Fine Art Gallery – art curators and sellers.

Aliases: Margaret Jerome, Mademoiselle Fahrney.

Notes: Good reputation for professionalism. Subcontracted to three jobs over past five years, all successful. Expensive but always delivers the desired results. Discreet. He has approved of her use.

"She looks interesting," he mumbled to himself.

Saacks left the warehouse and hailed a hansom. "Smythe's Fine Art Gallery, Chelsea, by the Victoria and Albert Museum," he told the driver. It was not a long trip. Just a little over twenty minutes if the bridge were down. He lit another cigarette and breathed in the relaxing smoke, expelling it in a large cloud with a sigh. The bridge was down. He could just see the warehouse from the bridge. The hansom took him through the London streets and he was soon close to his destination.

"Drop me off a couple of streets down," he told the driver. "Here's a sovereign, wait here for me."

"Yes, sir!" The driver was looked happy, holding the sovereign.

Saacks walked the length of three streets and across the street from the art shop where Becca worked. From across the street, he looked. It was a typical shop to buy and sell art with a large store window containing framed paintings and statuary. He watched for several minutes, smoking a cigarette. He looked down both sides of the street and waited. He finished the cigarette, crossed the street, and entered the shop. A bell hung over the door and rang in a light tinkle, announcing his presence as he entered.

Inside it was not more than fifty feet deep and seventy feet wide. The shop contained more of what was in the window. The place had the feeling of an art museum. There was a young woman sitting in a chair towards the back of the store, in one of the corners, playing a violin. There was hot tea in a kettle made of fine china with matching cups. He poured himself a cup of tea with milk and sugar and sipped while he waited and looked around.

From a door in the back of the shop a woman entered the room. She was a beautiful woman. Even from a distance and in the conservative Victorian dress she wore, her dainty form was evident as she walked to a waiting customer by a painting, her feminine hands clasped in front of her. She stood with grace and confidence. There was an air of refinement about her. She turned and looked in Saacks' direction. Her face was small and dainty, her eyes were green, and shaped like almonds.

Becca appeared to notice Saacks as soon as she came through the door. As she spoke with an inane customer about the availability of a painting from a particular artist, she sent searching, quick glances in Saacks' direction. As she finished with the customer, she turned and walked smoothly toward Saacks. When she was still five feet away, she said, "Good morning, sir. Is there anything I can help you find? Are you interested in a particular style or school, or are you more inclined toward a specific artist?" Her green eyes were locked on his and her slight smile was friendly and inviting.

Saacks, in a voice just above a whisper so only she could hear it, said, "Mademoiselle Fahrney?" Becca stiffened slightly but then regained her control.

"Why?" she asked.

"A mutual friend of ours, a professor, has interest in commissioning a special piece of work and would like to retain you for the project. I am his agent for this purpose. Might you be interested?"

Becca stopped and titled her head looking curious. "Well, we do specialize in special commissions, and I would be happy to discuss it with you further. Such commissions are usually expensive. Does your friend, the professor, appreciate that aspect of the transaction?" She demurely leaned against a small desk and looked at Saacks with her tilted head.

"Yes, I am sure that he understands there will be a cost associated with his commission, but we get ahead of ourselves. When would you like to meet to discuss the details and work out the…arrangements?"

"I find my schedule quite open at the moment. I am happy to discuss the details and the terms at a time convenient for the Professor."

"I am afraid that the Professor's time is very valuable, and he is much in demand at the moment, which is why he has asked me to represent his interest in the matter. When can you speak with *me*?"

Becca's lips curled into a pout, and her face showed disappointment and sadness. Her eyes looked down and she said nothing for several seconds. Then she took a breath, heaving her shoulders first up and then down. "That really is too bad. It is my practice to meet with the client personally to ensure that we have an understanding concerning the details of the commission so as not to disappoint. I am afraid that I must insist on it." She reached out and lightly touched Saacks' forearm and her fingers ran down his arm to just above his wrist. "Why don't you speak with the Professor and come round again when he has agreed. Thank you for coming in. Are you sure I can't interest you in a vase?" With that Becca turned around and walked to another client who was looking at a statue, ending the interview.

Saacks stood silently not knowing what to do or say. Finally, he said, "Thank you Miss. I'll come back around when you are less busy and discuss the commission. Good day." Becca turned toward him slightly and gave him a dainty wave.

Becca had performed three jobs for the Professor without having met him. The Professor's reputation preceded him and Becca, like many members of the London criminal world, knew the name, the reputation, but not the man. It was a dangerous game she was playing at. Anyone trying to meet the Professor in person was gambling with their lives.

Chapter 10

Watson stepped out of the hansom, arriving at Baker street just after 9 o'clock in the morning. He wondered what kind of mood he would find Holmes in. He still had keys to 221B, so he let himself in the front door and walked up the stairs to Holmes's rooms. As he opened the door, he immediately noticed that the gas lamps had not been turned on and the fire was out. He lit the lamps and walked over to the fireplace to put some fresh coal in and start up a fire. Once that was accomplished, he walked quietly over to Holmes's bedroom and peeked in.

"Watson, I assure you that I am awake. I simply have not had the motivation to get out of bed yet. Now that you are here, that gives me the motivation I need." Holmes sat up and moved to the edge of the bed. He still wore his clothes from the day before and his grey robe.

"Don't get up on account of my presence, Holmes. If you need the rest, please carry on." Watson was looking at Holmes and it was clear that Holmes had had a late night.

"No, give me two minutes to wash up and I'll be right out," said Holmes with a rub of his face and head.

Watson walked back over to his chair by the fireplace and sat down. He had breakfasted already and was not hungry. "Do you want me to ask Mrs. Hudson to bring up anything for you to eat? Some coffee? Some tea?"

Holmes was washing his face from water poured in a basin. "Some coffee would be nice, yes. I ate late last night, so no breakfast if you please."

Watson stood and walked toward the door. As he arrived and opened it, he met Mrs. Hudson who jumped at his sudden appearance. "You scared the wits out of me, Doctor!" she said.

"I am sorry, Mrs. Hudson. I was just coming down to ask if we could get some coffee brought up?" Watson's face was all apologies.

"Certainly, I'll be right back up as soon as I catch my breath." Mrs. Hudson was holding her right hand against her chest and carrying a newspaper with her left. She handed the newspaper to Watson and turned round to go back downstairs. Watson thanked her and then walked back to his chair to look over the newspaper. Holmes walked in slowly and sat in his chair opposite Watson.

"Have you heard from Mrs. Watson and how her trip to the Continent is going?" he asked.

"Yes. When I arrived home last night there was a letter from her. Thank you for asking. She is enjoying her trip to Spain. Not as cold as here, of course. She is in the southern part of Spain on the Mediterranean, where the weather is comparatively nice this time of year. The trip is good for her health, and I suspect that she is taking in the waters while there. The fresh sea breezes should do her a world of good."

"Ah, well I am glad for that and glad that her absence means that you can be back in Baker Street, in your old chair, and helping me with this case." Holmes smiled warmly at Watson.

"You're in a good mood this morning, Holmes."

"Yes, despite a late night, I slept very well. A good dinner and a good night's sleep can do wonders. Did you happen to notice a blind beggar along Baker Street when you arrived?"

"No, Holmes. Should I have?" Watson was all curiosity about why Holmes asked the question.

"Here's Mrs. Hudson with the coffee. Thank you, Mrs. Hudson." Holmes stood and went to the table to pour himself a cup of coffee. "I noticed the blind beggar last night. I saw him twice, or rather I saw him once and the last ten inches of his white cane another time. It is just possible that our rooms are being watched."

"I am sorry, Holmes, but did I hear you right? A blind beggar is *watching* our rooms?" Watson looked at Holmes incredulously.

"Yes. He is known in the criminal world as Blind Bart. He is a flim-flam man who feigns to be blind and makes his living begging and occasionally a few petty robberies. He has been arrested once or twice, but never convicted. He seems always fortunate enough to have an excellent solicitor whom he could not possibly afford. He works for somebody else who pays his way, I should think. Right now, he is being paid to watch these rooms. I think he may have noticed that I took him from the window last night. He will be more careful today. I doubt we see him."

"Why would he be watching these rooms, Holmes?" Watson looked concerned.

"I think that our little Tynemouth case is gaining some attention in the criminal world. This is a much bigger game that we play than merely a stabbing in a lighthouse, Watson. Blind Bart's presence confirms that. No, this is a much bigger case. First Oberstein, now Blind Bart. My original suspicions are being borne out." Holmes stopped stirring his coffee and took a thoughtful sip. "What do you make of the case so far, Watson?"

"I must confess that I make little of it so far. Seems like a series of unrelated and perplexing events. There are a great deal more questions than answers at this point. What is clear to me is that Oberstein was stabbed in the lighthouse by Dodd after a struggle over his dagger. Probably self-defense. A good solicitor should get him off."

"Humm, what do you make of Dodd's report that Oberstein yelled, 'The gruel. Drank it'?"

"Holmes, Dodd clearly misunderstood. No one in terrible pain and in the throes of death would possibly waste his last breaths in this world saying, 'The gruel. Drank it.' Dodd either heard wrong or Oberstein was stark raving mad. In either case, it seems to me that the phrase means nothing and could have no bearing on the solution to the case."

"For the sake of argument, assume that Dodd reported what he heard accurately, from his perspective. Tell me then, what do you make of it?" Holmes was playing with Watson and Watson knew it. He took another sip of his coffee.

"Holmes, if you have figured out what Oberstein meant, then please tell me. I can't make any sense of it." Watson was frustrated, but he knew Holmes liked his little games and the theatrics of revealing his conclusions.

"Not so fast, Watson. Follow me a little further. Assume that Dodd reported accurately what he thought he heard. Oberstein was German. Put those two facts together and what conclusions do you draw?"

"That Oberstein was mad and was yelling whatever came to his fevered mind, whether it made any sense or not. Holmes, in his physical condition, he must have been in great pain. A pain that drove him mad. Being German, perhaps he was merely saying the first English words that came to mind. Making no sense, but nevertheless, he yelled them. That is, assuming as you asked, that Dodd reported what he heard correctly." Watson looked at Holmes with a frustrated and blank expression.

"I see that you are in no mood to be contemplative. I will explain it to you then. But I will do so with a series of questions and see if you make the same deduction I did early this morning sitting in that chair. Agreed?" Holmes looked amused.

"Yes, of course Holmes. It's not that I am not contemplating the case, it's that the case presents nothing from which I can deduce anything helpful." Watson took a long drag from the cigar, blew out the blue smoke, and settled in his chair, shaking off a feeling of frustration and embarrassment.

"Watson, I assure you that it's an exceedingly difficult question. Your inability to see through the fog and arrive at the light is perfectly understandable. I admit that my solution to the question is likely one of the best deductions that I have made in some time. Let us start. What language did George Dodd speak?"

"Well, English of course."

"Yes. What was Oberstein's natural and first language?"

"Being German, I would assume German."

"Good so far. When a man is angry, frightened, in pain, near death, and wishes to communicate, does he naturally speak in an adopted language or in the language of his birth?"

"Well, usually a man tends to revert to his native tongue when in a heightened emotional or physical state. If suddenly surprised or if in great pain. If in terrible fear or in shock. I have seen many patients and even Indian soldiers on the battlefield when shocked or wounded revert to their native tongue, thus becoming perfectly incapable of communicating what is wrong with them." Watson was now interested and curious where Holmes was going with his logic.

"Exactly, Watson. Given his physical state, as you pointed out before, in great pain, near death, in what language would you expect Oberstein, a German, to be speaking when in such a state?"

"I see what you are getting at Holmes. Oberstein would have reverted to German. As I remember it, Dodd said he thought he was speaking German. But clearly attempting to communicate with Dodd, who only knew English, Oberstein said the only words in English that came to his fevered mind. But it made no sense."

"Did he, Watson? Is it not more likely that he never uttered a single English word and that his entire soliloquy was in German? Is it not much more likely that Dodd, who was attempting to make sense of what Oberstein was yelling, heard the only phrase that his mind thought was English and that is what he reported?" Holmes had a twinkle in his eye and a smile on his face. He finished his coffee and put the cup down on the table.

Watson sat in silence contemplating what Holmes was suggesting. "Holmes, if what you say is true, and Dodd reported what he heard accurately, then we need to find some German phrase or phrases that correspond to the sounds, 'The gruel. Drank it.' But that might take days or weeks."

"Very good, Watson. You have arrived at the first step along the path to understanding this part of our little mystery. I do not think however that it will take days or weeks. I did it in a matter of a couple of hours last night." Holmes looked at

Watson from the corner of his eye, his face set in a smile of pride and accomplishment.

"Tell me, Holmes. What does it mean?" Watson sat on the edge of his seat.

Holmes walked from the table to his chair across from Watson and sat down. He picked up his pipe from the floor where he had left it the previous night, emptied it, filled it with tobacco, and began the slow ritual of lighting it.

"Holmes! Do not keep me in suspense. Tell me!" Watson was all excitement now.

"Oberstein was indeed yelling only in German, Watson. Dodd, who knew only English, was trying to make sense of it in English. But what made no sense to Dodd or to us in English, makes perfect sense in German. Oberstein was yelling, 'Der grune drache,' or in English, 'the Green Dragon.'" Holmes took a deep drag from his pipe and let out a triumphant cloud of smoke.

Watson sat there for several seconds staring at Holmes in dumbfounded disappointment. "But, Holmes, that makes no more sense than, 'The gruel. Drank it.' How does that possibly help us resolve the case?"

Holmes was let down by Watson's reaction. He turned his face away from Watson, looking at the fire and then turned back toward him. "Watson, when a man is dying and in terrible pain, and comes upon someone unexpectedly, his natural and overwhelming inclination is to tell that person the cause of what ails him. Remember this, Watson, when we finally resolve this case, there will be a critical fact associated with the reference to a green dragon, either figuratively or metaphorically." Holmes stopped. His mood had changed. He was disappointed by Watson's reaction to his brilliant piece of deduction.

Watson sat quietly for several minutes trying to understand what Holmes was saying and what it meant, if anything, to the case. Both men smoked but did not converse. Watson was not confident that what Holmes had concluded was correct, and even if correct, that it meant anything other than the mindless delusions of a mind made mad by pain, injury, and terror. He looked at Holmes who was looking into the fire and tapping the arm of his chair with the fingers of his free hand.

"Holmes, I am sure that you are correct that Oberstein was yelling in German and never uttered an English word. I am also sure that Dodd, trying to make sense of what he was yelling, interpreted the German phrase assuming that it was spoken in English. Given the closeness of the English phrase to the German, I will concede that it is probably true that Oberstein was yelling, 'Der grune drache.' But I do not see how that helps us resolve the case. I am sorry."

Holmes looked up from the fireplace at Watson. "Thank you, Watson. I expect too much, I am sure."

Watson exhaled in frustration and went silent again. Holmes reached over and picked up the newspaper that rested on the floor in front of Watson and began to look through it.

Both men stayed silent for some time. The silence was interrupted by Mrs. Hudson's soft knock on the door.

"Yes, Mrs. Hudson," said Holmes.

Mrs. Hudson walked into the room holding an envelope. "A message for you Mr. Holmes. It's from the Foreign Office." She stood just in front of the door on the other side of the settee holding the envelope as if it were a national secret. "The messenger is waiting downstairs for your reply."

Holmes stood and walked to Mrs. Hudson and took the envelope. He opened it and read it quickly. He held the paper and envelope down by his left leg and moved his right hand and forefinger to his lips. He was thinking.

As Saacks walked out of the art shop, he was thinking about Becca. She was confident in herself, there was no doubting that, but he had to decide whether he would suggest a meeting with the Professor. Was she worth it? He lit a cigarette as he walked back to the hansom. He took his time, walking slowly. As he got to the end of the first block, he felt a tug at his left elbow and turned around to see Becca standing there.

"Whatever commission you have, I can do it. I want in. I have skills. I am smart and professional. I have the advantage that I am a woman, and no one suspects women of being capable of doing what I can do. You tell our mutual friend that he needs me. That I can bring whatever he has in mind to fruition. You tell him, I want the job!" Becca's eyes had changed. They were not seductive. Her eyes were menacing, and her voice was determined and cold.

Saacks nodded, and with that she turned and walked quickly back to the shop. He stood, watching her walk back. He turned and continued his walk back to the waiting hansom. All his doubts were gone. She was worth it.

"What does the message say, Holmes?" Watson looked both curious and concerned. Holmes handed Watson the message and he read it. The short letter was on the official Foreign Office stationery, and read as follows:

> I received your telegram informing the Foreign Office of Gustav Oberstein's death. I appreciate the information. We have been watching Oberstein for some weeks and our man lost him two weeks ago. We had no idea he was in Tynemouth and have no idea why. We want to speak with you on a matter involving the security of Her Majesty's kingdom. I would like to visit at a time convenient for you. Please let the messenger know when you are available, and I will endeavor to be at Baker Street at that time.
>
> Sincerely,

Sir Trelawney Hope

Foreign Minister to Her Majesty

"Holmes, you were right. This case does have much larger repercussions than I at first expected. I am sorry for ever doubting you." Watson held the letter in his right hand and placed his left on Holmes's forearm.

"That's quite alright, Watson." Holmes moved to his writing desk and took a pen and paper out and wrote a quick note, folded it, sealed it with wax, and handed it to Mrs. Hudson. "Please give this to the messenger. Thank you, Mrs. Hudson." Mrs. Hudson turned and walked quickly out of the room.

"What did you write?" asked Watson.

"The only thing I could write, Watson. I invited Sir Trelawney Hope to visit Baker Street this afternoon at 1:30. I warned him that our rooms may be watched and asked him to take appropriate precautions. It is a quarter past eleven now, that should give us time to prepare for his visit. Do you remember him, Watson?" Holmes was rubbing his hands together.

"Well, yes of course. He and the Prime Minister engaged us in the matter of the missing letter from the foreign potentate. As I recall, you solved the case and saved his wife's honor. Though he is unaware of the latter."

"Yes, indeed. He has risen in the world since then. A knight of the realm and the Foreign Minister. I dare say my little part in the affair surely had a positive effect on his career.

Well, from charwomen to the Foreign Minister in the same week. These walls have certainly seen their fair share of interesting people." Holmes walked back to his room while he took off his robe. "Could you tidy up a bit in here while I get ready, Watson?"

"Certainly, Holmes." Watson began picking up newspapers, Mrs. Hudson walked in with a broom, dustpan, and feather duster. "Mrs. Hudson, you are truly indispensable. Thank you."

"Well, it's not every day that we have the Foreign Minister making a visit. We must tidy up." Mrs. Hudson began to sweep up ash, spent pipe plugs, and spilled tobacco from the floor as Watson organized newspapers and tried to put things in order.

Saacks arrived back at the warehouse just before noon. He had two hours before the afternoon meeting with the Professor where he would report on his meeting with Becca and make a recommendation regarding whether the Professor should allow a meeting. He sat at his desk, having missed the morning meeting of the "generals" and looked over the handwritten notes of the "generals'" reports. He smoked a cigarette and drank a cup of tea. He could not focus on the meeting notes; instead, his mind was focused on what to do about Becca.

Saacks left his office and retrieved Becca's biographical dossier from the file room and returned to his desk to read it. Rebecca Saint John, a/k/a Margaret Jerome a/k/a Mademoiselle Fahrney, was an accomplished killer and seductress.

Though she had been hired on contract to perform three assassinations for the syndicate, she had perfected her craft on several other men before that. She had never been arrested and had not ever been suspected in any of the crimes. She was adept at using disguises and clearly planned her projects to the last detail.

Becca was a graduate of the Royal Holloway Academy where she had obtained a degree in European art history and literature. Any woman who was educated to that degree was either of high society or very unusual. The way she planned her murders showed a keen mind, a talented thinker, and someone who left nothing to chance. She was perfect for this job.

Holmes and Watson waited for the arrival of the Foreign Minister. It was almost half one and his arrival was imminent. Holmes stood at the window looking out at Baker Street. He could not see Blind Bart, but it was just as likely that the blind beggar was on this side of the street, so it was possible he was close but could not be seen from the window. As Holmes looked out a black carriage bearing no coat of arms or identification pulled up in front of 221B and almost immediately a man in a hooded black cloak descended and walked to the front door. Holmes heard the bell and the sound of the door opening almost immediately. Clearly Mrs. Hudson had been alert and waiting as well.

Holmes turned and nodded to Watson who was seated by the fire. At Holmes's nod Watson stood up at attention and waited for the Foreign Minister to arrive at the door. Sir Trelawney Hope arrived at the open door a few moments later. Mrs. Hudson escorted him in and carried the minister's cloak, coat, hat, and gloves.

"Sir Trelawney Hope to see you, Mr. Holmes," said Mrs. Hudson and with a slight curtsy she left the room, closing the door behind her.

"Sir, it is a pleasure to see you again. I trust that you and Lady Hope are doing well. Please, have a seat and tell me what I can do for you." Holmes was formal but smiled and motioned for the minister to take a seat on the settee.

"It is indeed good to see you Mr. Holmes. I still remember and I remain most grateful for the assistance you provided me in locating the letter that was taken from my dispatch box." Holmes looked at him with surprise. "Yes, Mr. Holmes, I say 'taken' because I am sure that it was. You have your reasons for not telling me how it was returned, and I will not inquire further into the matter. Dr. Watson, it is good to see you as well." The Minister gave a nod of his head to Watson, who answered the nod with one of his own. All three sat down in their respective chairs, Holmes and Watson waiting for the minister to sit first.

"I must say that I found your response to my telegram, curious," said Holmes. "I knew that there was more to the death of Gustav Oberstein, but I had no idea that it involved a matter of the security of Her Majesty's kingdom. Please tell me more." Holmes sat in his chair leaning forward, his elbows resting on each knee, with his hands together as if in prayer.

"Mr. Holmes, I don't believe for a minute that you did not have some inclination that Oberstein's death was of some national importance to the Crown. Such is my faith in your abilities." The minister smiled knowingly as he looked at Holmes.

"Well, perhaps I had an inclination that the death was of significance, but I assure you, I had drawn no firm conclusions on the subject. Please, tell my why you are here." Holmes answered the minister with a wry smile of his own and sat back in his chair. Watson took his notepad and pencil from his jacket pocket, opened it to a blank page, and was ready to take notes.

"Gentlemen, I can assure you that what I am about to tell you is a secret of the Crown. Doctor, I request that you not take notes and that neither of you reveal anything that I am about to tell you. I am afraid I must ask for your word as gentlemen." The minister looked serious and solemn.

"I give you my word," said Watson as he closed his notepad and replaced it in his jacket pocket.

"And I as well, Your Lordship. Now, please tell us what we can do for Her Majesty." Holmes was growing impatient with the formality.

"Quite right, Mr. Holmes. We have been hearing rumors and chatter for the past two months from our agents on the Continent about the potential for a new weapon coming on the market. The weapon was being developed by private actors not by another government. That much we know, but little else. I ordered that all known agents of European governments and free-lance agents in England be followed. They were followed and watched day and night. Gustav Oberstein was one of the foreign agents we had under surveillance. Only a handful of people in the government knew about our intelligence and fewer still knew that we had foreign agents under surveillance and who they were.

"Gustav Oberstein was of particular importance because we had reason to believe that Germany was especially interested in buying this new weapon. Several bank transactions we became aware of were made between German banks and Mr. Oberstein's bank accounts in Switzerland. Transfers were made from Mr. Oberstein's Swiss banks to his bankers here in London. The amounts were quite large and made in the name of one of Mr. Oberstein's known aliases. The transfers occurred a little over two weeks ago. Shortly afterward, the men we had watching Oberstein lost him, and we did not know of his whereabouts until your telegram, Mr. Holmes."

Holmes's face looked both concerned and excited. "You say that the transfers from the Swiss accounts to

Oberstein's London bankers occurred a little over two weeks ago?"

"Yes. Is that of significance, Mr. Holmes?" asked the Minister.

"Possibly, yes. Oberstein had been in Tynemouth for about ten days before he met his end at the lighthouse. It is very possible that he was negotiating a purchase and was on hand to assure himself that the weapon was worth the price. Having assured his principals he could purchase the weapon, and having received the money to do so, he wanted to be sure of the weapon's efficacy and value before completing the transaction." Holmes's eyes had a faraway look about them as his experience and imagination toiled and his deductions flowed from his mind's work. He sat silent for several minutes and then said, "I am sorry, Your Lordship, please continue."

"Well, there is not much more to tell, Mr. Holmes. I was hoping that you could tell me what you have discovered." The minister crossed his legs, placing both hands on the crossed knee and looked with anticipation at Holmes. Watson looked at Holmes in anticipation as well.

"You have no information about what kind of weapon is being developed? How it will be deployed? It's explosive yield, assuming it's an incendiary or bomb?" asked Holmes.

"No, I assure you all we know is that it is a new kind of weapon, and it is thought to be quite deadly." The minister looked concerned. His face was a mask of worry and anxiety.

"Well, I can tell you nothing more until my investigation is more mature, Your Lordship. I will of course inform you immediately of the results of any inquiries I make or developments in my case. Am I to assume that if I can arrange to buy the weapon on the open market, that Her Majesty would fund such an effort?"

"Yes, of course. If it means that we have exclusive possession and that the parties involved are silenced. I am sure that the Prime Minister would recommend such a course of action and that the Queen would agree." The minister sounded more confident than he looked. He was clearly committing himself further than his current mandate allowed. "But, Mr. Holmes, we have tried that already. Whoever is selling the weapon has very good intelligence and our agents, posing as potential buyers, have been rebuffed in their efforts. It is a path that we have abandoned."

Holmes looked at Watson and then at the minister, "That is useful information, Your Lordship. It means that the persons involved are highly organized and well-informed. That significantly narrows the possibilities. In fact, it may narrow it very much."

The minister uncrossed his legs and lightly slapped each with his hands, "Well then gentlemen, you will proceed along your chosen course, and we shall proceed on ours. I propose that we each keep the other informed of progress." The minister stood and prepared to leave. "By the bye, Mr. Holmes. Why do you think your rooms are being watched?"

"Because I noticed the man who is watching them. It appears likely that the person involved in developing this new weapon is concerned by my presence in Tynemouth and so is keeping me under surveillance."

"You said, 'person,' Mr. Holmes. If I had to guess, I think you already have somebody in mind." The minister stood looking at Holmes intently.

"Ahh, Minister. We all have our little secrets. I am not yet prepared to reveal mine. In good time. In good time." Holmes smiled and shook the minister's hand. Watson gave a respectful bow, and the minister left the room after Mrs. Hudson, who had apparently been waiting on the landing, helped him with his hooded black cloak. Holmes and Watson walked to the window in time to see the minister quickly get in his carriage and drive away. Watson noticed that the windows were covered in black shades.

"Well, what do you make of that, Holmes?" asked Watson.

"The case grows more complex, Watson. Complexity usually means enlightenment. It is the mundane that is difficult. The complex reveals itself to the careful observer." Holmes walked back to his chair, retrieved an old clay pipe, filled it, lit it, and began to smoke. "I would appreciate two hours of silence, Watson. There is much here to think about."

Watson raised both arms in front of him, palms out, in a gesture of acquiescence. He walked to his own chair, retrieved the newspaper from the table along the way, got a cigar, and sat down to read and smoke in silence. Holmes, legs crossed and sitting in his chair like a great Buddha, was in deep thought, smoke encircling his head and chest.

Saacks sat at the conference table with the other "generals" and the Professor listening to the reports from the others and awaiting his turn to discuss the Tynemouth project and Rebecca Saint John; consumed by his own thoughts. The Professor seemed his normal self this morning and was not particularly angry or disagreeable. His turn came and with a deep breath, after clearing his throat, Saacks began. "As you are aware Professor, we have had some setbacks with our project in Tynemouth. We lost the scientist, the buyer's representative, and the only viable batch. We still must clean up the mess at the lab from the accident, and recruit and motivate a new scientist. We can't go down into the lab for a few more days to be safe. I have sent Bob three additional men to help with the clean-up and they will remain until Bob's replacement has arrived, and they are ordered to return.

"I have ordered my man off watching Holmes, and Blind Bart is continuing in that role at present. We haven't received a report from him yet, but we are confident that if anything out of the ordinary occurs, he will send a report through one of our messengers in the area.

"As for Bob's replacement," Saacks hesitated, "I have researched suitable persons and have gone out to meet the one that I believe to be best suited to the circumstances. I am recommending that we retain Rebecca Saint John, who has served us well as a contract assassin with three successful kills. I have met her and researched her experience and given the situation that we find ourselves in, I am certain she will do well. I have spoken with her, and she is eager to assist us, but with one prerequisite."

"Please remind me about Miss Saint John's work for us?" asked the Professor. Saacks went through Becca's history. "She sounds like a formidable contractor indeed. What is the prerequisite?"

"Professor, she doesn't want to take the job under contract, but wants to join the syndicate as a member, and she wants to meet with you personally." Saacks gulped, making eye contact with the Professor on the last part of his sentence.

The Professor sat in thought for several minutes as the rest of the room remained perfectly quiet. It was a bold request from someone who was not yet a member of his team and coming from someone who, though experienced, was still new to the profession. Moriarty's anonymity was treasured and protected. A female member of the inner circle was something that he had contemplated before, but no one had yet met the requirements, the demands, or his expectations. He cleared his throat.

"Interesting proposition, Bill. When one of my most trusted 'generals' endorses a new addition to the syndicate, I am loath to disagree. Especially when she is so apparently qualified for the work. But, as you know, my anonymity is sacrosanct. Nothing must put it in jeopardy. Still, she seems interesting and from what you have told me here today, she has enormous potential. This project will be the test that she needs to pass before being given full membership.

"As for the meeting," the Professor paused more for effect than indecision, "I will meet with her, but under conditions that protect my anonymity. Bill, please inform Miss Saint John. She is to be at Kennington Park, tomorrow at three o'clock sharp. She is to come in a hansom and pull up beside the carriage that will be parked along one of the less traveled side paths. The carriage will have drawn curtains and the driver will be wearing a red scarf. She is to alight from her hansom, sending it on its way, and immediately enter the carriage without a word. You will be in the carriage to receive her. I will be dressed as the driver, and we will communicate through the small trap door in the roof of the carriage. You will come armed, Bill, and you will train your pistol at her chest as we speak. One false move or quick gesture and you will fire. Is that understood, Bill?"

"Yes, Sir. Thank you, Sir." Saacks looked relieved.

"If she still doubts that I am who I say that I am, well we will deal with that when the time comes. Is she aware of the tattoo on my right forearm?" The Professor had a tattoo of two snakes entwined in battle on his right forearm. The existence of the tattoo was part of the mystery and folklore that surrounded him, and he knew that many in the criminal world were aware of it.

"I don't know sir, but I will be sure to tell her that if she has doubts, she may ask to see the tattoo." Saacks looked nervous and he clearly wanted the interaction with the

Professor to be over. It was always better not to be the subject of his attention.

"Good. Then we are decided about the meeting. As for Tynemouth and the lab, the accident there along with the presence of Holmes has made that area of operation too dangerous. I agree, Bill, that it needs to be cleaned up and we need to salvage what we can of the equipment and raw materials. Your plans along those lines are fine. But I will need to think about a new location to finish our work. Perhaps one closer to base. I will also contact our network in Germany to ensure the buyers are still interested.

"Thank you, gentlemen. That will be all for this afternoon." The "generals" stood and began to leave. "Bill, if you could stay a minute." Moriarty was staring at Saacks with dead eyes as he made the request for him to stay behind. Saacks sat back down, but the professor did not speak for what seemed like several minutes. When he finally spoke, his voice was low and menacing.

"I will hold you personally responsible for the security of this meeting and for my continued anonymity, Bill. Make no mistake about it. You will pay for any mistakes with your life. Do we have a clear understanding?"

"Yes, Sir. I would expect nothing less. I give you my word that I will take every precaution and I am confident that Becca, uh Miss Saint John, is worth the risk and that I would not make this request if I did not believe that the success of the Tynemouth project was at stake, Sir." Saacks's voice quivered despite his best efforts to remain in control. The professor's eyes never left Saacks's eyes. He stared at him as if to underscore his point. Then the professor's face changed and formed into a smile, and his eyes softened.

"I have confidence in you, Bill. I am certain that you will do everything in your power to ensure the success of this most important project. Come, let us have a drink." As he spoke the professor stood up and he and Saacks walked into the library and towards the small bar. "Tell me what you think of young Miss Saint John, Bill. How has she impressed you?" The Professor poured Scotch into two glasses handing one to Bill.

"Well, sir, she is quite beautiful and can control almost any man, I should think."

"Is she controlling you, Bill?" The Professor's question came in his most gregarious of voices and with a friendly smile on his face.

"No sir. I must confess that like any man I was affected by her raw sexuality, but I have also seen her hard face, her determination, and her danger. I am not affected by her charms, and she does not influence the recommendations that I have made. She will be a good addition to the syndicate, and I believe her sex, her talents, her intelligence, and her looks will serve you well." Saacks drank his Scotch in one gulp, setting the empty glass back down on one of the small reading desks. He wanted to leave.

"Make certain that this continues to be true, Bill. Make certain that remains positively true." The professor's face and voice had taken on their menacing character. Saacks looked pale. "This setback of Bob's has cost me time and materials. It will very probably shake the buyer's trust in our professionalism and ability to deliver. Moving forward, Bill, this is your success or failure, not Bob's and certainly not Miss Saint John's, although she will share in your responsibility. Do I make myself clear, Bill?"

"Yes, Sir. Very clear, Professor."

Chapter 11

Holmes had been sitting, thinking through the problem of the Green Dragon for more than two hours. He had smoked four pipes and the air around him was foul with smoke. He opened his eyes and I looked at Watson who had fallen asleep in his chair, the newspaper on the floor and a book on his lap. It was late afternoon and Holmes looked at his pocket watch. It was almost half past four. Holmes still had things he needed to accomplish, and the afternoon was fading quickly. He stood and took a step toward the sleeping Watson.

"Watson! Watson, wake up," Holmes said with a humorous sound to his voice. He walked past Watson on the way to his bedroom.

Watson awoke with a start and a snort and almost knocked the book off his lap. "Yes, Holmes? Where the devil are you?"

"I am in here. I will be leaving for three hours at least. I have some errands to run. Are you in the mood for dinner at Simpson's? If so, let us meet there at eight o'clock. Is that satisfactory?"

"Yes, Holmes. Very satisfactory. Where are you going?" Watson looked happy to be going to Simpson's..

"I have to send a telegram and stop by the university library for some research. I would ask you to come, but the rest of the afternoon will be spent with my nose in books I'm afraid." Holmes came out of his bedroom with his coat on, his top hat on his head, and putting on his gloves while he held his walking stick in the gloved hand. "I may receive an answer to a telegram before I return. If you would be so kind to tip the messenger and retrieve the telegram for me, I would be grateful." With that Holmes left the rooms and walked down the seventeen steps to Baker Street.

Holmes hailed a hansom telling the driver, "Take me to the telegraph office, driver." He sat in the hansom for the short drive to the telegraph office, asking the driver to await his return. Holmes went into the telegraph office, took a form, and began to address and write the telegram. The telegram was to Inspector MacDonald in Tynemouth and was direct, just one inquiry, "Have you received unexplained reports of missing cats? If so, provide dates." Holmes paid the telegraph officer and walked back to the hansom telling the driver, "University of London Library, if you please." Holmes leaned back in the hansom for the trip to the library lighting his pipe as he went.

It was early evening and Watson was dozing again. He had been sitting in his favorite chair in front of the fire and reading the afternoon newspaper. He heard the bell downstairs and it awakened him. He heard the muffled voices of a man and Mrs. Hudson. He endeavored to be awake, alert, and presentable for Mrs. Hudson's expected arrival. She did not disappoint. Watson had already given Mrs. Hudson some change to give to the anticipated messenger. As Mrs. Hudson walked into the room, after knocking twice, he stood and accepted the telegram from her.

"What are your plans for dinner, doctor?" Mrs. Hudson asked.

"Holmes and I are having dinner at Simpson's this evening at eight. Thank you for asking." Watson looked happy to deliver the news.

"Oh my. I hope that you both enjoy it. I hear that dinner there is excellent." Mrs. Hudson beamed a smile at Watson.

"Thank you, Mrs. Hudson, perhaps I will bring you back some dessert!" Watson was beaming as he made the promise.

"Oh, Dr. Watson, I am not used to such delicacies, but thank you." There was a twinkle in her eyes.

Watson looked at the folded telegram in his hands. He looked like he was about to open it and read it, but hesitated. He laid it on the end table next to his chair. He sat down and began to focus on the newspaper he had been reading before dozing off. Several times he looked over and around the newspaper at the telegram laying on the table. After several minutes of internal battle, he finally picked it up and read it. The telegram said:

FROM: INSPECTOR HAMISH MACDONALD, TYNEMOUTH. STOP. TO: MR. SHERLOCK HOLMES. STOP. REGARDING YOUR INQUIRY ABOUT MISSING CATS. STOP. YES, WE HAVE HAD REPORTS OF FIVE UNEXPLAINED

MISSING CATS. STOP. FOUR PETS, AND ONE VENERABLE CAT WHO, THOUGH FERAL, WAS LOVED BY THE COMMUNITY AND WELL TAKEN CARE OF. STOP. THE ABSENCES OCCURRED DURING THE LAST THREE WEEKS. STOP. NO EVIDENCE OF WHO IS RESPONSIBLE HAS BEEN FOUND. STOP. THANK YOU. INSPECTOR MACDONALD. STOP.

Watson read the text of the telegram with incredulity. "Missing cats? What is Holmes up to? What in God's name could missing cats have to do with the investigation?" he said to himself. He folded the telegram and put it in his jacket pocket. Only Holmes could explain why he had sent a telegram to the inspector with a question about missing cats.

It was now 7:30, and Watson was ready to leave for the restaurant. He put on his coat, his hat, and gloves. He picked his heavy lead-weighted walking stick and left the rooms descending the stairs. As he exited the building, he looked for a hansom. About two streets away, on the same side as 221B Baker Street, stood a blind beggar with his white cane. Almost immediately, he receded into the shadows.

Watson arrived at Simpson's just before eight, walked in after paying the hansom driver, and was greeted by the maître d'.

"Ahh, Doctor Watson, welcome. Are you dining alone tonight?"

"No, no, it will be dinner for two tonight," said Watson.

"A fine lady no doubt, hey Doctor," the maître d' said with a knowing smile.

"No, I will be dinning with Mr. Sherlock Holmes. He should be here presently. By the way, I am married now, so no fine ladies that aren't Mrs. Watson." Watson was red-faced that his reputation had preceded him.

"Fine, we are all perfect discretion here at Simpson's, Dr. Watson. Would you care to wait, or would you like to be seated now?" The maître d' clearly had a reservation as he checked his list while addressing Watson.

"I think I will be seated and enjoy a before-dinner drink while I wait," said Watson.

"Very good, doctor. Please follow me."

He led Watson to a table for two by the window, "What may I get you to drink, Doctor?" he asked.

"I think that I am in the mood for a good Scotch. Surprise me with your choice," Watson said. The maître d' gave a smile and walked away to get Watson's drink.

Watson enjoyed his smokey Scotch while he waited for Holmes. He took the telegram out of his jacket pocket and placed it on the table just as Holmes arrived.

"Good evening, Watson. Is it not good to be back here at Simpson's?" Holmes sat down in the chair across from Watson.

"Yes, Holmes, very good indeed. How was your afternoon of research?"

"Not without its revelations. Is that the answer to my telegram?"

"Yes, the answer came just before I left Baker Street. I must say that it is a bit of a puzzle to me why you asked the inspector about missing cats." Watson looked both amused and curious.

Holmes picked up the telegram and read it. "It was a flight of fancy really. Just an idea I wanted to test. It appears that my intuitive guess was correct as cats are missing in Tynemouth. Well, Watson, what should we eat?" Holmes began to look over the short menu while Watson did the same.

"I am curious, Holmes. What did you research at the library?" Watson leaned into the table placing his forearms on the edge.

"Humm, and if I told you that I spent my time in the medical section of the library, what would you conclude from that Watson?"

"I should think that you were researching potential causes for the blisters and red skin on Oberstein's body. Not to mention the condition of his lung tissue and mucosa."

"Very good, Watson. Yes, that and a bit more. But our waiter is here. Let us order dinner, shall we?"

Holmes was in one of those moods that Watson knew well. It was apparent to anyone who knew him well that

Holmes needed a break from the case, wanted to enjoy a good dinner at his favorite restaurant, and he did not want to reveal his thinking or conclusions.

This evening Holmes talked about bees. It was amazing at what he knew about the subject. He talked about segregating the queen, the wonderous organizational structure of bee society, and the best blossoms for the most aromatic honey.

"Watson, we have much to learn from the bees," he said solemnly. "I fear that the world is on the brink of some great cataclysm, so bent on self-destruction are we. So selfish in our motives. It may not be this year, or the next, but I fear that in the next few years, England will be dragged into a European struggle, the likes of which will make all past conflicts seem tame in comparison. We are on the verge of great discoveries. New inventions come every other day it seems. But we are so volatile a species, we must learn to manage our emotions, our animalistic tendencies, and our baser instincts. Yes, we have much to learn from the bees." Holmes fell silent staring down at his wine, turning the glass in the light, watching the light play off its colors.

The mood had changed. "Well, not tonight anyway, hey Holmes?" Watson put on a happy tone and a big smile. Holmes looked up with weary eyes and nodded with a forced smile.

"Well, I promised Mrs. Hudson that I would bring her dessert. Waiter!" The waiter quickly responded.

"Yes, sir?"

"May I have a crème brulee to take home, please?"

"Of course, sir. I will have one wrapped for you shortly. Remember to pour a little brandy over it and light it with a match before you eat it." The waiter left to complete Watson's order.

"You obviously see more than I have in this tangled web, Holmes." Watson was growing worried and anxious.

"I doubt that Watson, but I probably deduced a lot more. You remember the case we had a few years back that involved Mr. Douglas of Birlstone Manor?"

"Yes, very well. Why?"

"Do you recall that I talked to you and the inspector briefly about evidence that I had gathered over the years of a central hub in the criminal world? A singular mind and presence that was behind many crimes. A mind that seemed to organize half of what was evil in London and almost all that was undetected."

"Yes, Holmes. You said his name, if I recall, is..."

Holmes held up his hand and Watson stopped. "No names here, Watson. It is very possible that he has agents, even here. No, we can talk more about it tomorrow. I am tired Watson. Let us retreat to Baker Street, back to the fire and my violin."

It was Saturday afternoon and Saacks was at the warehouse. He had his revolver in his coat pocket and was waiting for the Professor. Saacks had gone that morning to tell Becca that a meeting had been arranged and what she needed to do. He warned her that a meeting with the Professor, though she desired it, was a dangerous thing. "Be careful what you wish for. Be respectful and be cautious. Do not contradict him in any way. Now that you are in his gaze, you will feel the heat" he had advised her. She had wanted to know more about the project, but he had told her that details would only come after the meeting and the Professor accepted her. She had seemed confident and fearless.

Shortly after 2:15 in the afternoon, the Professor entered the conference room. He was dressed as a carriage driver and carried his hat and gloves. He also carried a large red scarf that Saacks presumed was to cover his face and to act as the prearranged signal.

"Bill, good afternoon. Were you able to meet with Miss Saint John and arrange our meeting?" Moriarty sat down, looking a bit impatient and frustrated by the whole thing.

"Yes, sir. She understands the protocols and will follow them."

Saacks and the Professor sat in silence. Moriarty's head oscillated from side to side. His eyes were focused on the desk in front of him. His face was chiseled in a scowl. They each sat at the table for several minutes without speaking. "A drink before we go?" asked Moriarty.

147

"Yes, sir. That will be welcome. I'll bring the drinks over." Saacks stood and walked into the library and poured two glasses of Scotch. He walked back and handed the Professor his glass.

Moriarty lifted his glass and said, "To our success." Both Moriarty and Saacks drank their glass in one gulp. Moriarty took out a handkerchief and wiped his mouth. "Shall we go?"

Moriarty drove the carriage through the park gates and proceeded toward the back of the park and to a less used side road. Because it was winter, the park was not crowded, and there were few people on the front of the park and none in the back. Moriarty parked the carriage along the side road and waited. He did not have to wait long, within a minute a hansom pulled up and a young lady descended, paid the driver, dismissed him, and opened the carriage door and stepped inside.

When Becca stepped inside the carriage it took a minute for her eyes to adjust to the darkened space and as they did, she recognized Saacks and she recognized a revolver pointed directly at her chest, barely two feet away from her. She instinctively recoiled at the surprising sight of the pistol but recovered very quickly. Her eyes were aglow with anger and her hands were closed into fists. Had she not been wearing gloves her nails might have cut into her hands. She regained her composure.

"Mr. Saacks, I don't find this a very warm welcome. What do you mean pointing that pistol at me in such close quarters?" she asked.

"It's just a precaution, Becca. Don't fret about it. If you mind yourself and follow instructions, all will be fine." Saacks tried to sound both menacing and reassuring at the same time.

"Where is the Professor?"

"We have a protocol about these things, Becca. What'd you think, he would invite you to his rooms for tea?" With that Saacks tapped on the small roof door that allowed communication between the occupants and the driver and opened it. "Professor, allow me to introduce Miss Rebecca Saint John."

"Miss Saint John, I have heard a great deal about you. Bill's description of you does not do you justice. You are indeed a beautiful woman." Moriarty was speaking through the opening in the roof of the carriage down to Becca.

"I'm sorry, but how in God's name am I supposed to know whether the driver is the Professor? He is covered in coat, hat, and scarf. I cannot tell who he is?" Becca looked suspicious.

"Miss Saint John, how would you know it was me had my face been twelve inches from your own? You have never seen me before and would not be able to pick me out of a crowd. My time is valuable, so let us get on with it." The Professor sounded impatient.

"I have heard through the grapevine that the Professor has a tattoo of two fighting snakes on his right forearm. Show me that and I will be satisfied." Becca's voice was more demanding than the situation called for.

Moriarty shifted in his seat and the entire carriage moved on its springs. A minute later and a bare forearm was shoved through the opening in the carriage roof revealing a tattoo of two fighting snakes. "Are you satisfied Miss Saint John?" asked Moriarty.

Becca's entire demeanor changed. "Yes, Professor. I am sorry for doubting you, but I needed to be absolutely certain that it was you I am talking to." Becca's personal became that of an obedient, feminine figure of perfection. "I am flattered that you have chosen me for this special project. I will not disappoint, no matter what the project entails, sir."

"I haven't chosen you for anything yet, Miss Saint John. You must first prove yourself to me by successfully completing two tasks in short order with little fuss and no one the wiser. Are you prepared to do that before I consider you for the project?"

"Yes, sir. I am happy to add to the three jobs I have already performed for you, each of which had very satisfactory conclusions. What would you have me do?"

"Bill will give you the details later, but I wish for you to retire one of our own who recently failed me, and use your talents to recruit, convince, and motivate a young scientist to join the project that has so far foundered in failure and disappointment. When you have accomplished both tasks in a timely manner and to my satisfaction, I will decide whether you are invited in, and, as Bill suggested, meet me over tea. These two things will of course be done by you as a sign of good faith, free of charge, and willingly given. Are we agreed?"

"At my own expense?" Becca looked at Saacks who still had the pistol pointed at her breasts. Saacks pursed his lips and shook his head silently.

"Perhaps you did not hear the part about 'willingly given.' If that is a problem, we will end the interview now, and I will decide whether you live to see another day." Moriarty's voice was cold and sharp like steel.

"It will not be a problem at all, Professor. I willingly give of my talents, skills, and time to serve you and the organization. If it means a chance to be admitted, I will willingly and gladly serve at my expense." Becca's voice was a pitch higher than normal, and her words were said in rapid succession.

"Good, good. Now Miss Saint John, if we can drop you off closer to the hansom routes, I will be happy to do so, or would you simply like to be left here?"

"Thank you, Professor, but I can find my way. You can leave me here." Becca looked eager to exit the carriage as quickly as possible.

"Bill will be in touch with you tomorrow. In the meantime, have a pleasant afternoon." With that, the door shut with a muffled bang.

Saacks put the revolver in his inside jacket pocket over his heart. "I'll stop by the shop tomorrow at 10:30 in the morning and we can discuss the details. Don't be late."

"I look forward to it." With that Becca opened the door and exited the carriage. Almost immediately it lurched forward and bolted off. She stood still, her hand over her heart, and caught her breath. She had taken her first step into a whole new world of criminal opportunities and riches.

Chapter 12

Moriarty had just finished his Sunday morning breakfast and Lilith was clearing away the dishes. He was still in his nightshirt and black dressing gown. He took a fresh cup of tea and walked into the small study in his apartment.

The project in Tynemouth had failed miserably. It was not that the science had failed but Bob had failed. Bob's failure was down to the way he had managed the project. Sloppy work and a lack of discipline were to blame. Bill did not escape a measure of responsibility either, and would be dealt with after the project was completed. The project would essentially need to be started anew.

But what was particularly disturbing to him was Holmes. Holmes had come dangerously close to making a full discovery of what he was doing in Tynemouth. It was not the first time Holmes had interfered in his plans, but the majority of the other examples had been on minor projects. Simple matters in the course and scope of his business – except of course for the matter of the French bullion. That had been a major blow to his potential profits, but he had other projects, though smaller in scope, that he put in place and made up almost seventy percent of the lost profits he expected from that one spoiled project.

This Tynemouth project was different. This was a wholly new venture. International in scope and potentially global in application. It would return profits for years to come and sow the seeds of chaos so deep in the soil of European politics that the fruits of his labors would be felt for perhaps decades to come.

Moriarty's immediate attention must be focused on two matters: Germany and a new location for the lab. He took out paper and began to write a telegram. The telegram would be addressed, put in proper form, encrypted, and sent to his contact in Germany via the syndicate's resources. His secretaries would take care of those details. He had to draft the substance.

Moriarty put his pen down and read through what he had written. "This is sufficient," he said to himself. His resources at the Foreign Office would ensure his telegram was sent surreptitiously via official channels to the appropriate people in Berlin. Moriarty stood and stretched, he walked to the entrance of his working office and called Lilith. She appeared almost immediately. "Can you get me a drink and one of my cigars please?"

Lilith set his drink down on his desk on a coaster and prepared his cigar. She cut it deftly, rolled it in her hands to give it uniformity, and lit it for the Professor handing him the lit cigar. Moriarty could taste the wetness of her mouth and lips on the end of the cigar as he placed it in his mouth. "Thank you," he said as she glided away.

Moriarty paced his office. Holmes had interfered in his plans in Tynemouth and he had to find a place closer to London to put the new lab. He needed a place that would be unexpected and secure. He needed his people to have access to it without raising suspicion or the attention of curious eyes.

He needed it to be contained to avoid unwanted exposure, not because he cared one wit for the public's safety, but because he wanted to avoid both detection and publicity. He needed it closer to his center of gravity to ensure better controls and tighter management. "Where can I move the lab at or near London?" he whispered.

He sat down behind his desk, opened one of the drawers, and took out a detailed map of London, spread it out on the desk, and began to look it over with a magnifying glass.

Becca stood in the middle of her apartment, having just finished her meeting with Saacks. She now knew her assignment. She had a target in Tynemouth by the name of Bob Whitaker, and Saacks had given her his general description and the address of his rooms there. According to Saacks, Whitaker considered himself a lady's man. He also told her that he could be found most evenings in the pub attached to the inn in the middle of town. Saacks gave her a general description of the town, the pier and lighthouse, and the old fort and abbey.

When discussing the matter with Saacks, they had decided she would need to travel to Tynemouth incognito and get a room at the inn in her disguised persona. She needed a disguise that would make her above suspicion and provide a reason for her visit. Becca was accustomed to using disguises and had several at the ready. She told Saacks that she would travel in the guise of Sister Mary Brendan, an aging and retired nun who came to Tynemouth to paint the lighthouse and the old abbey.

Becca stood and walked to her bedroom and to her dresser, opening one of the drawers. The drawer was full of theatrical makeup, theatrical glues, temporary hair dyes, powders, and various facial prosthesis. She looked through her choices and picked a fake nose, mole, and selected various jars of makeup carrying them to her makeup table.

She pulled her hair back and held it in place with a ribbon. She looked at her face in the mirror. She used her skills to place wrinkles, creases, and age spots on her face with the makeup. She applied the fake nose with the theatrical glue and smoothed the seams with additional makeup. Even though the makeup added age to her face, her bright green eyes still looked back at her in the mirror. They did not match the age her made-up face now showed.

She walked back to the dresser and found a pair of darkly tinted small square glasses and put them on her face. "Yes, that will do nicely," she said to herself. She arranged her hair in a tight bun and applied white powder to the edges to create the impression her hair was whitening. As she looked at herself in the mirror, she had transformed into the persona of an old woman. She hunched her shoulders. Once she put on the full habit of the nun, the disguise would be complete. She knew from experience that no one would suspect a beautiful young woman was under the nun's habit and makeup.

Moriarty had examined the map of the inner circle of the Metropolitan Railway and Underground. It was well known amongst the criminal classes that while workers were digging the tunnels for the main line, they had made dead-end offshoots that were used as work areas and staging areas for the mainline. One of these offshoots was relatively long in comparison to the others on the north end of the inner circle just under the intersection of Midland and Euston roads just south of the main terminus and cattle yards.

While Moriarty studied the map, he stopped and pointed with his finger at the offshoot at the intersection of Midland and Euston roads. Moriarty called Lilith, "I need to get dressed. Please also have my hansom ready for me downstairs in forty-five minutes. I will need one of the guards to assist me, and we will both need dark lanterns filled with oil and ready to use."

Chapter 13

It was Tuesday morning and Holmes was fully clothed and in his grey dressing gown looking out the window at Baker Street as the morning sun cast shadows and brought bright yellow light down the street. He was in deep thought, puffing slowly on his first pipe of the morning and humming to himself. Holmes's thoughts were interrupted by Mrs. Hudson bringing up breakfast as she began to set the table. At the same time,   Watson stepped through the door of 221b and walked up the steps to the familiar rooms.

"Everyone is in a good mood I see. Yes, breakfast! Thank you, Mrs. Hudson!" Watson took off his coat, gloves and hat and hung them from the hooks just outside the door to Holmes's rooms. He rubbed his hands together and sat at his place at the table and began to spoon large portions of eggs and beef on to his plate.

"Leave some for Mr. Holmes, Doctor," said Mrs. Hudson as she left them to their breakfast. Watson smiled and Mrs. Hudson could be heard mumbling to herself as she went downstairs.

"You were quite busy yesterday, Holmes. You spent a great deal of time at your writing desk, drawing something. I only caught a couple of glances. It looked like some complicated machine with gears and springs. Part of the case?" Watson was eating and clearly enjoying his breakfast.

"Watson, you were spying on me," said Holmes.

"No, no, not spying. Just curious. I left early yesterday because you were in no mood for company, obsessed as you were with your work. Care to share your musings with me this morning?"

"Well, perhaps some of them. The case grows clearer and clearer, Watson. What have you concluded?"

"Well, Holmes. You are not the only one who can conduct research at the library. I have concluded that the cause of Oberstein's death was exposure to a poisonous gas. From the condition of the body, the lungs, and the mucosa, I would say some variant of bis-2chloroethyl sulfide. A deadly gas that causes blistering of the skin, chemical burns, and destroys the lung tissue and mucosa when inhaled. But how he came in contact with such a gas is a mystery to me."

"Watson, you have truly outdone yourself. Excellent. Your research and conclusions parallel my own exactly." Holmes looked at Watson with both pride and admiration. Watson beamed at Holmes's praise and sat up straighter in his chair. "I believe dear Watson that you have hit the mark exactly. But I know where he encountered the gas and how!"

"Really, Holmes. Tell me!"

"Not so fast. Give an artist his space to display his art, dear Watson."

Watson laughed and almost choked on his toasted bread and jam. He took a drink of hot tea and slowed the pace of his eating. "Okay, Holmes. Tell me in your own way and at your own pace. I am all attention and excitement."

Holmes, who was sitting at the table with his back to the windows, steepled his fingers with his elbows on the arms of his chair. He looked satisfied and happy at Watson's interest. He looked like a man about to unravel a complicated yarn and was going to enjoy every minute of the telling.

"It is clear to me now that Professor Moriarty is behind an elaborate plan to develop a deadly gas weapon and sell it first to Germany and then to whatever other country that may want it. It is likely that he would sell it to any anarchist who wishes to sow confusion and destruction in the peaceful countries of the world, Watson. Quite literally, the fate of thousands may rest on our ability to stop the Professor before his weapon is deployed." Holmes was serious and solemn.

"Holmes, we must tell Scotland Yard and arrange for Moriarty's immediate arrest!"

"On what evidence, Watson? What can we prove? Nothing. As the Inspector in Tynemouth is so fond of saying, on its face the case seems a simple one. We have the death of a man in a lighthouse in the middle of the night. Stabbed through the heart by a man who admits it."

"But we have the evidence of the blistering and the chemical burns to the skin, Holmes. Oberstein's body."

"True, but how does that link him in any manner to the Professor? No, Watson, we must get the device itself, bring the light of justice to the place where it is being manufactured, seize the lab books and other materials, and then we will have stopped this scheme before it comes to fruition. Stopping the plan is far more important than getting Moriarty. That is his genius. He never leaves any evidence that one could trace back to him. His people act. He thinks, plans, schemes, designs, then issues orders, and sits back."

Watson suddenly looked depressed. He stopped eating and looked at Holmes from across the table. "But Holmes, when will this end?"

"Only when Moriarty is dead, I am afraid. That death may come at a high price. A very high price indeed." Holmes stood and walked over to his chair by the fire and sat down. Watson followed and sat in his chair opposite Holmes.

"You were going to tell me how Oberstein came in contact with the poisonous gas?"

"The facts as we know them and the information we learned from the Foreign Office, lead me to the following conclusions. Oberstein was Germany's agent. He traveled to Tynemouth, likely after dealing with one of Moriarty's men, to complete the transaction. But, before he did that, he wanted to see the effects of the gas himself. You were confused by my asking the inspector about missing cats. Has it become clear to you now, Watson?"

"Of course. Moriarty's men used the cats to test the potency of the gas in their lab. They needed several, as they conducted multiple tests. But why cats, Holmes?"

"Cats are ubiquitous. They are for the most part silent. They could not use dogs, as dogs bark and howl. Dogs are also much less clean and harder to keep than cats. Cats were perfect for what they needed. So much smaller. Easier to grab off the street when their unsuspecting owners let them out for the night. They could grab a cat, stick it under their coat and walk away."

"I see. So Oberstein went to their lab, expected to see a test of the gas on a cat, and the test went horribly wrong, and he was exposed to the gas. But how did he end up at the lighthouse, Holmes?"

"You were there with me, Watson. You saw the tracks. What do you deduce from the boot marks?"

"Oberstein walked through the abbey and the yard in front of it on his way to the lighthouse. Nothing else, Holmes."

"But where did Oberstein walk from, Watson? For surely, he came directly from the lab to the lighthouse. As Dr. Philby said, he was near death. Just minutes away from dying, so he could not have traveled far. What does that tell us, Watson?"

"That the laboratory was very close to the abbey. But we have been there, Holmes. There is no laboratory anywhere near the abbey." Watson was confused.

"My first inclination regarding the location of the lab came from the condition of Oberstein's shoes and the knees of his trousers. In addition to mud, the shoes and knees had a caked white, chalky powder residue on them. Dr. Philby told us that naturally occurring chalk was several feet underground in the area. There was none on the surface, and we both saw that there was none around the abbey, the old fort, or the lighthouse."

"I begin to see," said Watson. "The lab is underground! But where?"

"I am almost certain that the lab is in the caves under the old fort and abbey, Watson. The caves give access to the sea and are an excellent hiding place for a lab. The capstone we both observed, the starting point of Oberstein's boot marks, serves as both the foundation for the old altar and to cover the burial vault under it. The burial vault used by the old church to bury the holy relics that made the ground sacred. I am convinced that the burial vault connects to the caves and gave Oberstein access to the abbey from underground. It is from under the capstone that Oberstein emerged that night. It is likely Moriarty's men used it as an entrance and exit in the dark of night."

"Holmes, we must go back to Tynemouth immediately and break into that vault, find the lab, and end this!" Watson was standing ready to leave that moment.

"Watson sit down. This accident has made the lab incapable of occupation and it will remain so for at least a week, possibly longer. We have time. Neither Moriarty's men nor we can go down into the lab at present. Any residue of gas would have the same effect on us as it did on Oberstein. Only the passage of time and the sea winds moving through the caves will make the lab habitable again."

"But we must make the Foreign Office aware, Holmes."

"I have nothing to tell them but my deductions, Watson. We must have more concrete evidence before alerting the Foreign Office. They are men used to dealing with facts, not the armchair deductions of this subject of the Crown. For that is what they will think. Soon, Watson. Soon."

Watson sat back down with an air of exasperation. "Then what are we to do in the meantime?" he asked.

"I plan to spend the rest of the day in a laboratory at London University, studying the chemical composition of the crystals that I took from Oberstein's clothing. I cannot do the experiments here. Too dangerous. You are welcome to join me, Watson."

"Holmes, chemistry was my least favorite subject in medical school. As I recall, I barely got through the class with the help of a fellow sufferer. Is there anything that I can do while you are at the university?"

"Humm, yes. You can look over the plans I drew yesterday while, as you put it, I was engrossed in my work." Holmes stood and walked over to his writing desk and picked up a large piece of paper and walking back, handed it to Watson.

"Holmes, this is amazing. The world lost a talented engineer when you turned your mind to solving crime. I will be happy to look it over. What am I looking for?"

"Study it, Watson. Learn it. Tell me if I have left anything out or if there is a problem with the design. And, more importantly, see if you can determine a safe and quick method of disarming it. I am sure that Moriarty's design will not be far from mine. Studying my design, may help us when we encounter his. Two sets of hands and two keen minds may be required when the time comes."

Holmes had walked to his bedroom and emerged with his coat, gloves, and hat on, carrying his walking stick. He stopped at his small chemical table just outside his room and picked up the folded square of brown paper that contained the crystals he had scraped from Oberstein's clothing.

"I may be gone for some time, Watson." With that Holmes left the rooms and walked down the steps to hail a hansom.

Watson, moved to Holmes's writing desk where the light was better; picking up one of Holmes's magnifying glasses, he began to study the machine drawn on the paper. It was mostly a complicated arrangement of gears, a glass cylinder, and a perforated copper cylinder. It looked to be no larger than a solicitor's rectangular briefcase, one that he carried to court. Watson hunched over the drawing. This was going to take some time.

Sister Mary Brendan arrived by train at Tynemouth in midafternoon with her numerous bags, her easels, her brushes, and her paints. It was a cloudy and dreary day, with gusty winds and occasional sheets of drizzle coming in from the

North Sea. Three porters helped the aging nun with her bags as she attempted to get her umbrella to open while trying to step off the train and on to the platform without falling. Two men on the platform waiting for their train helped her make the crossing from train to platform.

"Oh, dear me. Thank you both very much. I don't know that I would have made it without your kind assistance. May God bless the two of you! In the name of the Father, the Son, and the Holy Spirit!" Sister Brendan performed the sign of the cross for each man, as they held their hats in front of them in a squall of wind and drizzle. Both men replaced their hats and with head bows, walked toward another part of the station.

Sister Brendan walked slowly into the station, hunched over with cane in hand, to the station master. "Dear sir, how may I get a carriage to take me and my bags to the inn in Tynemouth?"

"Yes, mam. There's usually a couple of locals ready to make a quick farthing or two just outside the station. I'll just step out and see if I can find one for ye." The station master took his hat off as he spoke to Sister Brendan and with a slight head bow walked out of the station on the side facing the town and gave a loud whistle and a wave to a man with a suitable, if rickety, carriage who drove up to the station. "I have a fine old woman who has taken the vows, if ye know what I mean, who needs taking to the inn," he said with reverence in his voice. "Come down and help her with her things."

The two men walked back into the station and with the help of one of the porters moved Sister Brendan's bags and things to the carriage, as she followed them out. "Oh, bless you, all. Thank you so much. I have come to paint the lighthouse and the old abbey. I sure hope the rain stops and the sun comes out. I want so much to capture the North Sea and the lighthouse with the light of the sun shining upon them."

"Yes, mum. I hear ye wants to go to the inn in town. I can take ye there," said the carriage driver.

"Thank you, sir. How much will it be?"

"No charge, mum. I be happy to do it for such a fine lady. No problem atoll." The carriage driver helped Sister Brendan into the carriage and climbed up to start the horses just as another gust of wind and drizzle hit him in the face.

Watson had been studying Holmes's drawing for some time. He had taken a break during the noon hour, gone out for lunch, and stopped by his house to take care of a few things. He arrived back at Baker Street just before three in the afternoon. As he got out of the hansom, he was met by a messenger from the Foreign Office with a message for Holmes.

"He is not home at present. I am his friend and colleague, Dr. Watson. I can take the message, and I will ensure that he receives it when he returns." Watson held out his hand.

"My instructions are to deliver this to Mr. Holmes himself, Doctor." The messenger, a young man who clearly took his job seriously, looked worried and perplexed about just what to do next. "I will be asked when I return to the Foreign Office the particulars of my delivery, and I do not want to tell them I gave the message to a man on the street, sir."

"I understand. Please, come with me." Watson took out his key and unlocked the front door to 221B Baker Street and let the young man in first. He knocked on Mrs. Hudson's door.

"Dr. Watson, is everything alright?"

"Oh, yes. This young man has a message for Mr. Holmes and is concerned about giving it to me on his behalf. Can you give him assurances that I am who I say I am?"

"Young man, this is Dr. John Watson. He is a past, and now sometimes, lodger and a good friend and colleague to Mr. Holmes. I assure you that you can put your faith in the good Doctor. He will deliver the message to Mr. Holmes when he returns." Mrs. Hudson smiled at the young man, and while she talked, she placed a hand on his shoulder.

The young messenger appeared to think about it for a minute and then with a nod of resignation handed the message to Watson. "I am counting on your discretion and your word that you will give this to Mr. Holmes when he returns."

"I promise," said Watson as he took the message from the young man and closed the front door as he left. "Thank you, Mrs. Hudson. I do not think he would have given the message to me without your assurances."

"My pleasure, Doctor. Have a nice afternoon." Mrs. Hudson closed the door with a smile as Watson walked up the steps to Holmes's sitting room.

As Watson sat smoking and thinking, he heard the bell ring signaling that someone was at the door. He heard Mrs. Hudson's muffled voice followed by quick steps up the stairs and a hard knock on the door. Watson stood.

"Come in."

"Are you Doctor John Watson?" asked the young messenger.

"Yes, I am he. Why?" Watson looked very concerned. Even without Holmes's skills at reading people, he could tell something was seriously wrong. As he took two steps toward the messenger, Mrs. Hudson walked into the room just behind the messenger. The messenger took his hat off and said:

"I have been sent to tell you that Sherlock Holmes has been taken to hospital near death, sir. There was an accident at the University lab where he was working. I have a hansom outside to take you directly to hospital. Please come with me."

Mrs. Hudson let out a little scream both hands going to her heart and Watson felt his heart sink in his chest, his mouth went dry, and the room seemed to spin.

Chapter 14

As the coach stopped in front of the inn, Sister Mary Brendan was helped down from the carriage and after thanking the driver, she walked into the inn and asked for the landlord. Seamus greeted Sister Brendan and she inquired about a room.

"I am here to paint the lighthouse and the abbey. I cannot stay longer than three to four days, so I really hope that the weather improves," she said.

"Oh, these little squalls blow over. In a couple of days, it will be clear and sunny. You'll see Sister. I've given ye a room with a window that faces the lighthouse. Ye may be able to paint from there if it doesn't stop raining."

"Thank you, sir. May I get some help with my baggage? It's quite a lot for three days, but I need all my painting materials with me to paint properly."

"Yes, mum. The driver and I will carry things up to ye. Ye just go on upstairs and ye bags will be up presently."

Sister Brendan went slowly up the stairs and to her room. As soon as the door was shut, Becca stretched her back and legs. All the stooping and hunching were taking their toll. She sat on the side of the bed and waited for her baggage. It was not long and there was a knock at her door.

"Come in, please."

"Here's ye baggage, Sister. Would ye be needing anything else?" asked Seamus.

"No, and landlord, I will not require any assistance or maid service for the duration of my stay. As you can imagine, I have gotten quite used to doing for myself. So please tell the staff to just let me be. Thank you."

"Of course, Sister. Thank ye." With that Seamus left the room, closing the door behind him.

As soon as the door was closed, Becca got up and locked it. So far, her plan was playing out as she expected. Tonight, she would need to do some reconnaissance of the house where Bob was staying and make certain preparations for when she would retire him. She obviously could not go out as Sister Brendan, so she decided to look around the inn for a back door. She assumed her bent posture and walked out the door, looking as if she were lost, she searched around the second floor and found a back door and some steps leading to the back of the inn. "This will be perfect."

After returning to her room, she took out her makeup kits and organized her disguises. She would go out as a man this evening. A man with a mustache, beard, hat, and glasses. She arranged the clothes she needed for the disguise, along with the mustache, beard, and glasses. All she had to do now was wait for nightfall, ensure that Bob was in the pub, and walk to the house where he was staying.

———————————————

Moriarty was sitting in his office on the second floor of the warehouse, having just completed the afternoon meeting. He had a drink in his hand, sat back in the chair, and reviewed his work in the Underground. He had given the necessary orders to his generals to obtain an engine and car, move the same to the Underground, and begin transforming the car into a makeshift lab.

As the Professor was going over his actions, deep in thought, there was a light knock on his door. "Come in," he said.

"Professor, a telegram from Berlin for you sir."

"Thank you, Roger. Bring it to me, please."

Roderick "Roger" Stapleton, a middle level manager of sorts in the organization, who was responsible for communications, walked gingerly to the Professor, and handed him the telegram. "It was in our code, Professor. I have taken the liberty of decoding it for you, Sir, and I typed the decoded message myself. I didn't feel it should be trusted to the secretaries to type."

"I appreciate that. Thank you. You may go."

Stapleton left the room with a slight bow of his head, closing the door behind him. As he walked back to his workstation, he tried hard to conceal his worry from his eyes and face. Prostitutes, gambling, robbery, and the like were fine with him. He could even accept an occasional murder to keep the citizens in line and reinforce the Professor's authority. But this was wholly different. What the Professor and the Germans were planning was wholesale murder by the hundreds. He sat at his small desk and let out a sigh. He opened the bottom right drawer of his desk and took out his flask. He needed a drink.

Moriarty opened the telegram and read it. It was short. The Germans remained interested and agreed that a test of the gas and its delivery system was required before they would finalize the purchase. It was not necessary to send an emissary. They had confidence in the Professor despite the setback. Moriarty was pleased. He now had to think about a location for a test of the gas and its delivery system, one that he had designed himself. It was no bigger than a solicitor's briefcase.

The test site could not be in England. The repercussions would be too great, and he would immediately be suspected by Holmes, if not the police and the government. It certainly could not be in Germany; they were his clients after all. France, Belgium, and Spain all came to mind. They were relatively close and could be gotten to quickly. The Basque anarchist were always a willing group and eager to take credit for atrocities committed in the name of political separation from Spain. They would gladly use the weapon in a village in Spain and aggressively take credit for the effects, taking any suspicion of British origin or his involvement off the table. "Yes," he said to himself, "Spain may be the perfect place."

Sister Brendan had been sitting in the pub for more than thirty minutes, and Bob had yet to appear. She had had two glasses of wine and was about to order her dinner. Locals began to come into the pub and order drinks. She decided to order.

"Waiter," she called. He came over. "I will have fish and chips please."

"Yes, mum."

The talk amongst the locals was about the weather and the coming trial of a local man named Dodd who had stabbed a German in the lighthouse. The majority opinion seemed to be that it was self-defense, but a vocal minority thought Dodd was getting what was coming to him. Dodd was not popular. She listened to as much as she could. Many of the locals looked her way and gave a respectful nod in her direction, and she gave a sign of the cross in return.

The fish and chips were passable, but that was all. But, as she ate, Bob came into the pub and sat at a table in a dark corner. He was soon joined by three other men, all of whom she believed were from the Professor's crew. If it were going to be four of them, it would make her job of seducing Bob more difficult. She stood, made a show of finding it hard to get started, and then walked up the stairs to her room.

Becca quickly took off her disguise, including the cumbersome pillows she used to hide her figure. She sighed, relieved to be rid of Sister Brendan for the evening. She decided to only glue the mustache and beard onto her face, not changing the Sister Brendan make-up to hurry things along. Given that it was only wrinkles and a mole, she thought it was fine the way it was. She put on her man's shirt, tie, and waistcoat after she used thick gauze to hide her breasts, as best she could. Then she put on the jacket, coat, hat, and glasses. In the dark, she was a passable man. She had a second identical disguise and she folded that and put it in a briefcase. She would need that disguise after she retired Bob and came back to the inn. She would need to find a place to hide the extra disguise somewhere inside the house, until she was finished with Bob.

She left her room and walked to the back door that led to the back stairs. She opened it and walked down the steps. She walked around the building to one of the cross streets and made her way in front of the inn and pub. As she passed, she looked in to ensure that Bob was still at his table, and he was. She walked quickly to the address. The streets were dark, and the gas lights were few. She was glad for that.

She arrived at the address and stood across the street from it, smoking a cigarette. She did not smoke and even feigning to smoke irritated her nose and eyes. The house was dark except for some lights upstairs. She crossed the street and walked to the front door. It was locked. She took out the locksmith tools that she had carried with her in the briefcase and easily picked the two locks on the door. She walked inside very quietly.

Bob's rooms were immediately to the left. That door was locked as well, but it succumbed to her talents easily. She was inside. There was a smallish sitting room immediately inside the door, which led to a small dining area and kitchen.

Beyond that was the bedroom. She made her way there. The bed was large, and it was covered in a skirt so that she could not see under it. Becca decided to place her extra disguise under the bed, pushing the briefcase so that it was in the middle and toward the top of the bed. It was a risk, but it was the best that she could do. There was no private privy. Obviously, Bob shared a privy with another lodger and that would complicate things a bit. There was no place to hide her blade. She would have to put it in her purse and try to get to it somehow during or before the amorous parts so that she could reach it quickly and dispatch Bob without a sound. She would have to improvise.

She walked around the rooms learning where everything was and the relative position of everything vis-à-vis the bedroom. She was satisfied. In all she spent less than ten minutes in the rooms. She left, careful to lock both the door to Bob's room and the outer door. She felt a sense of relief as she walked back toward the inn, her reconnaissance completed.

Chapter 15

Watson was almost too shocked to move. Mrs. Hudson was staggering in her disbelief. Watson went to her and putting his arms around her said, "I am sure it is not as bad as the young man makes it sound. I will go and see for myself. I will send you word as soon as I can."

"Thank you, Doctor. Oh, I shall pray like I have never prayed before!" Mrs. Hudson was in tears.

"Thank you, Mrs. Hudson. Yes, pray." Watson nodded to the messenger and followed him downstairs and to the waiting hansom. The trip to the hospital, located just off Guilford Street, the closest to London University, did not take long, but it could not happen fast enough for Watson. When the hansom arrived at the hospital, Watson leaped from his seat onto the street and ran ahead of the messenger to inside the hospital. The messenger caught up to him and took Watson to the emergency ward. Watson introduced himself as Holmes's doctor and was taken to a private area in the ward where Holmes was apparently being treated.

Before he entered the private ward, Watson could hear a man coughing and laboring to breathe. His lungs, even from this distance, sounded ragged and crackling. When he entered the room, he saw Holmes in a bed, propped up with pillows. The head of the bed had been moved next to an open window and a nurse stood by his side constantly fanning the air to increase its volume where Holmes was lying. Holmes's face was bright pink and there were four prominent blisters around his nose and mouth.

"Holmes, I am here. My God man, what has happened to you?" Watson was near tears. Another doctor who had been off to the side writing in a hospital chart walked up behind Watson and tapped on his shoulder. As Watson turned, the doctor introduced himself.

"I am Dr. Smiley, and I am the attending. You are?" he asked.

"I am Dr. Watson, Mr. Holmes's personal physician. What has happened to him?"

"Mr. Holmes encountered a very noxious gas while doing experiments in a chemistry lab at London University. I do not know what kind of gas or what chemicals were involved, and he will not tell me. A young chap at the lab had just opened some windows creating a through draft, and very probably saved this man's life. His lungs, bronchial tubes, trachea, and the mucosa of the throat, mouth, and nose are all affected. They are acutely inflamed and swelled; thus, his trouble breathing. We have washed out the nose and mouth with saline and believe that we have that under control. As for the lungs, bronchial tubes, and trachea only time will tell. We are treating the pinkish color of the skin and the blisters with a salve and his skin is responding well to that treatment, though he has only been here a little over an hour."

"Is his life in jeopardy?" asked Watson.

"I should think that if he were going to die from his injuries, he would have done so already. He has been with us for over an hour, and there has been some slight improvement. No, I should think that the next twenty-four hours will be critical to determining if there will be any long-term lung damage or other affects. I really cannot say at present."

"May I examine him?"

"Well, yes, Doctor Watson. I would be happy to have you render a second opinion. Please borrow any of my instruments that you may need. My bag is over on the table beside the bed."

"Thank you." Watson walked over to where Holmes was lying and coughing. He brought over a light and with the help of a mirror, he investigated Holmes's mouth and nose. They were indeed inflamed and swollen, but they were not closed. That was good news. The fact that Holmes was coughing was also a good sign, because it meant that his lungs were getting sufficient air to cough. Watson examined the whites of Holmes's eyes, the color of the skin under his fingernails, and the color of his gums and lips. All appeared to be getting sufficient oxygen. The blisters and redness of the face and hands were superficial and would recover in time. Watson listened to Holmes's heart. It was beating very fast, but it was regular. He listened to his lungs and there was a persistent wheezing, and every cough sounded like broken glass in his chest.

Watson walked back to Dr. Smiley and said, "From my examination, I would agree with you, Doctor. He is getting enough air at present, but his breathing is labored, and his heart rate is very rapid. I would normally recommend a little laudanum to help him relax, but given his difficulties breathing, I would not recommend any kind of sedative at this time. What think you?"

"Oh, I concur, Doctor Watson. I am afraid he will simply have to suffer through it for the next few hours. I am of course going to keep him here under observation." At this Holmes began to wave frantically at Watson and shake his head. It was clear that Holmes did not wish to stay at the hospital.

Watson walked over to Holmes's bedside. "Holmes, they will give you the best of care here. You really are not out of danger and as the doctor says, the next twenty-four hours will be critical. You should stay here."

Holmes shook his head harder and between coughs said, "Baker Street, Watson. Baker Street."

"But Holmes, I must advise against that. You really must stay here overnight. They will give you the best of care, and I will stay with you as well."

"Not safe. Baker Street." Holmes was adamant. Watson looked at Holmes for several minutes and finally shrugged his shoulders and walked back to Dr. Smiley.

"He is insistent that I take him home, Doctor. As his doctor I promise you that I will not leave his bedside for the duration. I will apply the salve to his superficial injuries. I think too that a chamomile vapor from the steam of boiling water may help as well. If you will discharge him to my care with whatever instructions you think necessary, I give you my word that I shall treat him accordingly."

"Doctor Watson, you put me in a difficult position. Do you give me your word that you will bring him back here, straightaway, if there is a worsening of his condition overnight or tomorrow?" Dr. Smiley was stern and direct.

"Yes, of course." Watson gave a sympathetic and assuring smile.

"Well then. I will write up some instructions and release him to your care if you countersign the orders and the chart indicating that you are accepting responsibility for Mr. Holmes's treatment. Agreed?"

"Yes, agreed, Doctor Smiley." Watson was relieved. He walked back over to Holmes who, with the assistance and protestations of the nurse, was putting on his shirt, jacket, and coat. He continually coughed but was able to breathe. "You must take it slowly, Holmes. You really are not out of danger, and you must promise me to go straight to bed and stay there for at least twenty-four hours. Do you promise me that, Holmes?"

Holmes nodded and Watson helped him walk out to the still-waiting hansom. The messenger stood beside it. "I didn't want to send him away in case you needed to go somewhere quickly," he said.

"Thank you very much." Watson helped Holmes into the hansom and wrapped his coat and the blanket around him.

"221B Baker Street, driver," Watson ordered, and the hansom set off on the short trip. "Holmes, you really must be careful. Very, very careful."

Holmes spoke hardly above a whisper with a hoarse voice interrupted with frequent coughs, "I need you to go to the lab tonight and get what's left of the crystals I had wrapped in brown paper. Stinson, the lab custodian, will direct you to where I was working. Destroy everything else there and bring back my notes."

"But Holmes, I must care for you. Can't this wait until morning?"

"No, it must be done immediately. Take me home, get me in bed, let Mrs. Hudson do what she can, and you leave for the university and do as I ask."

"Yes, Holmes."

The hansom had no sooner pulled up in front of 221B then Mrs. Hudson flung open the door and was at Holmes's side. "You are alive! Thank God," she said. "Let's get him to bed, Doctor." They both helped Holmes up the stairs and into his bed.

"Mrs. Hudson, please bring a pitcher of cold water and a glass and make sure that he drinks at least one glass of water every hour. If you can, please put some burning coals in a pan, place a kettle over it filled with chamomile and water and let that boil and steam his room. It will help him breathe." Watson was buttoning his coat.

"And where the devil do you think you're going, Doctor?" Mrs. Hudson was none too pleased that Watson was about to leave his patient unattended.

"I must run an errand on Holmes's behalf. He was most insistent. I shall return presently." Watson put his hand on Mrs. Hudson's elbow and gave her a knowing look. She nodded and went downstairs to carry out Watson's instructions. "Holmes, I shall return as quickly as possible. Mrs. Hudson is here and will care for you in my absence." Watson turned to leave but Holmes reached out and took his arm.

"I am eternally grateful for you, dear Watson. Thank you." Holmes had tears in his eyes and his affection was warm and genuine.

"Of course, Holmes. Now rest." Watson patted Holmes on his chest. He was touched by Holmes's gratitude as he turned to carry out his request. As he walked down the steps, Mrs. Hudson was on her way up with a pitcher of water and a glass.

By the time Watson returned to Baker Street it was dark. He was tired from the stressful events of the late afternoon. When he entered Holmes's bedroom, he could see that Mrs. Hudson was as good as her word. The room was steamy and smelled of chamomile. Holmes was propped up in his bed and she had him drinking a glass of water. Holmes gave Watson a look that seemed to beg. Watson almost laughed at the scene. Even though Holmes's condition was serious, the scene was comical. The great detective, laid up in bed, with Mrs. Hudson forcing water down his throat.

"Mrs. Hudson, thank you so very much. You have done wonderfully. I am afraid it is my shift now. If I need anything, I will call down for you."

"Doctor Watson, do you promise to call me, no matter the time?" Mrs. Hudson looked like a scolding schoolteacher, pointing a finger at Watson's face.

"I give you my word, Mrs. Hudson."

Mrs. Hudson gave Holmes one last examination, straightened his covers, and refilled his glass before slowly walking out of his bedroom, mumbling to herself.

"Thank you, Watson. I don't know which is worse, the pain in my chest and the coughing or Mrs. Hudson's attentions." Holmes's voice was hoarse, but his coughing was less often and not as deep or harsh sounding. "Did you retrieve the crystals and my notes?"

"Yes, Holmes. I laid them on your lab table. I also broke any glass beakers and pipettes that you were using. I cleaned the whole area and all is fine now. You mentioned at the hospital that you were in danger. How?"

"These rooms are being watched and I am being followed. I did not wish to be in a hospital where I would have been easy prey to assault and an easy target for murder. One plunge of a needle in my arm and no one would be the wiser. Death by lab accident." Holmes put his glass of water down. "I am waterlogged, Watson. I can drink no more."

"Holmes, the water will help your body flush out the poisons and help your tissues stay hydrated and heal faster. You must drink," Watson pleaded.

"Mrs. Hudson put three glasses of water in me in as many hours. I need a break. I will drink more after I begin to pass what's already in me."

Watson shook his head. "All right, Holmes. Now lay down and try to get some rest. Get some sleep." Watson helped Holmes settle into his bed, his head propped on pillows to make his breathing easier. Watson walked quietly out of the bedroom and sat in his chair by the fire.

It was a long night for Watson. He checked on Holmes almost every hour, refilled the teapot with chamomile and water twice, and brought in more hot coals to keep his bedroom misty. Holmes had several coughing fits, but for the most part he slept. Mrs. Hudson came up twice during the night to check on Holmes as well. By early morning it seemed that the worst had passed and though Holmes's lungs, bronchial tubes, and trachea were painful, his cough was only intermittent. He was pale except for a few remaining patches of red skin on his hands and cheeks.

"Watson, you look very tired. You should go upstairs and get some sleep." Holmes's voice was still hoarse and cracked as he spoke.

"I am fine, Holmes. We doctors have learned to get by on very little sleep. I napped earlier for about an hour and I can assure you that I am fine. It is you who needs to rest."

"I will rest, Watson. But I would rather sit by the fire than lay here in bed any longer." Holmes got up. "I will change into my nightshirt and robe and join you by the fire presently."

Watson sat in his chair by the fire and Holmes joined him. He looked haggard, pale, and weak. "You had a very close call, Holmes. Why did you put yourself at such risk?" Watson looked both concerned and a little angry with Holmes.

"I took all possible precautions, Watson. I used only one of the crystals at a time to experiment with. I was trying to find a reagent that would activate it. I found it, carbolic acid or phenol activates it, turns it into a gas and reacts with it making it even more deadly. I was not exposed for more than two seconds I assure you and it did this to me in that short a time."

"Did you at least learn its chemical composition?"

"Yes. The crystals are an amalgam of bis2chloroethyl sulfide, nitrous oxide, arsenic, and other chemical bonding agents. It is quite deadly and corrosive. The more so when introduced to liquid phenol, which reacts with it turning the crystals directly from a solid to a gas. Watson, although there was only a brief puff, the gas was green!"

"So, we know to what Oberstein was referring when he yelled 'the Green Dragon' in German. How did it make you feel mentally?"

"For a full two minutes I did not know where I was. I was convinced that I was being hunted and would be attacked by some unseen force. I simply wanted to run and escape. The young man in the lab had to hold me down while another went for help. I would have run into the street had I not been stopped. Acute paranoia, Watson."

"Yes, I think there were some lingering effects that caused you not to want to stay at the hospital."

"No Watson, that was me, not the Green Dragon. We are being watched and I can only assume that I am being followed. I simply did not want to take the risk. I am feeling comparatively better now, though I doubt I will be going out for a couple of days. Is it Wednesday, Watson?"

"Yes, Holmes. It is Wednesday."

"Any developments while I was indisposed?"

"Oh, I almost forgot. Yes, you received a message from the Foreign Office. I will get it for you." Watson got up and walked to the table, picked up the message, and brought it to Holmes. "I had difficult time getting the young messenger to leave it with me. But here it is."

Holmes opened the message and read it carefully. "It appears that the Foreign Office has intercepted an unauthorized telegram sent on official channels to Berlin. They let the message go through to its intended recipient but were able to copy it. It is in a complex mathematical code that their code breakers are working to decipher. Moriarty has people working even there, Watson. It was being sent in the middle of the night between this past Monday and Tuesday.

They aren't sure who was sending it but have put in place additional safeguards."

"What do you think it means, Holmes?"

"It means that Moriarty is communicating with his buyers in Berlin. He is probably informing them about the accident and making assurances." Holmes went silent as he began to think. "If it were me, Watson, and Moriarty is my intellectual equal, I would evacuate the lab in Tynemouth and relocate it elsewhere. The risk that I will discover it is too great given the investigation that we have performed to date. When he learns of my accident at the lab, I am sure he will move the lab after that, if he hasn't already ordered its relocation. We will find nothing in the caves, I assure you. It is Wednesday, as you reminded me, they will likely not be able to clean and relocate the lab until Friday or Saturday. Unfortunately, I am not in any condition to travel and won't be until probably this weekend. Any search of the caves will only serve to confirm what we have already deduced. Perhaps a trip to Tynemouth this weekend, Watson?"

"That will depend on your health, Holmes. Your iron constitution notwithstanding, as your doctor, I will be the sole judge of that."

Holmes smiled and resigned himself to three days of boredom sitting in his rooms at Baker Street, recovering. He heard Mrs. Hudson coming up the steps and from the sound of her footfalls he knew that she was carrying up breakfast. There were two knocks on the door, and she came in carrying a tray.

Chapter 16

Moriarty left his rooms and went down the tightly winding metal staircase and unlocked the "door" that led into the library below. He went directly to his office and looked for any overnight telegrams or messages that required his attention. There were a few, but nothing pressing. He scribbled instructions and decisions in the margins and moved the telegrams and messages to the outbox on his desk. His personal assistant would come in shortly and take his handwritten orders to a secretary who would ensure that they went to the appropriate parties. As he sat at his desk, there was a light knock on his door. "Come in," he said.

"Professor, I have some news about Holmes."

"Oh, have there been developments?" Moriarty motioned for his general to take a seat.

"Yes. Blind Bart has reported that yesterday Holmes was taken to the hospital after having suffered a serious injury while conducting experiments in a lab at London University. He was taken back to Baker Street by hansom in the company of Dr. Watson. He is there now."

"What kind of injuries?"

"We are getting the details, but it seems he was injured by a poisonous gas. We learned that much from the hansom driver who took him back to Baker Street. The driver learned this from the young messenger who spoke with him as he waited for Holmes and the doctor before taking them back to Baker Street."

"Do you suspect that the gas was ours...from Tynemouth? The Green Dragon?"

"Yes. The young messenger told the driver that a friend of his, who works at the lab and was present when Holmes went down, described the gas as green and the effects on Holmes – blisters, red skin, and difficulty breathing – are consistent with it being the Green Dragon, sir."

"How the hell did Holmes get access to it?"

"We don't yet know, Professor. It is a good thing that you decided to move the lab and that our men are in Tynemouth and will be able to clean-up the lab this weekend."

Moriarty sat silently staring down at his desk, his head oscillating from side to side. His eyes were dead and cold, his face frozen in cold hatred and fierce anger. "What of Miss Saint John?" he asked.

"All we know so far is that she left London for Tynemouth and should have arrived yesterday afternoon."

"Confirm Holmes's condition. Will he live? Will he require several days to recuperate? What is his timeline? He will go back to Tynemouth now, I am certain. It is only a matter of when. Anything else?" Moriarty stared.

"Yes, Professor. One more thing. Holmes received a message from the Foreign Office yesterday afternoon. Blind Bart recognized the messenger. Our sources say the message came directly from the Foreign Minister, so we do not know what it said. The timing of the message from the Foreign Minister is concerning, coming on the heels of our own coded message to Berlin. It may be that the Foreign office is aware that we surreptitiously sent a message to Berlin using their official communication channels."

"They will never break our code. It is too complex for their codebreakers. I designed the mathematics behind it myself. I am not concerned about their learning what it said. I am more concerned that our contact there may be compromised. You will check on him, learn what mental and emotional state he is in. If he is a threat to our security, deal with him accordingly. Understood?"

"Yes, Professor, I will deal with it personally. Anything else, sir?"

"No. Thank you for the report. Can you send in Bill? I wish to speak with him."

"Of course, Professor. I'll see if he is in." The general stood and left the office. An opportunity to undermine a worthy competitor for the Professor's attentions. He would take his time sending Bill in to see the Professor. Twenty minutes should suffice. He smiled to himself.

Moriarty waited impatiently for Bill to come in. At length he did. "What the devil took you so long?"

"I am sorry, Professor. I only just learned that you wanted to see me, and I came straight away." Bill was not happy.

"Sit down, Bill. What progress on establishing the lab in the Underground?"

"We have an engine and a car set aside for us. The men are down in the tunnel as we speak removing the materials necessary to put the engine and car in place. Should be completed by the end of the day."

"Good. Holmes has been meddling about. We need to be quick, and we need to be careful." Moriarty was pointing his finger at Bill.

"Yes, sir. I heard about Holmes. The men in Tynemouth will go into the caves very early Saturday morning, first thing, and have it cleaned out and the materials we need boxed and on a boat before the end of the day. No one will be the wiser."

"Make sure of it!" Moriarty was angry, and Bill did not want to be in his presence when he was. "I want Bob retired before Thursday night and Miss Saint John on the train back to London. I want the lab cleaned out, and the car ready for the materials from Tynemouth no later than Saturday evening. I want the materials transferred to the new lab in the Underground and the lab operational by Sunday afternoon. I will give you and Miss Saint John until Tuesday evening next to have a scientist at the ready. I will stand for no more failure. You are to see to everything, and I will hold you personally responsible. Understood!"

"Yes, Professor. I already have a scientist in mind. A lonely young chap who frequents our girls and likes his cocaine. Miss Saint John will be just the ticket for him, I assure you. Will that be all, sir?" Bill was already standing to leave.

"Yes," came Moriarty's cold, flat, and barely audible reply. He stared down at his desk, head oscillating more than unusual. "Holmes will have to be dealt with. He stands down or he dies!" he said to himself. Nothing could get in the way of the Green Dragon. Not his generals. Not incompetence. Not science. Not Holmes. Nothing.

Becca got ready quickly. She was practiced at getting into character and disguise and she was soon Sister Brendan again. Her preparations were complicated only by her period. She took one of the soft linen strips that she had for the purpose and folded it many times into a small rectangular "ball." Tying it in place with a string she inserted it to prevent the escape of her flow and to absorb it. "A menopausal old nun should not be flowing," she said. "No room for error." She added a "pad" she made of a washcloth she had brought with her and tied it in place with strings. Not very comfortable, but it would work. She looked at herself in the mirror. She was Sister Brendan again. She had the whole day and nothing to do. She went downstairs to the pub and sat and looked outside watching the drizzle and the occasional passerby.

The afternoon passed slowly, and she went between sitting in the pub watching the rain and her room to nap. By dinner time, she was ready to get on with it. She ate dinner as

Sister Brendan and waited for Bob to arrive. He did. When Bob arrived, Sister Brendan walked slowly up the stairs to her room. Once in her room, Becca began to take off the awful disguise and clean-up. She would go back downstairs as herself. She dressed immaculately in a form fitting, pale yellow dress that showed plenty of ankle. The pale-yellow dress had small violet flowers sown in and white lace along the neck and wrists. Her story, she had decided, was that she was an out-of-work actress on her way to Scotland for a part and was staying with friends for a couple of days in Tynemouth. She was bawdy, aggressive, and loved men. That was her character for the evening.

Becca left her room, careful that there was no one in the hallway to see her and walked down the back stairs of the inn to one of the main streets. She had put on dark blue cotton gloves, had an animal fur stole around her shoulders, a dainty umbrella that matched her dress, and a handbag, just large enough to carry the blade she needed for her work. She walked down the street and to the front of the inn, to make it appear as though she had arrived from outside and not from upstairs. As she walked into the inn, she made a show of closing and shaking out her umbrella.

"Does it do nothing but rain in this town?" she asked to no one in particular.

The landlord came over immediately. "Good evening, Miss. May I show you to a table or would you prefer to sit at the bar?"

"Oh, I will sit at the bar presently, but will want a table later for dinner," she said as she looked around the pub. There were several locals, some with wives, others by themselves. Bob was sitting at his usual table, this time by himself. She gave him a slight coquettish side look and walked to the bar. She sat at a stool, and let her dress come up a bit to show her calf. "I'll have a glass of gin, please, landlord."

"Yes, Miss. I haven't seen ye here before. What brings ye to Tynemouth?" asked Seamus with a broad smile and a frown from his wife as she cleared a table.

"Just visiting friends. On my way north for a part."

"Oh, are you an actress?" Bob had left his table and was sitting beside her at the bar.

"I am, and who might you be?" Becca looked at Bob starting at his face then down to his belt and back up again.

"I'm Bob, the best fellow you'll find in this pub. I haven't seen you here before. When did you arrive?"

"My, aren't you sure of yourself."

"Just trying to get to know you, that's all."

"So, you want to get to know me, do you? Lots of men have tried and so few have succeeded. What makes you think you will succeed?"

"I have me ways about me. You'll want to get to know me, I can assure you."

"Well, aren't you a cheeky fellow. Buy me a drink then?"

"You've got one."

"Not anymore," with that Becca drank the gin down in one gulp, to the satisfaction of a couple of the locals who gave her a "that's our lass," and a clap at their knees.

"What are you drinking, then?"

"I think I'll have a black and tan with a shot of whiskey."

"Landlord, give the lady what she wants and put it on my bill." Bob was all smiles. He was drinking with a beautiful woman who seemed interested in him.

Becca entertained the locals and Bob for several hours. It was now half past ten and some of the locals were beginning to leave for the night. Bob was glued to her side. Becca feigned drunkenness and this just spurred Bob along. He leaned over to her.

"I have some rooms rented a short walk from here. Care to come with me? I have absinthe in my rooms!" he whispered in her ear.

"Well, Bob! Are you threatening to undo my virtue?" Becca practically hissed the message she sent Bob, her eyes dreamy and seductive.

"If you'll let me!"

"Let's go then. Pay the landlord. I'll meet you on the street on the other side of the building. A girl has to keep up appearances," she whispered in his ear. "Well, gentlemen, I have to go back to my friend's. It's been a wonderful evening. Thank you!" she announced as she stood and began to leave. The locals, that were left, hooted, and hollered and applauded as she walked out the front door of the inn and around the corner. Bob couldn't pay the landlord quickly enough. He was out the door in less than half a minute with the locals shouting, "You ain't gonna get nothing. Sit tight!" as he left.

Becca waited for Bob in a darkened part of the street away from a streetlamp. He ran to her, and she had to laugh to herself. Bob passed her not seeing her in the dark. "Where you are going, lover?" she asked. He stopped and walked back to her. She embraced him and kissed him deeply. She could feel his arousal as he pressed his body against her. They walked arm-in-arm to his rooms rented in the local house. Becca feigned drunkenness and stumbled as she walked several times. Bob always caught her and helped her along. She stopped several times and kissed him passionately.

When they arrived at his rooms, he unlocked the outer and inner doors and invited her in. She walked in slowly never taking her eyes off his. He dropped the keys and immediately took her in his arms. Kissing her wildly and touching her all over.

"Slow down, Bob. We have all night. Where is the bedroom?"

"It's over there," he said with a jerk of his head in a husky voice.

"Let me get out of a few things and then we have the whole night," she said looking at him with knowing, lusty eyes.

"Yeah, go ahead. Let me know when you want me to come in."

Becca went to the bedroom and shut the door. She took her blade from her purse and hid it under one of the pillows on the bed. She took off everything but her chemise and called for Bob. He came to her quickly. His eyes were all over her body. "Been a long time has it, Bob?" she asked.

"Longer than usual, my love. Oh, so much longer than usual," he said as he went to her.

"I've had my visitor this morning. Does that bother you?" she asked.

"Visitor?" Bob was too lost in lust to understand.

"Yes, my monthly visitor came this morning. Does that put you off?" she asked.

"No! Nothing will put me off. You are so beautiful," he said barely able to get the words out as he held her.

"Slow down, my love. Plenty of time to enjoy me. I am so ready for you." Becca was moving slowly toward the bed as he caressed, kissed, and fondled her. "Bob is a good boy. He is going to get everything he wants," she said.

"Oh, yes. Please!" Bob began to take his clothes off as Becca lay on the bed and looked up at him. He could not take his clothes off fast enough, throwing them on the floor around the room.

"Oh, my look at you," she said. "Come to me and take me. Take me!"

Bob went to her and laid on top of her grinding his hips as he did. She kissed him and scraped her nails against his back. He was wild with passion. As he lost himself in his desire, she slid her hand under the pillow and grabbed the blade. She moaned and then in one swift motion her arm came from under the pillow and the blade went easily through the back of his neck and into his brain. Bob's back stiffened. His face was a mixture of pain, confusion, and agony. He went limp on top of her. Death came quickly as she moved the blade back and forth pivoting at the point where it pierced his skin. He was dead in seconds.

"Get off me you vile man! You filthy, stinking man. Get off me!" Becca squirmed under Bob and rolled him over onto the bed. In the process he had pulled the linen plug out of her and there was blood on the bed. She grabbed the linen plug and laid it on the floor beside the bed. Her flow was continuous from the removal of the plug and the stimulation Bob had provided. It went down the inside of her leg and a little pool formed on the floor.

Becca was on her knees getting the case that she had left the evening before from under the bed. She had nothing to stop the flow and simply put the plug back inside her hoping for the best. She took out the men's clothing and gauze from the case and folded her clothes and put them inside the case. She dressed quickly. She didn't bother with any makeup but put on the moustache and beard. She walked to the nearest window and tried to look at her reflection. It would have to do. She stopped and caught her breath. She looked over at Bob dead on the bed. She walked over to him and covered him in the sheets. She folded his clothes neatly and laid them over the foot board of the bed. She looked around. All her things were in the case. She walked out of Bob's rooms, out the front door, and onto the street. She remembered to walk like a man.

Chapter 17

Inspector MacDonald was at the pub with two constables after making their morning rounds about town. It was late Saturday morning and the rain had finally stopped and it was a sunny, if cold, day in Tynemouth. Each of the police officers was taking advantage of the free tea and light breakfast that Seamus offered them on such occasions. The inspector was careful not to take advantage of it, coming to the pub just every couple of weeks. It was a plum amongst the constables, whom the inspector would bring with him. They were all at work every other Saturday morning waiting to see if the inspector would finish his rounds at the pub and whom he would take with him. Tea, scones, biscuits, and whatever was left over from the inn's breakfast service was on the menu.

While the inspector carried on a conversation with Seamus, one of the young girls who helped the charwomen clean homes in Tynemouth came running into the pub out of breath and clearly agitated. "Inspector! Inspector! The lodger at Mrs. Collins' house was found dead in his bed just a little while ago while we were going in to clean. Ye need to come quick." The young girl was scared and excited and her frantic message stopped the men's conversation immediately.

"Now slow down and tell me again, young lady. Who found what where?" The inspector had moved away from the bar and was walking toward the young girl who stood at the door. "Tell me again slowly and carefully."

"Me mum and I were cleaning Mrs. Collins' house. The one she boards out to gentlemen. One of the men who lodges there is dead. Mum and I found him dead in his bed. Mum said he was, 'deader than anything,' and that I should come and get ye as quick as I could. So, I ran to the gaol and the constable said ye was here. So are ye going to come with me now or not?" The young lady was frustrated and impatient.

"Yes, I will follow ye over to Mrs. Collins' house. You two constables come with me." The inspector tipped his hat as a thank you and a goodbye to Seamus. "Does ye mother know who the man is?" the inspector asked as they walked out of the pub and into the street.

"She said his name was Bob. That's all I know. I've told ye everything I know. Am I going to be a witness, Inspector? Will I be at the assizes? Because, if so, I'll need a new dress."

"We'll see. Let's not get the cart before the horse, young lady. Lead on. Lead on." The young lady's interest in a new dress gave the inspector a bit of a chuckle as he patted the girl on the top of her head and followed her to Mrs. Collins' house. "Probably was nothing. Just a man passed out from drink. There just couldn't be two suspicious deaths in Tynemouth in as many weeks," he said to the constables following him.

It had taken all of Watson's and Mrs. Hudson's efforts and cajoling to keep Holmes at home and resting these past three days. Holmes had announced that he and Watson would take the morning train to Tynemouth on Sunday and resolve the issue of the hidden lab beneath the altar at the old abbey. Holmes was packing. His face and hands were almost healed, the blisters had diminished, and he coughed only rarely. Watson agreed that he was well enough to travel. Mrs. Hudson did not agree with his diagnosis.

"This country needs a good weather prediction service, Watson. Imagine how helpful that would be. I do not know what to bring to Tynemouth but must take clothes necessary for cold and rain. I do not like packing this much, but I have no choice. We may be there for two or three days. It all depends on what we find." Holmes was in one of his more energetic moods, putting his unspent energy from lying about for the past three days into his packing. Watson, on the other hand, was in a lethargic mood. Ignoring Holmes, he smoked his first cigar in three days and read the paper in front of the fire with his legs stretched out in front of him.

"Why the devil aren't you packing Watson?"

"What did you say, Holmes?" Watson had not been listening to anything Holmes was saying.

Holmes walked into the sitting room from his bedroom. "You need to pack Watson. We are leaving tomorrow on the 7 a.m. train for Tynemouth. Really, Watson. You can be such a lazy dullard at times."

Watson yawned. "I will pack later. I must go home to do so. Just don't want to go out in this cold at the moment. We have time, Holmes. No rush. It's only three o'clock."

As Watson said this the bell rang downstairs. "Oh, what now?" asked Holmes. Mrs. Hudson's muted voice and then her footfalls could be heard on the steps as she came to the door. It was open, so she walked in carrying a telegram.

"Telegram for you Mr. Holmes. It is from the inspector in Tynemouth. Perhaps it will save you a trip?" Mrs. Hudson rather hoped that it would keep Holmes at home for one more day of recuperation.

Holmes leaped over the settee and took the telegram from Mrs. Hudson and tore it open. As he read it his face changed from frustration to excitement. "Well, well. Looks like our trip to Tynemouth is fortuitous Watson. Look at this." Holmes walked over to Watson and handed him the telegram. Watson read it.

"Another suspicious death in Tynemouth. He says the dead man's name is Bob. Could it be the same Bob you noticed in the pub when we were there last?"

"The odds are against it being anybody else, Watson. It has to be Bob Whitaker." Holmes sat in his chair by the fire thinking. "Looks like Professor Moriarty is cleaning up a mess in Tynemouth."

"But the telegram says the death looks to be of natural causes. No marks on the body or signs of foul play. The inspector says only a small spatter of blood on the floor, away from the man – unrelated most probably since there are no marks on the body. What do you make of that?"

"Watson! What are the odds of one of Moriarty's men dying of natural causes in his bed less than two weeks after Oberstein is killed in the lighthouse? No. Natural causes just will not do. They simply do not know what to look for. So much for your Dr. Philby." Holmes got up and walked to his writing desk and began to compose a response to the inspector's telegram. "They must keep everything as it is. It is probably wishful thinking, Watson. I am sure they have walked all over the scene and moved everything about. But still. We must make a valiant attempt to find what we can."

"So, you suspect murder?" asked Watson.

"Indeed, Watson. Indeed. Mrs. Hudson!" Holmes called down the steps. "I need you, please." Mrs. Hudson came upstairs and Holmes gave her instructions to send a messenger to the telegraph office with his telegram. "This couldn't have come at a better time, Watson. We will be there fewer than thirty-hours after the discovery of the body. There may still be some evidence left." Holmes's eyes gleamed as he rubbed his hands together.

"Holmes, you must be the only man in England happy to be going to see a dead body and a crime scene," Watson said shaking his head. Holmes just chuckled in reply and then grew suddenly perfectly still. His eyes had a faraway look. He stood and walked swiftly to his bedroom. He came out five minutes later in his coat and hat, putting on his gloves.

"I have to go to the Foreign Office, Watson. Do not wait up for me as I will likely be late. Do not forget to pack. I suggest we meet at the station tomorrow morning at six thirty, sharp." And with that Holmes walked quickly down the stairs carrying his walking stick and out into Baker Street.

Watson stood in front of his chair dumbfounded by the swift and sudden change of events. He looked around the room as if not believing what had just happened. He fell exasperated with an exhalation of air into his chair. "Holmes, you are a very frustrating, infuriating, and incomprehensible man!" he said out loud to no one in the room.

Becca sat in her rooms in London in front of the fire thinking. She had arrived back in London Thursday evening as Sister Brendan. She had hired a coach to take her back to Chelsea to her rooms above the shop. But just as the carriage was arriving, she instructed the driver to go around the block twice. As he did, she gazed out the windows of the carriage and looked for persons who did not seem to belong. Persons who were only loitering. She saw three potentials. Two which she recognized as drunkards and common beggars. The third she did not recognize. "That would be whom the Professor has watching my rooms," she said allowed to herself. She made a quick mental note of what he looked like. He had made the mistake of standing near a light.

The carriage dropped her off and the driver helped carry her baggage into her shop, with a rather confused look on his face about why he was dropping a nun off at an art shop in Chelsea after eight o'clock at night. But Becca was confident the tip she gave him would keep him quiet.

The next day she opened her shop at half past ten and it was a quiet morning. When she was about to close-up for lunch, Saacks walked in.

"Well, how did it go?" he asked.

"It's done. Bob is retired. Died in his sleep it seems." Becca looked taken aback by the sudden visit. "You are having me watched, Saacks. Why?"

"We had to know when you returned from Tynemouth so I could stop by and have another little chat. Bob was only half the assignment if you remember. We still have more work to do."

"I haven't forgotten. Join me for lunch down the street? There is a nice Indian restaurant. You can buy." Becca gave Saacks a girlish look as she swung her coat over her shoulders and pointed to the door. Saacks opened the door for her and closed it behind him. Becca moved him aside and locked it. "Shall we go my dear?" she said, putting her hand through his arm and walking in the direction of the restaurant.

Becca got up from her chair and walked over to the window overlooking the street below. She was thinking about what Saacks told her at lunch. The Professor needed her and Saacks to recruit and motivate a chemist to perfect and concentrate some crystals and then design a process to produce great quantities of the same. The perfection and concentration being the priority. Saacks would not tell her any more than that. He would not tell her what the crystals would be used for, only that the process was dangerous and required an experienced chemist to perform the work. Saacks had also impressed upon her the absolute secrecy of the project and that the lab where the chemist would work was underground.

Saacks already had a scientist in mind. A young chemist named Anthony Poe. It seems Poe had a problem with cocaine and frequented women under the syndicate's employ. Through these women Saacks had learned that Poe was addicted to cocaine and from an examination of the files he had access to, had learned that five years earlier Poe had failed to show-up for his final exams to obtain his degree in chemistry. Through the information provided by the working ladies, the syndicate had provided Anthony with counterfeit transcripts and a counterfeit degree.

Poe had been on the list of potential blackmail targets at the syndicate. But using him in the project was more valuable than any blackmail. Poe lived in fear that the university where he worked would learn his secret and he would be ruined. Saacks was convinced that between what they had on Poe – addiction to cocaine, frequenting prostitutes, and the fraudulent degree and bona fides provided by the syndicate – combined with Becca's beauty and determination – they could get the scientist to cooperate. Becca disagreed.

"What we need, Saacks, is a more feasible plan to get him to want to work with us. Let me think this over. Come back Saturday after five and I should have something in mind by then. In the meantime, we should cut him off the cocaine. I am assuming that the Professor has the power to order that no one affiliated with the syndicate selling cocaine should sell to this man. His hunger for his cocaine will grow strong and his physical condition will deteriorate making him more susceptible to our plans. Agreed?"

"A good idea, but he is likely to find a fix before next week," said Saacks.

"I don't know, from what you told me he is not likely to take the risk of sourcing from different people than those he is used to. If he succeeds in getting a little here and there before next week, he will still be malleable to our influence not having received his normal dosages. If what you say is true and he takes a ten percent solution intravenously twice a day and more on weekends, even slowing down his supply will have the effect we want."

"So," Becca whispered to herself, walking back to her chair, and sitting, "Poe will be desperate. How do we use that to our advantage and how can I use it to manipulate and control him?" She smiled to herself, "Yes, my plan will work." As soon as Saacks showed up, she would share it with him. They could get started on Monday late afternoon. Mademoiselle Fahrney was the perfect character for the job. She loved speaking in a French accent. That would be the icing on the cake.

Chapter 18

Holmes and Watson arrived in Tynemouth, midafternoon on Sunday. Holmes had been silent about his visit to the Foreign Office. Whenever Watson tried to approach the subject, Holmes avoided answering or changed the topic. His mind was clearly occupied most of the trip. Holmes looked tired as if he had not slept the evening before their journey. As they were walking off the train onto the platform, Watson looked around for the inspector. Holmes's telegram of the day before surely told the inspector when they were arriving.

"There ye are. Good afternoon Mr. Holmes. Dr. Watson. I fear that ye may have made a trip for nothing." The inspector took one of Holmes's bags and directed them to a waiting open carriage. "It looks like the man died of a stroke. There is some evidence of blood in his ears and the small puddle of blood beside the bed is likely from a nosebleed that preceded the stroke he had in his sleep. But ye'll be able to see for ye selves shortly."

"Thank you, Inspector. I would like to go to Bob Whitaker's rooms first please, after we drop Watson off at the undertaker's home. I am assuming Mr. Whitaker's body is at the undertaker's?" Holmes sat in the open carriage with a commanding demeanor.

"Of course, Mr. Holmes," the inspector gave the instructions to the driver. "Yes, his body is there and Dr. Philby will likely be waiting there for you, Dr. Watson. How do ye happen to know the man's name, Mr. Holmes?" The inspector looked at Holmes sideways in distrust.

"Because I saw him and another man in the pub the evening we were here. I sent their descriptions to the Yard and learned their names. You should really be more curious, Inspector." The inspector said nothing in response.

"How has the weather been, Inspector?" asked Watson trying to lighten the mood.

"Typical winter here. Lots of rain. Today is nice though as was yesterday. Ye happen to get lucky picking good days to be here. I say, Mr. Holmes, why did ye send me a telegram asking about missing cats?"

"Ahh, we will get to that tomorrow, Inspector. I hope you have nothing planned for the morning. I will need you and as many constables as you can spare for a little cave exploring?" Holmes chuckled to himself.

"Cave exploring? Ye certainly have strange methods Mr. Holmes. A man dies in a lighthouse and ye search an old fort and abbey. A man dies in his bed in a house, and ye take me to caves." The inspector shook his head in disbelief.

Holmes let out a scoff, "It is never boring with me, is it, Watson? All will be revealed Inspector. I assure you." Watson nodded his head reassuringly to the inspector.

The open carriage first dropped Watson off at the undertaker's, and then just three blocks down the same street they arrived at the house. There was a constable standing guard at the front door. Holmes asked the inspector to wait in the carriage as he carefully let himself down and looked first at the road and then the front yard.

"Inspector, you and everyone else have made a mess of the entire scene. I cannot make any sense of the innumerable boot marks in the grass, nor can I make any sense of the carriage or horse tracks on the street. Let us go inside and see what we can find there." Holmes was not happy and walked toward the front door of the house without waiting for the inspector, moving the constable out of the way with a wave of his left hand.

Holmes examined the lock to the front door of Whitaker's rooms. There were no signs of forced entry. He opened the door slowly and looked carefully at the wood floor of the sitting room just inside the door, making his way into the sitting room.

"There is nothing to be gleaned from the door, the lock, or this hard wooden floor, Inspector. Is the bedroom toward the back?" The Inspector nodded his head and Holmes made his way to the back of the apartment and stopped just outside the bedroom. "The sheets have been moved about when the body was taken to the undertaker. Did you make any notes about what condition the sheets were in before the body was removed?"

"Eh, no, Mr. Holmes." The inspector was looking a bit embarrassed.

"Of course, you didn't! Why on Earth would an inspector inspect. I am sure that I expect too much!" Holmes was inpatient and angry.

Holmes looked over the wood floor in front of the bed carefully, but there were no discernable foot marks. He moved to the left side of the bed and examined the floor there and found the same. He then moved to the right side of the bed and immediately went down on his knees. "I see the small spatter of what looks like dried blood." Holmes took out a piece of brown paper and with a knife blade from a multi-bladed knife, he scraped half of the dried blood onto the paper. "If this is blood, and I will be able to conduct a test to tell, it is unusual blood. It appears very thin and weak. That is telling Inspector. Are you sure there were no wounds on Whitaker's body that might account for this blood?"

"Yes, he had no discernable wounds anywhere on his body that I could see." The inspector stood with his small notepad and pencil taking notes as Holmes narrated his examination.

Holmes put his face and nose within an inch of the pillow, sheets, and blanket on the right side of the bed. "There is a light smell of perfume on the pillow and just below it, Inspector." He examined the pillow carefully and withdrawing a pair of tweezers from his coat pocket, lifted what looked like two or three long hairs from the pillow, placing them in a folded piece of brown paper.

Holmes moved the blanket and sheet down and let out a little exclamation, "And, there are several small spots of blood on the sheet." Holmes took out a measuring tape and measured the distance between the middle of the pillow and the blood spots, making a note of it in his own notepad. He then moved to the left side of the bed and examined the pillow, sheets, and blanket on that side of the bed. "There is no smell of perfume on this side of the bed."

Holmes then took an oil lamp from the nightstand and lit it. He laid flat on the floor using the lamp to shine light underneath the bed. He got up quickly and moved to the right side of the bed and did the same. "A briefcase or small piece of luggage has been placed under the bed and then taken out. You can see where the act of withdrawing the briefcase has disturbed the dust under the bed, and there is a rectangular shape in the dust indicating where the briefcase rested." Holmes started to get up but stopped and looked back down at the floor where he had scraped the dried blood. He moved the lamp closer and took out his magnifying glass. He examined the floor carefully.

"In addition to the small spatter of dried blood, there is an oval shape in dried blood to the side. When viewed through my glass, it shows a very light pattern that looks like woven cloth. Interesting. There is a thin line of dried blood proceeding from the oval shape, and a smudge where it looks to have been picked up." Holmes was intrigued. He got up from the floor and walked over to the small dining table and sat. He looked all over the apartment from that vantage point. He got up and then lay on each side of the bed, looking around the room as he lay.

"There has been a woman in this bed with brown hair that has distinct shades of red or russet. She wore perfume and she lay down here on the right side of the bed. If I am not very much mistaken, it was her time of the month and the blood on the floor and sheets is from her. The oval of dried blood and the short line of dried blood proceeding from it, is likely the vaginal insert she used to collect her menstrual bleeding, which apparently fell to the floor, before she picked it up. She is roughly five feet, six inches tall and is not overweight, though I cannot say how much she weighs; she is quite likely petite. It was likely she that took a briefcase from under the bed, but that is speculation on my part, as the briefcase could have been moved earlier. Once I test this dried blood that I took from the floor, I will be certain both that it is blood and that it is menstrual blood."

"What? What do ye say, Mr. Holmes? How in the world can you tell there was a woman in that bed?" The inspector was incredulous.

"Several things lead me to that deduction. First, the smell of perfume only on the right side of the bed. The long hairs that I found on the pillow. The blood on the floor and sheets when there were no bleeding wounds on Whitaker's body. The cloth "sponge" she made and tied with a string that she used to collect her menstrual blood that was dropped on the floor and left its mark. These are obvious to the trained observer.

"Her size I deduce from the distance between where her head lay on the pillow and the spots of blood which define the length of her torso, along with some simple calculations referencing an ordinary woman's body ratios, these give me an idea as to her height.

"As for her weight, she did not leave a deep impression in the mattress, which as you can no doubt tell, is rather soft and filled with feathers, thus her impression would have stayed had she been larger and heavier. It could also mean that she didn't lay on the mattress very long, but given the other evidence, including her estimated height, I prefer to deduce that she is not heavy." Holmes gave his explanation in the detached, unemotional voice and demeanor of a bored expert being forced to explain his thinking to a child. "I would ask around town, the pub for example, if Whitaker was seen with a woman the evening of his death, Inspector."

"I can tell ye, Mr. Holmes, that he indeed was. Before we were called to the scene, I was in the pub. It was the last stop on me rounds. Seamus told me about a beautiful woman, an actress on her way up north for a part, who was staying in town with friends, and who entertained the folks at the pub just this past Wednesday evening. This man, Whitaker, was particularly taken by her and spent the evening trying to impress her. But Seamus said she left before Whitaker. She hasn't been seen since." The inspector was dumbfounded at Holmes's methods and conclusions.

"We will want to speak further with Seamus to get a detailed description of this woman." Holmes walked around the rest of the rooms but finding nothing else, indicated that he was ready to go. "Let us go to the undertaker's, Inspector. No need for the carriage. Let us walk over together. It will give me time to think before we arrive." Holmes and the inspector left the house and walked toward the undertaker's residence.

"Mr. Holmes, there was no reason for me to suspect any foul play. The situation presented itself entirely as a man who died in his sleep. There are no wounds on the body. He was found lying on his back with the sheet and blanket around him as if he had fallen asleep in that position. As you can see, there are no signs of a struggle. There are no signs of forced entry. Everything points to a man who died alone in his sleep. Until ye came and found what ye did, I had no reason to believe otherwise. Everything ye found is consistent with a man having brought a woman to his bed. They had intercourse and then she left. He fell asleep and died of natural causes while he slept. When we find and speak with the actress, if it was indeed her, I believe we shall find that my interpretation of the facts is correct."

"Inspector, to be fair, I know a great deal more than you do about what has been going on in Tynemouth. Still, as the local inspector, you should have more imagination and look for things that are not obvious. Especially when you have had two deaths in as many weeks, both very out of the ordinary for this area, and the one at the lighthouse presenting facts of a very suspicious and unusual nature. After our explorations tomorrow in the caves, I am sure that your conclusions will change. Now let us examine the body." Holmes walked rapidly and the inspector had difficulty keeping up. They arrived at the undertaker's home and rang the bell. Mr. Macmaster answered the door.

"Mr. Holmes and Inspector MacDonald, good to see you both again so soon after our last meeting. Please come in. Dr. Watson and Dr. Philby are downstairs with the body. You know your way. Make yourselves at home." The undertaker motioned Holmes and the inspector in. Both walked toward the back of the house and down the stairs to the basement.

"Dr. Philby, good to see you again. So, Watson, what can you tell me from your inspection of the body?" Holmes walked up to the body, laying on one of the porcelain tables under a bright lamp. Decomposition had begun and the body was already in poor condition. Mottled all over with dark blotches and large purple areas on the underside of the body where blood had begun to gather and congeal. The internal gases inside the body, caused by decomposition, had begun to make the body look bloated and unnatural. There was an odor of death and decomposition in the room. The inspector stood well away from the body with his handkerchief over his face.

"Dr. Philby should begin and then I will add any of my additional findings," said Watson.

"Well, Mr. Holmes, the official cause of death is yet to be determined, although after you hear Dr. Watson's findings and after my autopsy, that may change. As you can see, I have yet to conduct a formal autopsy. I have examined the body in detail however and I can give you a quick summary of my conclusions.

"From the condition of the body, I would say that Mr. Whitaker died sometime during the night this past Wednesday or very early Thursday morning. There is no bruising or lacerations anywhere on the body. The body is intact, no missing limbs or digits. The body is of a male approximately 30 to 35 years of age, five feet, eight inches tall, weighing 185 pounds. There are no signs of a struggle on the body. No ligature marks. The body presents as unremarkable.

"The penis and immediate area surrounding it shows signs of recent sexual activity. There is some slight pre-ejaculative fluid that escaped the penis, and the penis is covered in a light film of blood, likely from a menstruating female. The inner ears show signs of bleeding as there is the presence of blood. Blood in the ears is usually caused by a brain hemorrhage from a brain aneurysm or stroke, although I have yet to remove the brain and examine it. That is a summary of my findings so far, Mr. Holmes." Dr. Philby delivered his report in a quiet, even voice.

"And what can you tell me, Watson? Anything to add?" asked Holmes.

"Only this Holmes. When I was examining the face, head, and ears, I held the head up placing my fingers behind the neck and lower part of the skull to support the head while I made my examination. When I did so, the fingers of my right hand felt an indentation at the base of the skull where the skull joins the neck. Upon further examination, it appears that Mr. Whitaker experienced a puncture wound to the base of the skull. It could be from a long, thin bladed, knife. This would have separated the spinal cord from the brain stem, and may have damaged the medulla oblongata, causing almost immediate death. There is very little if any blood from a wound like this and such a wound is very difficult to find, as the skin and hair close the wound and can conceal it from inspection. My finding it was the merest of chance."

"Excellent! Very good Watson. You have outdone yourself. Really." Holmes lifted the head and with his fingers probed the area of the back of the skull that Watson had described. "Do you have a long probe, Dr. Philby?"

"Yes, we have already measured it, it is approximately six to seven inches in length and goes in at a slightly upward direction. In other words, the thin blade entered the neck and base of the skull at an acute angle rising upward toward the back of the skull," Watson explained.

"Consistent with a woman stabbing Mr. Whitaker from a prone position, lying on a bed on her back with Mr. Whitaker on top of her engaging in intercourse, and she stabbing the back of his skull with her right arm from behind his head?" asked Holmes.

"Yes, I think that theory would be consistent with our findings," answered Watson. "So, it's murder we are talking about, Holmes?"

"Yes, murder. Very refined and practiced murder. Not the usual tool or method of killing. A method designed to be difficult to find and one that mimics natural causes. Inspector, the number one suspect must be the woman at the pub. We must speak with those who were at the pub last Wednesday evening." Holmes looked over the body quickly to see if he could find anything additional.

"You say a woman did this, Holmes?" asked Watson.

"Yes. There is evidence to support the conclusion that a woman was in Mr. Whitaker's bed. She was menstruating and left blood stains on the sheets and the floor. I will be certain it is blood after I have conducted tests back at Baker Street but given the evidence Dr. Philby has provided, I am almost certain that the dried material I took from the floor is menstrual blood.

"From the condition of Mr. Whitaker's penis, I conclude that the woman killed him by stabbing him with a long, thin blade through the back of his skull, as she was lying on the bed engaged in intercourse with the unfortunate Mr. Whitaker. This is further supported by the angle of attack of the blade in the brain. It would help our investigation, Dr. Philby, if you would complete your autopsy, especially of the skull and brain, and report your findings to us tomorrow. We will be staying at the inn in town."

The inspector had remained quiet during this entire exchange standing away from the body, but as Holmes turned to leave, he stepped forward and said, "Mr. Holmes, I am familiar with your reputation, but I am still amazed by your methods and the rapid deductions and conclusions that ye make. As I am with your work, Dr. Watson. This is truly amazing. It is an honor to work with you both!"

"Thank you, Inspector. And if I have been a bit harsh in my comments and suggestions, it is only because I am anxious to move this investigation along and due to a recent illness that I am still recovering from." Holmes looked at the inspector with gratitude and warmth.

"Of course, Mr. Holmes. No offense taken. Shall we go to the pub and talk with Seamus?" the inspector asked.

Holmes nodded and the three left Dr. Philby in the basement to complete his work.

When they arrived at the inn, it was still too early for the dinner crowd and Holmes had an opportunity to speak with Seamus without distraction. Watson, Holmes, and the inspector sat at the bar and spoke with Seamus.

"The actress who was here last Wednesday evening was a beautiful woman she was," said Seamus. "She is a dainty lass, small-waisted and very much a woman to be desired. Her hair is a russet color. Her eyes are green. She carried herself like a lady. We were all smitten by her, but the dead fellow was particularly so. You say ye think that she may have killed the man?" The inspector nodded his head. "I don't believe it. There is no way that so dainty a thing could kill a man. It's not just her size either, gentlemen. I don't think a woman like her has that sort of thing in her. No sir, I don't believe it for one minute." Seamus threw the towel he had been drying dishes with over his shoulder in a sign of defiance.

"Well, Seamus, I appreciate the description nonetheless. Was there anyone else here this past week that was a stranger to the town?" asked Holmes.

"Yes, there was an old nun, she stayed here in the inn, she did. She came to paint the lighthouse and the sea, but the weather didn't cooperate, and she went back to London on the noon train on Thursday past. Don't go accusing no nun with murder, now gentlemen. No sir." Seamus was defensive and getting angry.

"No one has seen the actress in town except for that one evening?" asked Holmes.

"No sir. I never saw her before nor after."

"What about the nun?"

"No, Mr. Holmes. She was here for two nights and left for London."

Holmes sat in thought while Watson, the inspector and Seamus talked. Holmes did not listen. "How long was the actress here that night?"

"Oh, only for about three to four hours. She came around dinner time and left around ten in the evening I think," answered Seamus.

"And Bob Whitaker left right after she did?"

"Yes, sir. He paid for their drinks and hurried out of here quick like. We all laughed. It was clear he didn't want the bird to get way. I don't blame him."

"Did she ever say what family she was staying with?" asked Holmes.

"I don't remember. I don't think so, but I am not sure. I don't remember if she did." Seamus was getting inpatient with the questioning. "Anyway, gentlemen, I have me work to do. Will ye be staying with us, Mr. Holmes?"

"Yes. Watson and I will need our old rooms if they are available. Thank you, Seamus." Holmes was distracted and thinking.

"Well, Mr. Holmes, I need to be getting home for dinner. Do ye still want me here in the morning with two or three of me constables?" The inspector stood and was buttoning his coat.

Holmes did not answer him right away and the inspector was about to ask him again when he suddenly said, "Yes, yes. Can you be here with three constables at 9 o'clock in the morning? Please bring lanterns, and I suggest that you all arm yourselves." Holmes was smiling and looking at the inspector in a distracted manner.

"Certainly, Mr. Holmes. I will be here then. Good evening gentlemen." The inspector shook Watson's hand, but Holmes was in deep thought again. He turned and left the pub.

"Holmes, that was a bit rude. The inspector has been very helpful and patient with us. You should have bid him good evening and shaken his hand." Watson was embarrassed and disappointed in Holmes's behavior.

"Watson, it is the inspector who should be thanking me. If not for me this town would have two unsolved murders. He has bungled the entire thing. He is incompetent and what is worse, he is completely unaware of it. He has no imagination and no ambition. Who knows how many crimes have gone unsolved in this town because of the likes of him?"

Watson cleared his throat and stood up. "Well, I am going to go up to my room and freshen up before dinner, Holmes. Will you be joining me for dinner this evening?"

"Yes. Come down in an hour's time and I should still be here." Holmes stood and moved to a table set off from the rest of the room. He wanted quiet and time to think. He took his coat off, took out his pipe and pouch of tobacco and began to smoke. Watson took his bag from where it had been placed by the carriage driver and walked upstairs to his room.

Holmes sat and smoked and thought about the case for about thirty minutes. Seamus reentered the room from the kitchen and Holmes took the opportunity to ask him more questions. "Seamus, how tall was the nun?" he asked.

"Oh, hard to tell, her back was bent over, and her knees were bent. She walked with a cane. I didn't see a lot of her. She stayed to herself most of the time. She dressed in her full habit, and I really didn't look at her much." Seamus thought the questioning was over and was eager to move on.

"When the actress was in the pub at dinner time Wednesday past, was the nun here as well?"

"Uh, I didn't notice, Mr. Holmes."

"Think man. Think. Did you ever see the nun and the actress in the same room at the same time?"

"As I think back, no, I never did. But what of it, Mr. Holmes? Like I said, the nun stayed to herself. Mostly stayed in her room and just came down for dinner. She did sit here in the pub most of the day last Wednesday just sitting over there and watching the rain."

"Did she ever paint anything? Did she draw any sketches?"

"No, sir. I never saw her with any materials for painting. She had a lot of baggage sir, but no, I never saw her draw or paint anything."

"Thank you, Seamus." Holmes emptied his pipe and refilled it. He sat back in deep thought as the business of the pub moved around him.

Watson came downstairs for dinner and joined Holmes at his table. "Holmes, I am hungry. Are you going to eat tonight, or will you starve your body again, to feed your brain?" Holmes looked up at Watson as he sat down.

"I will eat something tonight assuming that there is something worth eating in this establishment. You look refreshed. Shall we get something to drink?" Holmes set his pipe down on the table and motioned to the waiter.

"Waiter, I will have an ale please. You, Holmes?"

"I will have a Scotch and soda please."

"Well, it has been an interesting day, Holmes. We now know that a woman, likely the actress who was in this very pub last Wednesday evening, killed Bob Whitaker by driving a long, thin blade into the back of his head as he attempted to have intercourse with her. What do you make of that and how does it fit in with what we already know about the case?" Watson sat back and waited to be enlightened by Holmes.

"Watson, before we left Baker Street, I said to you that the Professor was cleaning up a mess in Tynemouth, and I believe that is exactly what has happened.

Tomorrow when we go into the caves to find the lab, we will find very little. His people will have cleaned it up before we get there. Mr. Whitaker's death was a part of that clean up.

"Clearly the woman who claimed to be an actress was a professional assassin and she was sent here by the Professor to kill Whitaker who had failed him. As usual with the Professor, there is no proof of what I am saying. But I am as sure of that as I would be had I been there to hear the Professor give the order. This woman came, completed her assignment, and then she vanished. Her skills and her method of killing Whitaker have all the hallmarks of a professional and experienced killer. There were two women, strangers to the community, here at the same time. Do you not find that curious, Watson?"

"What, do you mean? The nun?" Watson looked at Holmes incredulously.

"Yes, I mean the nun. While you were upstairs, I spoke further with Seamus. The nun was here and gone as well. She claims to have come to paint the lighthouse, but she never made a single sketch and did no painting. That was blamed on the weather, but I believe it was a ruse. Why would a retired nun come here in winter, when the weather is particularly bad and unpredictable, to paint the lighthouse? Wouldn't such a trip make more sense in the spring or the summer, when the weather was warm?"

"I see your point, Holmes. Are you suggesting that the nun and the actress were in league together?" Watson took a drink of his ale.

"No, Watson. I am suggesting that they were the same person. Seamus has confirmed that the actress and the nun were never seen in the same room, at the same time. Each was here and then gone in short order. It is an easy disguise, Watson, and quite clever. The nun was described as hunched over with bent knees. I have assumed a similar posture when I want to disguise my height. A nun would be above suspicion. I believe that we are looking for a killer who is comfortable assuming different personas, adept at disguise, and skilled at her profession. Her beauty hides a heartless killer."

"But Holmes, her description is hardly helpful. A petite woman, five foot six inches tall, with brown russet hair and green eyes, could fit the description of hundreds of women in London. How will we find her?"

"You are correct, of course. Her description is very common. I am not aware of any active assassins who fit her description. She has remained undetected and unknown to me. I would be surprised if Scotland Yard has arrested anyone for murder who fits her description and demeanor. She is too good at what she does to have been caught by Scotland Yard, and the Professor would be careful not to use someone for so important a task who has a record with the Yard. She is unimportant for our immediate purposes. The question we must focus our efforts on answering is where did the Professor relocate his lab?"

The waiter came back to their table and asked if they wanted to order dinner. "We haven't looked over a menu yet, can you please provide two?" asked Holmes. The waiter came back with two menus.

"Holmes, it seems that we are at a dead end. How are we to find the Professor's lab in a country the size of England?" Watson looked over the menu.

"I have some ideas in that regard. Do you remember Porlock?"

"Yes, he sent you a coded letter in one of our past cases. You described him as someone on the inside of the Professor's organization. Are you planning to seek information from him?"

"Yes, but here comes the waiter again. Let us order dinner. Waiter, I will have the curry chicken and rice please."

"And you sir?" the waiter asked Watson.

"The fish and chips please." Watson was hungry and ordered his dinner with anticipation.

"Holmes, what did you do at the Foreign Office?"

"My efforts there did not bear fruit, Watson. We questioned the man who sent the Professor's telegram, but he knew nothing of the Professor nor anything about the coded message or what it said. He was paid to send messages from time-to-time and to provide information. His contact was a nondescript messenger who provided the messages he sent already coded and the payment in cash. He could not tell us if the Professor had any other agents at the Foreign Office. The minister sacked the man, and it is likely he will be charged with espionage and misuse of Her Majesty's government. He was arrested at the Foreign Office. At least that particular agent is no longer available to the Professor. I had not expected to learn much from this agent, but desperate times call for desperate measures. Though I was able to help the Foreign Office narrow their search for who sent the message, it was still not one of my finest hours. I advised the Foreign Office to use its network in Germany to track down and seize the persons there who received the message from the Professor. That will not be easy, but I advised them how best to locate the person or persons in Germany. I am hopeful that the German members of the Professor's syndicate will be captured."

Holmes seemed depressed. He sipped his Scotch and looked around the pub as if lost. He and Watson sat in silence for several minutes. The seriousness of the case and its significance to the Crown were clearly weighing on Holmes. Their investigation had come full circle. They were back where they had started and it was not clear what the next step was.

"Holmes, despite your best efforts to appear otherwise, you are only human. You are brilliant, diligent, devoted, and disciplined. You are capable of incredible insights, imagination, and your ability to observe and deduce is beyond my understanding. Still, you remain human. No one else in all of England, Europe and the Americas could have gotten this far. You have put your very health, body, and life on the line to solve this case. I frankly do not know what else could have been done." Watson reached over and patted

Holmes on the shoulder. "Drink your Scotch and let us enjoy our dinner."

"Thank you, Watson, but I fear that brilliance, diligence, discipline and devotion may not be enough to stop the Professor or the enemies of the Crown from using this horrible poison, this Green Dragon. I am in hopes that my work beyond this particular case may someday bring down the Professor and his organization. I fear the cost to myself and those around me may be high. Perhaps too high for some to bear. Still, a man's life given in the struggle against the evil that the Professor represents may truly be said to have not been lived in vain."

Watson looked at Holmes concerned and confused. "Holmes, you talk as if this case, this Professor Moriarty, will be the death of you. Come now, surely his reach does not come so close as to put your life in jeopardy?"

Holmes looked at Watson as if looking at an innocent child who does not understand the true ways of the world. "Watson, I dare say that if it were in the Professor's interest that I be dead, I would be and there is very little that you or anyone else could do to prevent it. But his interest has yet to be sufficiently disturbed to make my death worth his efforts and the problems that would rain down upon him for causing it. But that time is coming, and it is coming soon." Holmes looked tired and paler than usual. "You are right though, dear Watson. Let us enjoy our dinner and our drinks and forget about the Professor for one night. Tomorrow will bring new surprises and new problems to resolve." Holmes raised his glass, "To my good friend, Dr. Watson," and he smiled.

Chapter 19

The next morning, Holmes was up early. He dressed and went downstairs and outside before the light of day had dawned on Tynemouth. Holmes walked to the yard in front of the old abbey and looked out at the sea. The light from the lighthouse shone at first bright and then slowly melted into the mist of the sea. The air was clean. The sky was clear, and it was bitterly cold. Holmes knew that when they went to the caves that morning they would find nothing. It was highly probable that the Professor had already cleaned up his mess and relocated the laboratory. Whitaker's murder was proof enough of that. What he needed to discover was where the Professor had moved the lab. Holmes suspected that the Professor, having failed in his first attempt by the inability of his soldiers to carry out his orders, would naturally want to move the laboratory someplace closer to his control. Like a spider, he would move the laboratory toward the center of his web and that center was London. But, where in London would he move the lab?

The first beams of the rising sun came up in the eastern sky and Holmes stood and watched as the sun rose and shined its brilliant light upon the sea. He watched the waves come in and crash upon the pier and rocks. It was a new day. Another opportunity to tease the truth from the tangle of life and to resolve the problems laid before him. Holmes simply stood and watched the morning and the waves.

Holmes met Watson back at the inn ordering his breakfast and drinking a cup of coffee. The two sat and while Watson ate his breakfast and Holmes drank his coffee, they engaged in talk about anything else but the case. It was just before nine in the morning and in walked the inspector flanked by three constables.

"Mr. Holmes and Dr. Watson, good morning. I have kept me word and I am here with me constables. We have come with lanterns and each of us is armed. May I ask if ye are likewise armed?"

Watson and Holmes looked at each other and Watson said, "Yes, I am armed. Holmes does not always arm himself in these situations except with a heavy walking stick or sturdy hunting crop. Am I right Holmes?"

"On this occasion, I am not armed, Inspector. But I feel perfectly safe in the company of Watson, yourself, and these three constables. All will be well, I assure you."

"Good. Now, Mr. Holmes, would ye mind telling me why we are going into the caves? I have prepared a launch for that purpose, and it stands ready for us at the pier." The inspector sat down at the extra chair while he spoke.

"The launch will not be necessary, Inspector," Holmes said with a twinkle in his eye.

"Not necessary? Mr. Holmes, I am not going to climb down the sheer rock face and risk the tide and waves to gain access to the caves. No sir. I do not recommend that for either of ye." The inspector started to stand, but Holmes motioned for him to sit back down.

"The launch will not be necessary because we will be accessing the caves through another entrance. An entrance that has been staring you and everyone in Tynemouth in the face for these many years." Holmes was delighted that his little surprise was having its intended affect.

"Another entrance? Mr. Holmes, I can assure you that there are no other entrances to these caves except by sea. Ye are wasting all our time if ye think otherwise." All three of the constables nodded their heads in agreement with the inspector. "I have indulged your strange methods and little habits in deference to your reputation and results. But this is going too far, sir. There are no other entrances to the caves except their openings at sea. Of that, sir, I am certain."

"How sure are you Inspector?" asked Holmes.

"I am as sure as I am that I am sitting here before ye in the pub." The inspector folded his arms in defiance as the three constables did the same.

"Well then, Watson, if you are finished with your breakfast? Inspector, allow me to surprise and amaze you by taking you to an entrance to these caves just a few yards from where we sit." Holmes stood and Watson wiped his mouth and stood as well. The inspector scoffed, looked at the constables and stood.

"This, sir, is something that I want to see. Lead on!" The inspector was incredulous.

Holmes led them out of the pub and toward the yard in front of the old abbey. The sun was shining, there was a light wind coming off the sea, and it was bitter cold. Holmes walked toward the "inside" of the abbey, between the ruined walls and toward the capstone where the altar had been. As they approached the capstone Holmes stopped and seemed to be lost in intense thought. "Inspector, I may have unnecessarily had you bring your three colleagues." With that Holmes took out his powerful magnifying glass and fell prostrate before the capstone. To the amazement of the Inspector and his three men, Holmes crawled about the cold ground examining the edges of the capstone, all the while letting out little exclamations and mumbling to himself. After several minutes Holmes stood and brushed himself off.

"Watson, I have been an imbecile. After concluding that Oberstein emerged from underground and beneath this very capstone, I should have deduced a mechanism. If you would move aside gentlemen."

"What in blazes are ye talking about Mr. Holmes?" The Inspector looked dumbfounded.

"Move aside please. Now observe the results of deduction and careful attention to detail, Inspector." With that Holmes moved to the farthest shorter side of the rectangle formed by the capstone and with the fingers of both hands under the edge of the capstone he raised it up. As soon as Holmes removed his hands the capstone began to close. Holmes held it open with one arm and gestured grandly with the other.

"It's hollow underneath," said the inspector with amazement. "How the devil did ye know that Mr. Holmes."

"Because, I had eliminated the impossible and whatever else remained, however improbable, must be true. Oberstein had to come from somewhere, inspector. Constable, please hold this open." Holmes rubbed his hands together to get the dirt off. "Now if you can hand me a lantern, let us see what lies underneath."

Holmes took a lantern from one of the constables and shined it in the dark hole underneath the capstone. There was a ramp of stone underneath that went down into a tunnel. Holmes lowered himself into the hole and in a crouched position made his way down the ramp. "Please wait above until I call you down," he said. "Watson, there are large hinges, springs, and counter-weights making the capstone capable of being opened from the inside and close on its own."

Holmes stood at the beginning of the tunnel and breathed in the air. It was not stale but fresh from the other side of the cave system that opened to the sea. The air carried the dank, wet smell of soil and stone, and there was something else as well. Just under those aromas was the smell of death and decay. But it did not smell of chemicals and his breathing was normal and unrestrained. He turned toward the ramp and called up for the rest to join him. The inspector came down next, followed by Watson and then the three constables. The capstone slowly closed behind them leaving them in the dark save for the light of their lanterns.

"Well, I'll be damned, Mr. Holmes. This is incredible. The air is fresh down here and I can feel a draft of air coming from deeper down the tunnel. How in the devil?" The inspector looked at Holmes as if he were a magician.

"Yes, Inspector, I think that we will find that this tunnel leads to some catacombs and eventually out to the caves themselves and the sea. Please stay behind me and shine your lights in front and to either side of me as we walk." Holmes walked only three steps and then stopped. "The floor, Watson. Look at the floor." All five men shined their lanterns on the floor. It was white and chalky. Watson lifted his foot and looked at the bottom of his boot, it was already covered in a thin coating of chalk dust.

They walked only a few yards before they saw niches cut into either side of the tunnel with the old remains of those buried there. There were six niches in all, and each held old relics and remains, except for the last niche on the right that held a relatively fresh dead body, already decomposing. As Holmes neared it the smell of death and decay was thick.

The decaying body of the man was in bad shape. Rats and insects had infested it, and it was little but bone and decaying flesh covered in torn clothing. What flesh was still on the hands and one side of the face hung like strips of old rag. The eyes were missing. The nose had been gnawed away by rats. The cheek bones and teeth were clearly visible in the light, the white bone shining. The lips and tongue were gone and as they stood, transfixed by the bizarre image, one of the constables crossed himself and the other coughed and gagged.

"The dead scientist, Watson," Holmes said with a look of disgust upon his pale face. "Come gentlemen, there is nothing we can do for him."

As they walked a further few yards down the tunnel, two large square rooms cut out of the stone appeared on either side. Holmes went first into the room on the left. It was empty. "Stay back gentlemen. Let me examine the area first." Holmes walked in and shined his light around the square walls and corners of the room. The ceiling was only about six feet from the floor and Holmes had to stoop to move around. Holmes shined his light on the floor in a methodical pattern, back and forth. From where Watson and the others stood, Holmes looked like a ghostly figure, and his light created faint dancing shadows as it reflected off the white, chalky floor. Holmes stopped moving his lantern back and forth and stooped to one knee examining the floor.

"If I am not very much mistaken, there has been a bed set here on the floor. You can just see the marks of the four posts that supported its frame. Over here are marks of a table and several sliding marks where the chair was moved back and forth as the man sat and got up. There are marks from what looks like crates in this corner. I am assuming this is where the man slept and lived." Holmes moved over to a far corner of the room and brushed the surface of the floor lightly with his boot. "There is a hole dug in the floor and covered over with chalk dust and dirt. Where the man had created a makeshift privy."

Holmes left the room, passing the astonished inspector and his constables, and entered the other room slowly. "I need your lights in here gentlemen. Please stop at the door and each of you shine your lights on a different part of the room." The inspector, Watson, and the three constables complied. The room was lit up by their lights and Holmes began to move about the room methodically and carefully, several times on just his tip toes, and then bending low to examine the floor. At three points he stopped, knelt, and with his gloved hand picked up several pieces of something, holding the pieces carefully in the other gloved hand. Holmes covered the entire room carefully and stopped once more and picked up something else from off the floor.

"This is the room where the lab was, Watson. There is nothing more I can glean from this room. Let us follow the tunnel to the cave entrance at the sea."

As they walked further down the tunnel the floor turned gradually downward at an increasing slope. They followed the tunnel for almost twenty yards until it suddenly opened into a large cave at least twenty feet high, fifty feet wide, and several hundred feet deep. It was damp and moisture dripped in places. They could see the opening to the sea to their right as they entered the cave. Holmes stopped.

"Look here, Inspector. The moss growing on these rocks has been scraped and disturbed in several places. Something has been dragged here and over there. There are barely perceptible boot marks from several different men along the edge of these rocks. Watson, as I expected, the lab has been moved and the area cleaned out, except for these pieces of broken glass I took from the second room, and this cigarette butt. It bears the label of a tobacconist in London."

The inspector stared at Holmes in wonder as the three constables held their hats and scratched their heads.

"This is remarkable, Mr. Holmes. What is the meaning of all of this?" asked the inspector.

"Let us all return to the inn and I will explain, Inspector. There is nothing more that we can learn here." Holmes threw the pieces of glass and the cigarette butt into a small pool of water and led the way back up the tunnel toward the entrance under the capstone. Once out, the capstone closed of its own accord, sealing the tunnel underneath it again.

As they walked across the yard and back to the inn, Holmes said to the inspector, "I believe that you need to drop your charges against George Dodd, Inspector. He is guilty only of being blind drunk and unhappy in his job. Oberstein was under the influence of a powerful drug and completely mad when he exited the caves from underneath the capstone and ran toward the only light his nearly blind eyes could see – that lighthouse. In his madness, he attacked Dodd and would likely have killed him if Dodd had not defended himself. Oberstein's murder was justified self-defense. What was going on here has far greater ramifications than the death of one man. I am afraid that at this time, that is all that I can tell you."

The inspector stared at Holmes with his mouth agape. "This is remarkable, Mr. Holmes. Your reputation is certainly well-deserved. I have never seen nor heard of anything to compare to what happened this morning. What was the German fellow doing in those awful caves?"

"I cannot tell you more, Inspector. Suffice it to say that the caves are where Oberstein was exposed to the drug that made him mad. In his madness and pain, he was beyond reasoning with. There was nothing Dodd could do but defend himself. He is innocent of murder."

"I will speak at the assizes on his behalf, Mr. Holmes. If they agree, Dodd will be released by the end of the week. Ye have saved an innocent man from the gallows ye have, Mr. Holmes." The inspector, Watson, the constables, and Holmes stood in front of the inn. "May I shake ye hand, Mr. Holmes?" Holmes shook the inspector's hand, turned, and walked into the inn and up the stairs to his room, leaving Watson and the others alone at the front of the inn.

"Dr. Watson, that was the most remarkable thing that I have ever seen. Holmes is a remarkable man!" the Inspector's face was flushed with emotion.

"Yes, Inspector. He is."

Anthony Poe walked through the streets of London on his way to Chelsea to an art shop identified by one of the cocaine sellers who had refused to sell him cocaine, like all the others had before him. His skin itched. It was like a thousand pins and needles under his flesh trying to get out. His gut hurt. He could not eat without vomiting. His body was covered in a cold sweat. He was clammy. He was pale and had dark circles under his eyes. He could not sleep. He had to get to the art shop and put in his veins what he so desperately needed.

The thoughts in his mind were chaotic. He could not concentrate enough to think about anything for longer than just a few seconds before his mind moved to another disconnected thought or image. His hands shook and his breathing was short and shallow. He stopped for a minute in the street and leaned against a building. He felt dizzy as though he were about to vomit again. He steadied himself and closed his eyes. He as the very epitome of a ruined man. There was no reason to return to his job at the lab. He had missed too many days in the past six months and had not been at work the past Friday or this Monday. The lab's supervising chemist had told him that if he missed any more work, he would be let go. Even the working girls he frequented would not see him anymore. He was alone, desperate, and dying from three and a half days without cocaine.

He arrived in Chelsea and was only two blocks away from where the seller had told him the art shop was and where he could get his injection. He increased his pace looking wildly from shop to shop trying to find the art shop he needed. He finally saw it and almost ran to the door. As he opened the door a little bell sounded. No one was in the shop. He looked around and called out, "Hello? Hello?" From the back of the shop a beautiful woman walked out from behind a door.

"*May I help you, Monsieur?*" Becca feigned the French accent of Mademoiselle Fahrney.

"Yes, yes miss. I was sent here by Froggy Jones. He said that you could help me."

"Well, that depends on what you are looking for. We have paintings and statuary from several local artists and some fine works of Continental artists as well. What are you looking for in particular, Monsieur?" Becca looked at Poe coyly and demurely with her head cocked to one side.

"No, no. I am not interested in art, Mademoiselle. I was told that you sold other items to discriminating buyers in the back of your shop?"

Mademoiselle Fahrney looked at Poe closely. She could see that he was in a bad way and needed a needle quickly. *"You do not look well, Monsieur. How long has it been?"*

"Three days! I am accustomed to using twice a day and for three days I have had nothing. Can you please help me? No one else will sell me anything. I am at my wit's end."

"Well, I usually only sell to those I know."

"Please, Mademoiselle. Please! I will do anything to show you my gratitude."

"Anything? Really Monsieur, you must be careful what you promise." Mademoiselle Fahrney walked closer to Poe and put her hand on his forearm. *"You are shaking. You are in a very bad way. Come, come with Mademoiselle Fahrney and see what she can do for you."* Mademoiselle Fahrney put her arm through Poe's and led him toward the back of the shop. *"Oh, wait one minute."* Mademoiselle

Fahrney turned and walked back toward the front door to the shop and locked it. She put up a little sign that read, "Closed," and turned back toward Poe. *"We will want our privacy. No?"* She walked back to Poe and placed her arm through his again and led him to her back room.

"Thank you! Oh, thank you, Mademoiselle. You are quite beautiful. If I was in better condition, I would certainly be more presentable and better company. I am sorry for that."

Mademoiselle laughed. A wonderfully feminine and seductive laugh. *"It is no problem, Monsieur. I am sure that we will get to know each other much better now. You are young. You are handsome. Let me take care of you, and we shall see if you are not better company in a couple of hours. No?"* Mademoiselle took Poe upstairs to her apartment. He followed her like a cat follows its owner carrying a saucer of milk. He could not take his eyes off her. His anticipation of the needle and the relief it would bring were palpable. She opened the door and invited him in with a feminine wave of her hand, in the European style, with the palm down. He walked into the apartment in a daze.

"Sit, sit here by the fire. Let me take your coat. There, now take off your jacket and roll up your sleeve. Yes. Yes. Relax, mon amour." Poe did as she asked like an obedient child. Helpless. Desperate. He sat in a soft, cushioned chair in front of the warm fire and waited for the ecstasy to come in the form of the needle. It did not take long. Mademoiselle was in front of him again. She went down to her knees in front of him and looked at him with seductive green eyes. She laid the needle and the strap down beside her and with her

fingernails she stroked his forearm and veins. Poe laid his head back against the chair. He was aroused and needy all at once. She softly blew her breath against his skin, and he felt goose bumps all over.

Mademoiselle tied the strap around the top of his left arm, tight. She patted his veins and softly rubbed his arm with her soft fingers. Poe had his eyes shut and his head laid back. The ecstasy had already started, and she had not yet injected him. He was in a swoon of desire and chemical dependence. She took the needle and its accompanying plunger from off the floor beside her.

"Mon amour, Mademoiselle will make you feel so many different ways, but all pleasurable. Now take my love into your veins." She plunged the needle into his vein and released the contents taking the needle out slowly and skillfully. She folded his arm closed and stood in front of him, kissing him deeply on the lips.

He felt the surge of the cocaine go through his entire body. A wave of relief and pleasure. The ecstasy of desire fulfilled. He felt stronger. He felt virile. His body no longer craved. No longer shook. He sat in the chair with his eyes closed for what seemed like hours. And when he finally opened his eyes, she stood naked and inviting in front of him. He could wait no more.

Chapter 20

Moriarty sat at the conference table in the Warehouse during the afternoon briefing. He was anticipating the report from Saacks, who had yet to make it to the meeting. He only half listened to the other reports coming from his generals. His interest was only in whether, after she retired Bob Whitaker, Miss Saint John would also be successful in her plan to lure the new chemist to his work.

He had already learned of Holmes's visit to Tynemouth and his investigation of Whitaker's murder. He had already been assured by his informant in the police force in Tynemouth that though Holmes suspected a woman in the killing, he had no information from which he could identify her. He also learned Holmes had visited the emptied lab in the caves, and he had found nothing there to implicate him or the syndicate. Things were improving. The lab in the Underground was set-up and ready for the chemist to begin his work.

Though his informant in the Foreign Office knew nothing of him or the syndicate, Moriarty wasn't about to take chances. He had already spoken with Colonel Sebastian Moran, who assured him that Moran's political and legal contacts would eliminate that risk while the informant was in jail. Moriarty was pleased that Moran's influence amongst the powerful, the wealthy, and the connected had once again resolved a potentially risky problem before anyone was the wiser. The mess created by Whitaker's incompetence had been cleaned up and things were back in order.

Moriarty had also heard that the inspector in Tynemouth was going to speak at the assizes and was planning to dismiss the charges against the man in the lighthouse who had killed Oberstein. That man, George Dodd, might be a loose end that he would have to deal with later, but that was not his immediate priority.

Moriarty's main concern was getting the Green Dragon completed and ready to be tested. His organization in Spain had already identified a Basque anarchist leader in that country, one Senor Alejandro Vasquez, who was willing to use the Green Dragon in one of his attacks against the Spanish government. That test would informally announce to the world that he had such a weapon and would surely result in interest amongst several governments and separatist groups in Europe. The sale to the Germans would be only the beginning and he would need to scale up his production to meet the expected demand. As Moriarty was thinking, Saacks walked in the room.

"I'm sorry for being late, Professor. I wanted to confirm that Miss Saint John's plan was in motion. Her plan went off like clockwork, sir. She has the chemist in her apartment, and I am to meet them at the prearranged restaurant this evening at dinner to complete the deal." Saacks was out of breath and clearly excited.

"Good. Very good. If the chemist does not agree this evening at dinner, you know what to do?" The Professor looked at Saacks as his head oscillated from side to side.

"Yes, sir. I will retire both Miss Saint John and the chemist, and we will need to find someone else, but I am confident that her plan will work, Professor. This chemist is desperate, out of work, a fraud in his profession, addicted to cocaine, and hungry for the other things that Miss Saint John can offer him. He will agree." Saacks sounded more confident than he was. He had Becca's shop and her apartment above it watched around the clock, with messengers at the ready to deliver any news to him at a moment's notice.

"I trust it will be so, Saacks. It is you whom I shall hold responsible for the failure." The Professor held Saacks's gaze with a cold stare and a scornful frown upon his face. Saacks knew that if he and Becca failed, in addition to Becca and the chemist, he would be dead as well.

Poe was out of breath as he lay beside Mademoiselle. She was incredible and his lust for her, though satiated for the time being, would be with him forever. He knew that. As sure as the drug that flowed in his veins was with him forever, his desire for her was another addictive substance he knew he would not be able to be without and that he would want her again and again. He was amazed at how fate had brought them together when he needed her and what she supplied most desperately. She lifted herself on one elbow looking at him as she caressed his chest with her left hand. Those dreamy green eyes looking at him and her perfect lips moist and inviting.

"*I don't even know your name, mon amour,*" she said with a husky feminine voice.

"Oh, yes. I am Anthony Poe. I'm called Ant by those who know me. Please call me Ant." Poe, who was lying on his back, lifted his head enough to look into her eyes more directly. "You are incredible. I have never felt like that before. You are an angel of grace and beauty. I don't know how I can ever thank you." Poe looked into her green eyes and kissed her softly on the lips.

Mademoiselle Fahrney looked into his eyes, accepting his kiss. She cooed at his kiss and laid her head on his chest. "*You are just what I have been looking for, Ant. You have come into my life like a storm and now there is a quiet calm. You will stay tonight?*"

"Yes, of course. I will stay as long as you let me. I have nothing to go back to. My life will need to start again. Perhaps this is how it begins?" Poe was hesitant but he could not help himself, he felt that he could tell her anything. "What should I call you?"

She giggled and lifted her head from his chest and looking into his eyes said, "*You may call me Gigi. That is a little nickname that my friends in Paris used to call me when I was a little girl. Yes, call me Gigi.*"

Poe and Gigi left her apartment after cleaning up to go to dinner. Becca had arranged with Saacks that he would interrupt their dinner and give Poe the proposition to serve as their chemist. But, at the moment, she was just Gigi.

"I like Indian food very much, Gigi. It is a good suggestion," said Poe as they walked down the street, arm-in-arm.

"When will you need more, Ant? I have more back at the apartment when you need it." Gigi pressed herself against him as they walked.

"Oh, no I should be fine until morning. What you gave me was particularly pure and I am feeling myself again. It's a cold night. Are you warm enough?" he asked.

"Yes, my dear. You make me warm. Warm all over." She smiled as she looked up at him and continued to walk toward the restaurant. Becca knew that her rooms were being watched and suspected that Saacks too was in the shadows somewhere waiting for his time to play his part. She had thought of everything and so far, her plan was going just as she had expected. Unless she was very mistaken, Poe was completely enamored of her, her assumed personality, her beauty, the sex, and of course, the cocaine. He was out of work and desperate. The offer that would come from Saacks was sure to be accepted without question.

They arrived at the restaurant and were seated at a table near the window as Gigi had requested. While they were having a glass of wine, Saacks came into the restaurant and took a table within sight of them, but far enough away as not to be noticed by Poe. Before their dinners arrived, Saacks stood and walked over to their table.

"Mademoiselle Fahrney, isn't it?" he asked.

"Yes, Monsieur. And who are you?" asked Gigi.

"Oh, I apologize I thought that you would remember me. I visited your art shop a month or so ago and purchased a vase for my wife. A French vase. Do you remember?"

"Oh, yes, I remember you. Let me introduce you to Mr. Anthony Poe, my dear friend and escort for the evening." Poe stood and shook hands with Saacks who appeared a bit embarrassed.

"Oh, I am sorry. I didn't mean to interrupt a date. I can speak with you later."

"No, no. It is fine, Monsieur. Does your wife like the vase?"

"Yes, very much. That is what I came over to tell you. She loves the vase and we have been complemented on the fine detail and artistry many times. It enjoys a prominent place in our sitting room. Mr. Poe, I am sorry for interrupting you, please go on with your dinner." Saacks started to turn as if to leave.

"*Please, sir. Sit and join us for a drink before our dinner arrives.*"

"Well, that is very nice. Thank you." Saacks pulled up an additional chair and sat down. "What line of work are you in, Mr. Poe?"

"I am a chemist by trade, but I am afraid that I am between engagements. I worked as a research chemist over at the university, but I recently had a falling out and I am looking for work." Poe was a little embarrassed to admit it, but Gigi stroked his forearm and looked into his eyes.

"*Ant, I mean Mr. Poe, is a wonderful chemist. I am sure that he will find another posting very soon,*" she said.

"A chemist you say. Interesting. My employer has use for a chemist about now. Work of a highly sensitive nature. We recently lost our chemist, and I was tasked just this morning with finding another." Saacks looked at Poe as if examining him.

Poe looked at Saacks with interest. "What kind of work is it?" he asked.

"As I say, it is very sensitive. Can't really talk about it here. My employer would pay very handsomely for the kind of work that we need. The position wouldn't probably last more than a month or so, but the opportunity of further work is there, should my employer be happy with what you, or uh, the person we hire produces. Can't promise anything, you understand."

"Oh, Ant. What a wonderful stroke of luck for you! It seems today is a lucky day, for us both, no?"

"Now, Mademoiselle Fahrney, I haven't said that I would hire Mr. Poe. We are just talking over drinks, as it were. But if you are interested, I am sure that we could speak further."

"Well, yes. I am interested. When can we speak further?" Poe was leaning forward in his chair, both arms in front of him on the table.

"Let me think…tomorrow morning say around 10:30? I can meet you at the art shop. Will that do?"

"Yes. Very good. Yes, I can meet you then." Poe had a smile on his face.

"I see that your dinner is coming. I will bother you no more." Saacks stood and shook Poe's hand and kissed Gigi's hand and went back to his table.

"You are my lucky six pence, dear Gigi. How my life has taken such a turn for the better since I met you." Poe leaned forward and gave Gigi a kiss on the cheek as their food was placed in front of them. He felt that at last he was not alone. At last, his luck would change. He was happy.

Holmes had returned to Baker Street alone. Watson had gone back to his home to unpack and to address a few pressing matters. Holmes had slept well but got up early. The sun was just beginning to rise above London. He was full of energy and anticipation of the day's events. He was very concerned about finding the location of Moriarty's lab. He had concluded that it was most likely in London, but where in the great city was the question that haunted him. He was running out of time. He knew that Moriarty had likely recruited another chemist and was probably hard at work creating a new batch of the Green Dragon. Lives depended on him solving this case and preventing what could be an international disaster.

Holmes paced in front of the fire in his nightshirt and dressing gown. He had his long-stemmed pipe in his mouth and was thinking hard about the question – but he had no data. There was nothing left in Tynemouth for him to decipher and no clues as to the whereabouts of the laboratory. He had but one card left to play and that was Porlock. Holmes did not even know if he were still alive. It had been months since his last contact with him. But he had to try.

Holmes walked over to the bookshelf and took out his older copy of Whitaker's Almanac. He sat at his desk and wrote out the message he would send to Porlock. It read:

> I am aware of the Green Dragon. Aware that the lab in Tynemouth has been moved. Aware that the Germans are buyers. Am close to resolving the case but need location of the new lab. I know it is in London. Can you provide location?
>
> SH

Now he had to encode the message using the code that Porlock had first used in the case Watson published as, *The Valley of Fear*. He looked up the words of his message in the Almanac, counted the words before it, took note of the column and page, and carefully encoded the message to Porlock. The coded message would look like a series of numbers, nothing more. There were certain words he would need to hand write if he could not find them in the Almanac. He wanted to keep as few words as possible in handwritten form as they would be capable of being read by anyone who might intercept the message. The most obvious of which was "dragon." Holmes was able to find every other word he needed for his message in the Almanac. He kept looking for the word, "dragon," and found it in the astronomy section of the Almanac referencing the name of one of the constellations named by Ptolemy. He was relieved. No words would need to be handwritten.

Holmes folded the cryptic message around a ten-pound note, placed it in an envelope, addressed it, and placed it on his desk. He would need to wait for the post office in Camberwell to open. Holmes began pacing again. He knew that his rooms were being watched, and it was likely if he left, he would be followed. He needed to get to the Camberwell post office without being followed.

———————————————

Poe was downstairs in the shop a half hour before Saacks arrived. Gigi was busy cleaning the shop and adding some recently purchased inventory. The "Closed" sign was still up in the window and Poe thought Gigi was losing business.

"Should we open the shop, Gigi?" he asked.

"No, not yet Ant. After you meet with Mr. Saacks. I am so excited for you!" she said with a giggle.

"I am feeling good. Thank you for the, ugh, injection this morning. My whole outlook on life has changed since I met you." Gigi smiled at him and walked over and gave him a suggestive kiss on the lips. Her green eyes were alive and happy.

As Becca worked around the shop, she was also working hard to hide her disgust of Poe. It was not that he was undesirable and wasn't handsome, it was that she just hated the very sight and smell of men. They all wanted one thing – to use her and to take advantage of her. But enough of these thoughts. The sooner she was done with Poe the better. She hoped the Professor would let her kill him in some creative manner. But now she was Gigi, and Gigi loved Poe. She looked up as she heard a knock on the door and saw Saacks. "Okay," she thought, "time to be Gigi again."

Holmes was dressed, had the envelope with the coded message in his jacket pocket, and was putting on his coat when Mrs. Hudson knocked twice on the door and came in.

"Mr. Holmes, you are up and about early. I was just coming up to see if you wanted anything for breakfast, but I see that you are about to go out."

"Thank you, Mrs. Hudson, no breakfast this morning. I have some errands to run. Let Dr. Watson know that I will be back before lunch." Holmes walked past Mrs. Hudson and toward the stairs.

"Goodbye, Mr. Holmes." Mrs. Hudson shook her head as she began to tidy up the room.

Holmes walked out onto Baker Street and hailed a hansom. He waved the first one off. He waved the second one off. He stopped the third one and quickly got in. He called out to the driver, "Grosvenor Square, as fast as you can, driver!" Holmes sat back in the hansom and looked around him, he just saw Blind Bart on his left come out of the shadows of a building and motion for a hansom. He was being followed.

The hansom brought him to Grosvenor Square and Holmes having already paid the driver en route, leaped from the hansom and walked briskly south down Carlo Street, crossing Mount Street to Berkeley Square and hailed another hansom. This time taking the first that arrived. "Haymarket as fast as you can, driver!" he said in a quieter voice. He arrived at Haymarket within minutes, and repeating his process of before, leaped from the hansom and proceeded south to Pall Mall where he hailed another hansom telling this driver to take him to Camberwell Post Office. He was sure that he was not seen or heard.

Holmes arrived at Camberwell Post Office in the far south of London, having gotten out of the hansom two blocks before the Post Office. Holmes stood in the shadows of one of the buildings along the intersection of Camberwell and Waterloo roads. He waited several minutes to ensure that he had not been followed. He was certain that he had lost Blind Bart somewhere between Baker Street and Camberwell, but still he wanted to act quickly. He walked across the street to the post office and having entered went to one of the windows and handed the post office attendant the envelope with the coded message and said, "Hand delivery for Fred Porlock when he calls." Holmes then handed the attendant some change as a tip.

"Yes, sir. For Mr. Fred Porlock when he calls. Thank you, sir."

Holmes quickly left the post office and walked west toward Camberwell Road and caught another hansom home to Baker Street. Now, he just had to wait…and hope. As the hansom went northwest up Camberwell Road, he noticed another hansom at speed going southeast. He had managed to shake his follower and complete the process without Blind Bart knowing where he had gone. He chuckled to himself; it would not be a good day for Blind Bart. Holmes lit his pipe and sat back in the hansom relaxing. He had placed a lot of hope in whether Porlock was still alive, still checking Camberwell Post Office, and would be amenable to cooperating with his investigation. But at present, it was all he had to rely on.

"Well, as I said at dinner last night, this is a very sensitive matter. My employer requires absolute secrecy. You can't even tell Mademoiselle Fahrney the details, mind you." Saacks was pointing his finger in Poe's face as he said this.

"Yes, sir. I understand. But who is your employer?" asked Poe.

"Never you mind about that. Let's just say that your service to your country will be noted and may open doors for you afterward. We need you to review the lab books of the previous chemist, whom we lost in a lab accident. This is dangerous work, therefore the higher wages. We need you to recreate what the previous chemist did, test to ensure that it works, and then make a larger batch that will fit in a one-liter bottle and a half liter brass container. The brass container will hold crystals and the bottle a liquid. When mixed these two chemicals are highly poisonous and form a green gas. Do not under any circumstances mix the two without taking precautions and do not come into contact with the green gas or breathe it in. I will deliver to you the mechanisms I just described after you have recreated the two substances and successfully tested them. You will need to create a means to concentrate the crystals and the liquid so that less can be used with the same effect. If all goes well, we may offer you a position as managing chemist of a small factory making this material for us. Do you understand?"

"Yes, I understand. But I am sure that Gigi has heard us, and she can be trusted. I don't want to keep secrets from her." Poe looked at Saacks with concern.

"Well, if she must know, I will need to swear her to secrecy as well. You understand that I am taking quite a risk here?"

"Yes, I understand. But those are my terms. Where is the lab?"

"The lab, yes. I will take you there shortly. It's probably best that Mademoiselle Fahrney knows as well in case you don't come home one evening." Saacks looked up and motioned for Gigi to come to them. "Mademoiselle Fahrney, you and Mr. Poe are going to take an oath. An oath of secrecy. Please raise your right hands and repeat after me." Saacks, in a solemn and formal fashion, went through the oath of secrecy that now bound both Poe and Gigi. Gigi stood perfectly straight and serious as she repeated the words that Saacks said. Poe looked proud and serious.

"Right. That's done. We are counting on you, Mr. Poe. You are now a part of something much bigger than yourself. We are grateful for what you have agreed to do. Here is twenty pounds as a down payment as it were. I will be back late this afternoon to take you to the lab. You will be working nights. Is that acceptable to you?" Saacks was all business and formality as he handed Poe two ten-pound notes.

"Yes, sir. Thank you, sir. You can count on me. I will not fail you." Poe took the notes and shook Saacks's hand. Gigi had her arm around his waist and rubbed his right shoulder with her free hand.

"Good. I will see you late this afternoon." Saacks nodded to Gigi, turned, and walked out of the shop.

"What do you think it means, Ant?" she asked.

"I think it means that I am now working for Her Majesty's government in a secret capacity," he said. Poe looked down at her in awe.

"Yes, that is what I am thinking as well. We are servants of the Crown!"

Chapter 21

Holmes returned to Baker Street and as he walked into his sitting room, he noticed Watson was looking again at the plans he had drawn-up of the device Holmes expected Moriarty to use to deliver the Green Dragon.

"What do you think, Watson?"

"Holmes, you startled me. It is a diabolical contraption. If he succeeds in getting this completed and sold to the German government, the world will not be safe from anyone who can simply carry a case into a room and leave it to its deadly purpose." Watson was shaking his head and looked worried.

"Yes, that is his plan, of that I am certain." Holmes went to his bedroom and emerged with his dressing gown on over his waistcoat. He was all nervous energy and could not seem to be still, pacing and moving about the room aimlessly.

"Where have you been this morning?" asked Watson.

"I have been to Camberwell where I delivered a coded message to be delivered to Porlock when and if he calls. I was followed and so took precautions." Holmes stopped pacing and stood in front of one of the windows overlooking Baker Street.

"It seems we have solved the murder in Tynemouth, have discovered a much more sinister plot, have learned a great deal about that plot, but are no closer to solving it,

Holmes. What are our next steps?" Watson had walked over to the fire and was lighting a cigar.

"Watson you have summarized the situation succinctly. Porlock is the last piece I have to play. Unless he responds or something else breaks in the case, I am afraid I have very little hope of finding the new laboratory and stopping this disaster before it happens. I am in fear that the Professor has checkmated us. He has played the game well; my last piece must be played and my next move must be brilliant and quick, or I am afraid the game is lost." Holmes gave a quick glance at Watson and his eyes were filled with dread and despair.

Watson puffed at his cigar and looking into the fire said, "There is no one else who could have come this far Holmes. You have done and are doing all that you can."

"Yes, but it is not enough, Watson. Not even close. I do not think this case is one you will want to publish, for all sorts of reasons, not least of which is our apparent failure to solve it and avert a European catastrophe. I am not a cursing man, Watson, but at present if I allowed myself, I am afraid a tirade of curses would spill from my mouth such as would embarrass a sailor." Holmes left the window and resumed his pacing. "We can do nothing now but wait and hope that Porlock gets my message and responds before it is too late."

Watson did not know what else to say. He watched Holmes pace back and forth with a look of concern and pity. He had not seen Holmes in this disturbed a state in some time. There was nothing that he could do and nothing that Holmes could do but wait, and Holmes was not good at waiting. The pressure on him was enormous but greater still was the pressure he put on himself.

"Well, perhaps some lunch will make you feel better. It is still early, but I can ask Mrs. Hudson to bring something up."

"No Watson, I cannot eat. Perhaps some tea and biscuits. That is all I can imagine putting in my stomach at the moment. Thank you."

Watson left to ask Mrs. Hudson for tea and biscuits. Holmes walked over to his writing desk between the windows and opened the middle drawer looking down at his syringe and bottle of cocaine. He stood there arguing with himself regarding whether he should administer the seven percent solution and find reverie in its chemical embrace. He shut the drawer hard as Watson came back into the room.

"Do not go there for solace, Holmes. For God's sake!" Watson looked concerned and angry. Holmes looked over at him sheepishly and walked back to his chair by the fire. "Mrs. Hudson will be up presently with tea and biscuits. In the meantime, smoke your pipe, play your violin, but do not go back to that drawer," Watson pleaded. Holmes simply sat gloomily looking into the fire.

"I sometimes envy you Watson. Having a mind such as mine is both a blessing and a curse. I know there are many who would trade a great deal to have my gifts, but there are times Watson when I would trade much more not to have them. This is such a time. To have simply solved Oberstein's murder without having the ability to see behind it and beyond it. To simply enjoy a scene without dissecting it. To know the peace of stillness.

"I am afraid, dear Watson. Very much afraid that I shall fail in my task and that Moriarty will prevail. And even if I succeed in stopping this wretched crime before it happens, Pandora's box has been opened. Is man mature enough and moral enough to hold such power within the palm of his hand? What one man has invented surely another can discover. The age of reason has lifted us from the mire, but I am afraid it has only lifted us from that pit to kill us all with the sum of our own wit."

It was late afternoon and Becca was about to close the shop but was waiting for Saacks to arrive. Poe had received his second injection of the day – of both his cocaine and Gigi. He was upstairs getting ready. Becca had dressed down for the occasion, preferring more movement and less skirt to get caught on the things around her. Saacks had told her the lab was underground, but that was all. Her hair was up, and she was wearing the shortest heel that she owned. She was impatient to get started. As she dusted, Poe came downstairs and into the shop.

"My love. You look beautiful even when you are trying not to," he said as he approached her for a kiss.

266

"*You are not very objective, mon amour. I look hideous,*" she replied as she gave him a kiss.

"So, are you ready for our little adventure? I must say that I never thought that I would be doing secret work for the Crown. It is very exciting. I want to take you out for a wonderful dinner with the money they paid me already. We should enjoy ourselves a bit, don't you think?"

"*What a wonderful idea. Perhaps Friday night after you get a chance to start on your work tomorrow. That will give you two nights to study and one night off to rest and recuperate. I will also have something special planned for Friday night,*" she flashed him a seductive grin.

"How did I get so lucky to find you, Gigi? I am already looking forward to it. Tomorrow, if you don't mind, I will go to my apartment and get my clothes and other necessaries. I have very little of anything else there. I will pay off the landlord and set myself up here. Does that make you happy?" Poe was taking a risk and he was nervous about it, but he needed to know where this relationship was going.

Gigi stopped her dusting and looked Poe in the eyes, her green eyes welling up with tears, "*Yes, mom amour, that would make me very happy indeed. There is plenty of room upstairs. I had hoped that you would do so. The shop pays the rent, and we have enough money to live. Now that you have this wonderful job, we will do very well indeed.*" Poe walked to her and held her in his arms. He was emotional as well. They stood holding each other, Poe basking in his newfound happiness. The bell over the door interrupted his reverie.

"Are you ready?" asked Saacks. He was all business again. He looked at Becca's eyes. He wanted to determine, was she playing her part or was she falling for Poe? You could never trust a woman's emotions he thought. They were so quick to change sides. He would need to ask her.

"Yes, we are ready to go," said Poe.

"Good come along, I have a carriage outside to take us. I have brought lanterns as well."

"Lanterns? Are we going somewhere dark?" asked Poe.

"Well, yes, you'll see. Now go on to the carriage. May I speak with Mademoiselle for a moment? Seems my wife wants a painting to go with the vase."

"Of course. I will meet you both in the carriage." Poe walked out of the shop and stepped into the waiting carriage.

"This is a bit irregular, Saacks. What do you want to discuss?" Becca was alarmed and on guard.

"You and Poe seem to be getting along very well," he said.

"Yes, isn't that what is supposed to happen?" she asked.

"Are you, objective? Not falling for this man, are you?"

Becca was furious. She turned her back to the store front window and said, "Are you really asking me that? This entire plan comes from me. I have worked it and made it happen. What have you done? Nothing! The sooner we are finished, and I can kill that weak little man, the better. Don't you ever doubt my professionalism or my dedication. No man is going to weaken me or take me off task." She was working hard to regain her composure. Saacks was taken aback. "Now, come with me to the pictures on the wall over there so I can show you a painting to go with that vase." Saacks simply followed her as she suggested, saying nothing. They soon finished the charade and left the shop, Becca being careful to lock the door. Saacks helped Gigi into the carriage, and she sat next to Poe.

"I showed him two paintings that will go wonderfully with the vase," she said. *"Mr. Saacks has agreed to purchase one of the paintings tomorrow. I am so happy to have him as a client. He agreed to pay the full price."* Becca looked straight into Saacks's eyes. Sending him a very clear message.

Saacks wondered how he was going to explain the expenditure of forty pounds for the painting, but such was the cost of upsetting Miss Saint John. "Yes, Mademoiselle, and happy to do so. My wife will love it! Can you have it ready and wrapped for me at noon? I can come around during lunch to pick it up."

"Of course, Monsieur. It will be ready for you tomorrow at noon."

"Well, we must be off," said Saacks. "Driver, the corner of St. Pancras and Wharf roads by the terminus in front of St. Pancras Depot."

Becca was familiar with that area of London and knew that there was nothing there but the Underground and cattle yards. She became nervous. Her hair was up, and she held it in place with two long, metal hair sticks sharpened to a fine point, with decorative jeweled designs on each end. She wondered if she would need them to dispatch Saacks, or if he was being true to the plan? She looked at him in the dark carriage as it rattled along toward their destination. There was nothing in his demeanor to alert her.

She knew that the lab was underground and began to think perhaps it was literally in the Underground. The terminus of several lines ended there. There was the one depot, and people would be around that, but the rest of the area would be little inhabited, especially at night when Poe would be working. The location they were headed to was certainly "remote" for London and secure, but she decided to remain on alert. She held Poe's hand and rubbed her shoulder against him, more as an instinct than as anything she did consciously. She would be more secure when this trip was over, and she was back at her apartment.

The carriage arrived at their destination and Saacks got out first helping Gigi down from the carriage. He asked the driver to wait for them and taking up two dark lanterns, he handed one to Poe and then led them down Wharf Road. He made a sudden left turn into a dark alley and opened one of the shutters of his dark lantern casting a bright light in front of them. He worked a knob to focus the beam by adjusting the lens and proceeded into the alley. Becca stopped and did not enter. Poe, two steps in front of her, stopped as well.

"Is everything all right, my love?"

"No, I am frightened. Mr. Saacks, why have you brought us here? What do you have planned for us?" Gigi's voice trembled and as Poe put his arm around her, he felt her shaking.

"Mademoiselle Fahrney, I know this is irregular, but the secret lab is this way. It is underground, or better said, it is in the Underground. Please follow me. I assure you that there is no danger and you are perfectly safe. If it makes you feel better, I have a revolver. No one will harm you." Saacks did not know if Becca was acting or whether she distrusted him.

"It will be all right, my love. I will protect you. Nothing will happen to you as long as you are with me," Poe said with a hand on each of Gigi's shoulders. Gigi nodded and followed Saacks holding Poe's hand. They arrived close to the end of the alley and there on the ground was a maintenance hatch to the Underground.

"This is where we go down," Saacks said as he opened the hatch. "There are hand and foot rails, like a ladder, that will take us down. Please watch your step. I will proceed first, then Mademoiselle, and you last, Mr. Poe."

The alley was dark, but the hole leading into the Underground was even darker. Becca was not sure about this but decided to proceed as Saacks had instructed. He went down first and as soon as she could not see him anymore, she proceeded carefully down the ladder. She looked up and saw Poe's reassuring face lit by his lantern. He nodded to her. As her head went below ground level, she was immediately aware of a foul stench. The smell of oil, grease, stale water, and rats. Becca hated rats. She could smell their feces and urine. The filthy things with their beady eyes and long tails disgusted her. She closed her eyes for just a second and tried to calm herself.

Saacks was on solid ground shining his lantern at her feet to light her steps as she came down the ladder and stood beside him. Poe was soon down as well. Except for the light of their lanterns, it was pitch black in the tunnel. The ground was just that, compacted dirt. It was damp and she could hear the dripping of water. In places the brick walls of the tunnel were slimy and wet. Becca heard something move in front of her and froze. From the light of Saacks' lantern, she just caught a glimpse of a large rat run out of his light. She shivered.

"I do not want to be down here, Mr. Saacks," Gigi said. *"Can we hurry and get this over with as quickly as possible?"*

"It's not far now. We will have you out of here as soon as we are finished," Saacks said as he walked in front of her.

"It is all right, Gigi. I am here with you. Is it the rats?" Poe asked.

"Yes, mon amour. I dislike rats."

"I will scare any away that come too close. Do not worry, they are more afraid of you than you are of them, I think. You are being very brave. Follow me." Poe held her hand and walked beside and slightly in front of her shining his light in front of them. She followed.

The three walked a few more yards and came to a tunnel that branched off the main line toward the right. As they entered and walked further into the tunnel, their lights began to be reflected off two underground railcars.

"This, Mr. Poe, is your lab. The first car has the electrical power necessary to operate the lights in the second. The second is your lab." Saacks opened a door into the first car and stepped inside while Poe and Gigi waited outside. After a few seconds the first car started up and the lights in the second car came on. "Come in here, Poe and I'll show you how to start it up." Ant went on board, leaving Gigi outside with the second lantern. Saacks showed him how to start the first car and then they both exited the first car and, with Gigi in tow, walked over to the second car.

The second car had been hollowed out. On the walls of the car were lab tables bolted to the metal frame. There was an entire lab set-up inside the second car. Chemicals and lab equipment were stored in shelves on the far end of the car. Poe was impressed by the set-up.

"This is quite the kit," he said to Saacks. "I should have everything that I need, depending on what you want me to do."

"The lab books you need to review are on the desk to the back of the car," Saacks said.

"Good, I'll just take those with me to study back at the apartment," said Poe.

"No. You cannot take the lab books from the car. Under no circumstances are you to take anything from this car at any time. Do you understand?"

"Yes, I understand," Poe nodded.

"You will be watched as you enter and exit this area by other agents who will report back to me. Do not violate our orders and everything will be fine." Saacks looked Poe in the eyes and pointed.

"I do understand, Mr. Saacks. I will not take anything away from the car. When can I start?"

"Tomorrow evening. Plan to be here by 6 o'clock and work until 4:30 in the morning. A carriage will pick you up from the shop at twenty minutes before the hour and take you home each morning. Do not speak with the driver. There is a bag there on the lab table that contains several changes of workmen clothing. You are to wear those clothes and nothing else. You will blend into the area. We can't have you walking around too well-dressed for the surroundings. That will catch attention. Do not speak with anyone about what you are doing. If asked on the street, you are performing maintenance work on the line – that is all. Are these instructions understood?" Saacks again looked Poe in the eyes, his hands on his hips.

"Yes, sir. I understand." Poe picked up the bag of working clothes and slung it over his shoulder.

"Better not to clean those clothes. We have intentionally given you well-worn clothing. Do not look too clean. Remember, you are supposed to be a workman doing maintenance work on the line. Okay, that's all unless you have any questions."

"What am I going to be making here?" asked Poe.

"That will become clear when you study the lab books. Until then, there is no need for me to tell you more. Suffice it to say, you are making a liquid and crystals that when mixed, form a poisonous gas that's green in color. Be very careful. Your life depends upon it."

"It's cold down here, Ant. Mr. Saacks, are we finished? Can we please leave?" Gigi looked tired, cold, and scared.

"Yes, we're done. Let's shut off the first car and return to the surface." Saacks led them out of the lab car and back toward the first car. He got in and shut the car off. They then walked back to the ladder. "Do you remember how to get to the branching tunnel from the ladder?" Saacks asked.

"Yes, I have been careful to observe and to remember," Poe answered.

"Good. Do you remember how to get to the maintenance hatch from where our carriage parked?"

"Yes, and as we walk back, I will be sure to memorize any landmarks that will help me find it in the dark."

The three ascended the ladder and returned to the surface. They walked in silence back to the carriage. Gigi held Ant's hand as the carriage took them home. When they arrived back at the shop, Ant and Gigi descended from the carriage, but Saacks stayed inside.

"The carriage will be here to pick you up tomorrow at twenty minutes before six. Be ready and dressed as instructed. Thank you for agreeing to serve. Your work will be much appreciated. Thank you." With that Saacks closed the carriage door and the carriage started off down the street. Ant and Gigi stood in front of the shop watching the carriage disappear into the distance. Ant had his arm around Gigi's shoulder as she leaned into him.

Chapter 22

Roger Stapleton sat at his desk contemplating the communications that he had reviewed during the past several weeks. It was clear to him that the Professor had decided to create a horrible weapon, in the form of a gas that would kill thousands at its release – and kill them in a most horrible manner. Stapleton was comfortable with the ordinary vices of humanity: gambling, prostitution, drug use, petty theft, and even blackmail. But he was not comfortable with the wholesale slaughter of innocents in the name of power and wealth.

He thought of Holmes frequently and wondered if he should send him a coded message to warn him about the Professor's plans. But fear for his own security and life had prevented him from doing so. He played a very dangerous game each time that he notified Holmes of one of the Professor's plans.

It was 5:30 p.m. on Wednesday, and he was finished for the day. He felt tired and heavy from the burden that he bore. He left the warehouse and took a hansom to Camberwell Post Office, where he still went, once a week, to check to see if Holmes had left him a message. He did not know why he still went weekly. It had been months since the last coded message from Holmes. The post office closed at seven, and he usually arrived about six.

It had become a kind of touchstone for him. A part of his weekly routine. Something he looked forward to, even if there were never any messages. This weekly ritual gave him a sense of moral balance. Even if there were no message, his act of looking for one balanced what he did during the day. At least, in his own mind.

He looked about him as the hansom took him to Camberwell. He had not been followed; of that he was certain. He stopped the hansom several blocks away from the post office and walked the remaining distance to it. Being careful that he was not being observed. When he arrived in front of the post office, he stopped and looked all around him. He saw no one of interest.

He looked up at the post office and asked himself how much longer he would do this. He laughed to himself, for as long he kept up his life of moral ambiguity. Holmes was his touchstone. His compass. He needed this to feel good about himself despite whom he worked for and the communications he read daily. The fact that he had a morally unambiguous relief valve in Holmes, as it were, that he could use to help set things right from time-to-time, made what he knew easier to live with.

He climbed the steps to the post office door and walked in. He went to the first window to his right and said, "Are there any messages for me? Porlock is the name." He half expected the usual, "No," and even turned as if to leave.

"Let me check," said the attendant as he went to a wall of small niches organized in alphabetical order. "Yes, I have one message for you. To be hand delivered upon request. Here it is."

Stapleton held out his hand and took the envelope. He was shaking. "Thank you," he said to the attendant. He walked over to a high shelf that contained an oil lamp and looked at the envelope. It was white. It was neat. And it was addressed to Fred Porlock.

He wondered if he should open it here or wait until he was back home. He could not wait. He opened the envelope and took out the paper inside. A ten-pound note fell to the floor. He bent over and picked it up and put it in his trouser pocket. He unfolded the note and saw that it was a series of numbers in columns. He knew immediately that it was the code that he and Holmes used to communicate. He would not be able to decipher the message until he got home.

Poe was dressed in the old, used workmen's clothing given to him by Saacks and was ready to go outside and wait for the carriage. He had moved his clothing and some other personal items to Gigi's apartment. She had received him with open arms, and he was happy to be living with her. His lease was terminated, and he had paid off the landlord. He had stopped by the university lab to confirm that he was terminated for excessive absences and had taken with him what few personal items he had at the lab. He was beginning a new life with Gigi.

He was standing at the window looking down at the street and thinking about his addiction to cocaine. As he stood at the window thinking, the carriage pulled up in front of the shop. He moved from the window and went downstairs. As he walked into the shop, Gigi looked up at him and excused herself from one of the customers. *"Ready for your first evening at work?"* she asked.

"Yes, and I don't mind saying that I am a bit nervous," Poe replied.

"You will do wonderfully. I have nothing but confidence in you," she said. *"Wait here a minute."* Gigi walked back to the storeroom and office behind the shop and returned with a cloth bag and handed it to Poe.

"What's this?" he asked.

"It is some food to eat and a bottle of water to drink. You'll need it later."

"What would I do without you, Gigi?" Poe gave her a kiss and a quick hug and then walked out the door. He immediately got into the carriage and as soon as he was seated and the door closed, the carriage started off toward the lab.

Stapleton had arrived home and before eating his dinner he took the coded message out and using his older copy of *Whitaker's Almanac*, he worked on the message from Holmes. It took him some time. After decoding the message and reading it his blood ran cold as he realized what Holmes was asking.

Holmes already knew quite a bit about the Green Dragon and the Professor's plans for it. But Holmes needed him to identify the location of the lab. Stapleton knew the location of the lab in the Underground from the many messages that had passed through his hands during the acquisition of the two Underground cars and the one's transformation. But could he reveal that secret to Holmes without putting his own position and his very life in jeopardy?

This was not a request that he could easily grant. He needed time to think before he decided whether to answer Holmes's message with a coded one of his own. Time was short given the Professor's plans for development and testing of the Green Dragon. He knew that Senor Alejandro Vasquez in Spain was waiting and willing to test the Green Dragon for the Professor. Wheels were in motion and plans were coming to fruition.

Stapleton paced his sitting room. His stomach was in knots. His hands shook and his mouth was dry. This was by far the most dangerous request that Holmes had ever made of him. He went over to the fireplace and robotically made his preparations to start the fire. When done, he sat in his chair in front of the fire and stared off into empty space, shivering, not from cold, but from a deep fear.

Poe stepped out of the carriage back at the art store after a night of working in the lab. He had read through the lab books. He now understood that he was to recreate the work of the previous chemist and create two chemicals, one in a crystalline form and another in liquid from that when mixed formed a lethal gas of bis(2-chloroethyl) sulfide, nitrous oxide, arsenic, and other chemicals required to make the mixture atomize more efficiently in the air. He could do that easily. In fact, he could improve on the formula and make the mixture both more lethal and more easily atomized. The previous chemist had rather dramatically named the resulting gas, "the Green Dragon."

He had been in deep thought in the carriage on the trip back. He knew that he could complete his work in the next forty-eight hours and be ready to test the gas on a test subject, likely a small cat or dog. He suspected that the gas had military uses to the Crown and would be a very deadly weapon on the battlefield. It would save countless British lives in battle, so long as the wind did not shift and blow the gas over the British forces.

He wondered if he could make the gas light enough to be carried by the prevailing winds, but dense and therefore heavy enough to stay closer to the ground and make it resistant to changing direction and kill those who had deployed it. That was the problem that dominated his focus while riding in the carriage back home. He thought that it wasn't just a matter of density, but also perhaps making the resulting gas unstable enough to dissipate on its own after a few minutes.

He decided that he would make a more concentrated and effective version of the Green Dragon to test, while also working out how to make it denser, more likely to stay close to the ground, more resistant to the prevailing winds, and more volatile so as to dissipate after only a few minutes. That would take more experimenting and therefore take longer to achieve, but he was confident that he could accomplish it.

Stapleton sat at his desk at the warehouse and tried to work. He was having difficulty concentrating all morning. The generals were in their morning meeting with the Professor. He had heard them talking before the meeting and apparently the new chemist was working and had been observed spending the entire night at the lab. There was a strong feeling of confidence amongst the generals, especially Saacks, that the Green Dragon was back on plan.

Stapleton knew that he had to decide whether he was going to help Holmes. He did not think he was suspected of anything, too far down in the organization to be bothered with, but high enough to know what was going on. He was perfectly placed and in the perfect position to give Holmes help from time-to-time, but this request felt different. The Green Dragon was a key part of the Professor's overall strategy and an important project for the syndicate. If the Professor failed and he suspected someone had betrayed him, he would spare no effort to find out who the traitor was and, if failing in that, he would initiate a purge of persons in critical positions in the organization to kill the one who was guilty. He worried he might be caught up in the chaos and be eliminated along with a few innocent people he worked with.

Even without his help, he thought Holmes might stop the Green Dragon before it was implemented and the result for those in the syndicate, including himself, might be the same. No matter what he did, there was a chance he could be eliminated. There was only one way to save the most lives and that was to tell Holmes the location of the underground lab. It was the death of as many as several hundred innocent people weighed against the death of a handful of people in the syndicate, including himself. He knew on which side the scales tipped. The only question was: Did he have the courage to help Holmes and take the risk? As he was lost in thought, he was startled by the sudden appearance of one of the telegraph operators.

"Damn, Roger, I've been standing here trying to get your attention for almost a minute. What are you thinking about so hard that you couldn't hear me?"

"Sorry, I was daydreaming. What do you have for me?"

"I've got another coded telegraph message from Spain. I need you to decode it and give it to the Professor." The operator handed Stapleton the typed coded message.

"Thank you. I'll get right on it." Stapleton looked at the message and recognized one of the Professor's more complex cyphers. This would take some time to decipher, even with the key on his end. Intricate mathematical formulas were behind the code, and it took several complex steps to decipher. His counterpart in Spain, there was only one person in each organization with the job of decoding messages, had taken a message from someone in the syndicate or a report from outside, had coded the message, and sent it via telegraph to the warehouse. He worked for more than two hours to decode and type the message.

When he was finished, he read it. Senor Vasquez was planning to use the Green Dragon at a large festival in Spain to kill as many men, women, and children as he could in a political statement against the government. He needed the Green Dragon and the device that would deploy the gas within two weeks to be sure he had time to prepare and implement his scheme. Stapleton was shaken by the content of the message. Before he brought it to the Professor, he had to regain his composure. He did not need to think about it any longer, he would tell Holmes where the lab was located but would do so in a manner that would increase the odds that he would be protected.

———————————

Watson was sitting in front of the fire looking at Holmes sitting across from him in his usual place. Holmes was paler than usual, and he had dark circles under his eyes. His hair was uncombed and though it was noon, he still had not changed from his nightshirt and dressing gown. He was barefoot and the area around his chair was a mess of newspapers, his violin and bow, several spent pipes, and ash and tobacco flakes. The atmosphere in the room was heavy with strong tobacco smoke. The curtains were drawn, and the room was dark, except for the light of the fire and the turned down gas lights.

Watson had only just arrived and found Holmes in this state. He had barely acknowledged him when he entered, and Watson knew from long familiarity not to try to engage Holmes in conversation. As he studied Holmes both as a friend and a doctor, there were two knocks on the door, and Mrs. Hudson came in.

"Mr. Holmes! The place is a mess. You have not eaten in two days. I insist that you have something for lunch. Let me bring you some chicken broth, some bread with butter, and some good strong tea. I won't take 'no' for an answer!" Holmes looked up and dismissed her with a grunt.

"Holmes, Mrs. Hudson is right. You must eat something. Mrs. Hudson, please bring up lunch. I will have something more substantial, but what you propose for Holmes is perfect," Watson said. "As your doctor, I am strongly recommending that you eat and build up your strength. You are suffering from nervous frustration, depression, and fatigue. I must insist that you eat."

"You'll listen to Dr. Watson, you will," said Mrs. Hudson as she opened the drapes and cracked the windows to let in fresh air.

Holmes raised his head looking from Watson to Mrs. Hudson. "I suppose you are right. Thank you, Mrs. Hudson. I will have the broth and tea, but no bread please. You will do me the favor Watson of not eating in front of me at present. I do not think I have the stomach to watch."

"Pish, posh! I will be back shortly with your lunch Mr. Holmes. Dr. Watson, looks like you will have to wait." With that, Mrs. Hudson left the room, descending the stairs muttering to herself.

"Holmes, you must not lose hope. It has only been two days. Who knows what the afternoon post will bring?"

"I know, Watson. I know. But this infernal case has me at my wits end. I must know the location of the lab but have no way of deducing its location for myself. I am certain it is in or around London. But where? It could be across the street from these very rooms, and I would not know it. What a damnable position to be in."

"Why don't you go and wash up and get dressed? You will feel better for it. While you do that, I will tidy up around here."

Holmes gave Watson a sheepish look and went to his bedroom. Watson began picking up newspapers and tidying up as much as possible. He stopped and looked around him. It was better, he thought. He walked over to the window and closed it. Looking out the window the snow was gone. It was a bright sunny day. Not as cold as it had been. Watson thought a good walk in Regent's Park would do Holmes a world of good. He decided to suggest it.

Holmes walked back into the sitting room, looking better, but still pale and with the dark circles under his eyes. He joined Watson by the window. "It is a beautiful day. Perhaps a walk in the park?"

"Holmes, you are a mind reader. I was about to suggest just that," Watson looked at him incredulously.

"Well, it doesn't take deductive skills to know what you would suggest on such a day when I am in such a mood. I know your methods, Watson."

Mrs. Hudson came in with the broth and tea. "I want you to drink all this broth, Mr. Holmes. You need your strength."

"Thank you, Mrs. Hudson. Do we need to add doctor to your list of skills?"

"That will be the day!" she said leaving the room.

Chapter 23

Holmes and Watson were taking off their coats, having returned from their walk in the park, when Mrs. Hudson walked into the sitting room.

"The afternoon post came while you were out Mr. Holmes. You have several pieces of mail." She handed Holmes the letters and turned to leave.

"Thank you, Mrs. Hudson. I think some tea and something to eat would be nice. Nothing heavy, mind you, just something light. Your famous cucumber sandwiches, scones, and tea would be quite lovely about now." Holmes looked at Mrs. Hudson with a smile.

"Very good, Mr. Holmes. I see the walk in the park had its desired effect. I will bring it up shortly." Mrs. Hudson smiled back at Holmes, then turned and left.

Holmes threw the uninteresting mail aside until he came upon an envelope that bore his name and address in a handwriting that he immediately recognized. He stared down at the envelope for several seconds. "It's from Porlock," he said. Watson stopped his fidgeting and stood perfectly straight staring at the envelope in Holmes's hand.

"Well, open it, Holmes!"

Holmes walked over to his desk and sat. He examined the envelope carefully before opening it. There was nothing unusual about it. It was postmarked from a post office on the

East End. He took his letter opener and carefully tore the envelope open to reveal its contents. Inside was a letter on ordinary foolscap paper that could be purchased anywhere in town from two dozen paper and ink shops. Nothing there to reveal anything about its owner. The contents were type written on a Sholes & Glidden typewriter. Commonplace amongst typewriters. The message was the now familiar code that he and Porlock had adopted for their communications.

"Come man! Here is the almanac let's begin deciphering. You read the message slowly and I will look up the words in the Almanac and write them down. Come Holmes! What are you waiting for?"

Holmes sat back in his chair with the message folded in his hand looking at it as a fortune teller looks at her crystal ball. "But, of course, you are correct. Let's decipher it, shall we?"

Holmes handed Watson several sheets of paper, ink, and a pen. Watson sat at the table with the Almanac in front of him to the left. He waited for Holmes to give the first number that would signify the page. He leafed through the Almanac to the correct page and waited for the number that would identify the correct column. He found it. Holmes next said the number for the word and Watson counted down the column of words to the correct number and wrote the word down saying, "'The.' Not a very auspicious beginning, Holmes." So, it continued until Watson had what he thought was a full sentence. "It reads thus, 'The truth you seek is never far.' Sounds like a bloody poem, Holmes."

"Be patient, Watson. I had anticipated this. Remember the last time he sent us a message he failed to identify the Almanac; I think because he felt he was being watched or that Moriarty suspected him. Porlock is careful and he has likely built a kind of code within a code to tell us of the location of the lab without being too obvious. At least the first line is both comprehensible and clearly doesn't indicate his refusal to tell us. Promising so far."

Mrs. Hudson came in the room with the tea service, little cucumber sandwiches, and scones. "Put the refreshments on the table, Mrs. Hudson. Watson and I are engaged at the moment but will enjoy your little snack momentarily." Mrs. Hudson shrugged and left the room. Watson helped himself to one of the cucumber sandwiches, putting the whole thing in his mouth at once.

So, it continued for more than an hour as the two deciphered the coded message. Watson poured tea for them both and Holmes helped himself to a scone, while Watson counted and wrote between bites and drinks himself. Before long, the cucumber sandwiches were gone, and the crumbs from the scones littered the table and floor around both Holmes and Watson. The tea was cold and Watson, having eaten most of the cucumber sandwiches, felt like a nap.

"That was the last one, Watson. Read it back to me please."

"It's a bloody two stanza poem, Holmes. It makes no sense. I'll read it aloud to you:

The truth you seek is never far
It lies beneath your feet
The cold and dark the secret keeps
On rails of steel, it sleeps.

For to the rising sun, you face
The northern star sits idle to your left
Abandoned and unused the crypt
That hides the secrets you do seek.

I must confess that it means nothing to me, Holmes. It's a child's rhyme. It's meaningless. No help at all."

Holmes sat still with his eyes closed and his fingers steepled in front of his face. "Read it to me again, Watson. This time slowly, pausing between lines." Watson complied, reading the eight lines carefully and slowly, pausing between lines. Holmes sat still. Silently mouthing the words to himself. Eyes closed and hands before his face. He sat like this for several minutes as Watson watched and read the lines to himself several times. Perplexed.

Suddenly Holmes leaped from the chair and going to the shelf on the opposite wall began to throw papers to the floor looking for something. Upon retrieving what he was looking for, he began shouting, "Mrs. Hudson! Mrs. Hudson! Where the devil is she when you need her?" Mrs. Hudson could be heard coming up the stairs. "Hurry, Mrs. Hudson! I haven't all day!"

"Mr. Holmes, I am coming as fast as my old legs will take me."

"Clean this mess up will you? I need the table."

Mrs. Hudson began to clear the tea setting and wipe away the crumbs as Holmes towered over her repeatedly gesticulating for her to hurry. "There, Mr. Holmes. When would you like dinner?"

"At half past eight on Sunday. Now please get out of the way!" Mrs. Hudson turned and walked downstairs shaking her head and mumbling to herself.

"What do you have there, Holmes?" asked Watson.

"A detailed map of London. Now read me again the first four lines." Holmes had his magnifying glass out looking over the map. Watson complied. "Clearly Porlock is telling us that the lab is underground, that much is clear from the line, 'It lies beneath your feet.'" But where underground? Read me the last line from the first four." Watson read the line. "There is only one thing that runs on rails of steel, Watson, and that's the Underground. The lab is hidden in the London Underground. That narrows things a bit, but there are many dozens of miles of underground railway in London. We need more specifics. Read me the first line of the second four again."

Watson was not finished reading when Holmes let out a cry of excitement. "It's to the east of us, Watson. That is the meaning of facing the sun and north being to our left. It's east of Baker Street. Now, Watson, the last two lines." Watson read them. Holmes stopped and paced back and forth for several minutes.

Holmes mumbled to himself as he tried to divine the meaning of the last two lines. "The lab is underground. It is to the east of Baker Street. It is hidden in the London Underground. But where? 'Abandoned and unused the crypt,'" he quoted.

Holmes began to look over the map of London concentrating on the Underground to the east of Baker Street. Looking past Regent's Park where they had taken their walk earlier, he examined the area around the terminus at Somers Town, but that area was too populated and busy. There were no unused lines there. Then he looked at the terminus off Midland Road just before the much larger terminus and cattle yards. That area was fairly abandoned at night and if his memory served, contained many unused tunnels that had been active during construction but were no longer used except as maintenance back-ups and emergency turnarounds. An easy place to mill about without being noticed. They would have to gain access to the Underground by way of the surface, Holmes thought.

Holmes walked over to his chair by the fire and lit one of his clay pipes and sat. Watson followed and sat in his chair in front of him, lighting a cigar. "What do you make of it, Holmes?"

"This much is clear, Watson. The lab has been hidden in an unused, maintenance tunnel of the London Underground to the east of Baker Street. As I looked at the map the most likely area is the depot off Midland Street just before the much larger terminus and cattle yards further east and north of that location. The area is surrounded by workhouses and is an unsavory part of London. Just the kind of area that Moriarty would be comfortable using. People who frequent the area or who live there keep to themselves. They protect their own. 'Mum's the word' when outsiders ask questions around there. He could control that area. But I must be certain. I cannot waste time looking in the wrong place." Holmes sat in silence smoking his pipe, refilling it twice. An hour went by.

Watson was dozing on and off and his cigar had gone out. He was leaning back in his chair with his feet in front of the fire. He was awakened suddenly by Holmes quick movements as he rose from his chair and began making a mess of his desk.

"What are you looking for Holmes?" he asked with a yawn.

"Where the devil is my chalk?" Holmes asked as he emptied the contents of a drawer on the floor. "Ahh, here it is," and with that Holmes ran from the room and down the stairs.

Watson stood in alarm. Holmes had left without his jacket or coat. He looked at his cigar, only half smoked, and tossed it into the fire. Watson stretched and looked about him at the mess that Holmes had made. He walked to the desk and putting the drawers back in, began to fill them with the papers and other things Holmes had emptied on the floor. He was just finishing when Holmes walked back into the room.

"We should have a visitor in the next hour, Watson. Someone I believe that you will remember, Wiggins." Holmes looked at Watson with a knowing grin.

"What, the young lad who leads that group of street urchins you use from time to time on your cases?"

"Yes, Watson. The very same." Holmes walked over to the fire and chose his long-stemmed cherrywood pipe and began to fill it. "He and his gang of miscreants are my eyes and ears. They will confirm whether my deductions concerning the location of the lab in the Underground are correct. I wager that within twenty-four hours they will either have confirmed or disproved my conclusions."

"What on Earth did you need your piece of chalk so urgently for?" asked Watson, a bit exasperated that he had been left to clean-up the mess Holmes had made.

"To signal, Wiggins of course. I have made my mark on the sides of two buildings on either end of Baker Street. Wiggins frequents the area and always checks. Those marks will summon him to us unless he is busy elsewhere. He will be here within the hour and his gang of miscreants will follow."

It wasn't an hour but two before Holmes and Watson heard the bell at the front door. Holmes walked over to the top of the steps and called down to Mrs. Hudson, "Let Wiggins up please, Mrs. Hudson. The rest are to remain outside."

Holmes stood in front of the table as Wiggins came in. "Mr. Holmes, I came as soon as I saw the sign and could get the others," said Wiggins holding his battered hat in front of him. Wiggins had on several layers of clothing. His boots were secondhand, and the soles were separated from the tops in several places. His gloves were missing the tips of the fingers and his face was grimy. His hair was unkempt and though he was only in his teens, he was already missing two teeth.

"That's fine, Wiggins. You came as soon as you could. I have a very important assignment for you. We need to find the location of an underground rail car, possibly two, which are hidden in one of the old construction tunnels or a maintenance tunnel in the Underground. The most likely location is the terminus by the depot at Midland Street on the near East End. Do you know the location?"

"Yes, sir. You mean the one over by the cattle yards?"

"Yes, that is correct. Not the larger one, mind you, but the smaller depot to the west of the cattle yards. It is likely that the people we are looking for gain access to the Underground through a maintenance entrance on the surface."

"Mr. Holmes, I know of a hatch in an alley in that area, off Midland Street. Me and the boys go down there sometimes. It's not used any more, but there's a ladder that goes down into the Underground. If you're careful, you can get all over London from down there."

"Very good. I want you and the others to watch the area, including the hatch that you describe and tell me if anyone who doesn't belong in the area goes down into the Underground. I need to hear from you as quickly as possible. Normal scale of pay and a sovereign to the one that sees anyone use a hatch or other means to enter the Underground in that area. Understood?"

"Yes, Mr. Holmes. I'll report back to you meself as soon as we see anything."

Holmes handed Wiggins a handkerchief filled with coins, "This is a day's wages in advance. Make sure everyone understands that this is dangerous work, and they must be very careful. Now go on and report to me as soon as you learn anything."

"Yes sir, Mr. Holmes," Wiggins put his knuckle to his brow in salute and ran down the stairs and outside. There was a commotion of noise as the others followed Wiggins down the street going east.

"Can you really trust them, Holmes?" asked Watson.

"They have never failed me before. Wiggins can be trusted to keep the rest of them in line. If there is anyone gaining access to the Underground from Midland Street or the alleyways and streets around it, they will see it and report back." Holmes moved from the window where he had been watching the boys run down the street, his hands in the pockets of his dressing gown. "Fate is an interesting thing, Watson. Our ability to stop Moriarty's scheme, avert the death of possibly hundreds of people, and bring those responsible to justice, rests on the efforts of a dozen street urchins, you and me."

Poe had been working all night. He was very close to completing the first batch of the Green Dragon. He had adjusted the chemical composition to make it more lethal but was going to need more time to make it denser and to maintain its potency while making it volatile enough to disperse within several minutes. He was finishing up for the night, when he saw a light in the tunnel approaching the lab. He immediately turned out the lights in the lab and watched. As he looked into the darkness and his eyes adjusted, he recognized Saacks.

"Mr. Saacks, come in," said Poe as he opened the door to the car. "What brings you down here?" Saacks wasn't alone, there were two rough looking men with him who waited outside the lab as Saacks spoke with Poe.

"How is your work coming along, Poe?" asked Saacks.

"I have almost completed my first batch. Should be finished tomorrow night. I have improved on the formula, and I believe that the resulting gas will be more lethal. I want to work to change the density of the gas, so that it isn't as easily dispersed by the air and stays where it is released longer. I also want to make the gas more volatile so that its chemistry is unstable enough to breakdown to nonlethal constituents after several minutes. Those are safeguards against the gas coming back on those who disperse it."

"Very good. But at present, we just need you to complete a batch. We can work on improving it later. You say you will have a batch ready tomorrow night?" Poe nodded his head. "Good, you will need to test a small amount of the gas to ensure its effectiveness, correct?"

"Yes, Mr. Saacks. I will need a cat or small dog for that."

Saacks knocked on the window of the car and one of the men outside walked over to the door. "Give me the cat," Saacks said. The large man stuck his arm in his coat and pulled out a cat, holding it by the scruff of the neck and handed it to Saacks. "Here Poe. Use this cat. Put it in one of the empty crates for now and use it for the test tomorrow night. You look tired. Go home now."

"Yes, sir. I am tired. Thank you, sir."

"I will come back around tonight. I know working nights might have you confused, so let me be clear, it's Friday morning now. I will come by tonight or early Saturday morning. I'll check on your progress and the results of the test. If all goes well, I will discuss the next steps with you." Saacks put his arm around Poe. "You are doing very well. I am sure that when this assignment is over, we will be able to find you another more permanent posting. Would you like that?"

"Yes, Mr. Saacks. I would like that very much. A more permanent posting would allow me to make a steady income and help me support Gigi. I would like that very much." Poe was all smiles.

"Good, now go home. I'll lock up here. The carriage should be waiting for you upstairs. Give my best to Gigi." Saacks lit a cigarette as Poe left the car and walked down the tunnel. Things were going very well. Even a little ahead of schedule. There would be plenty of time before they needed to ship the Green Dragon and the device to Senor Vasquez in Spain. There was nothing to worry about.

Wiggins had stationed himself on one of the rooftops of an old warehouse overlooking the alley where he knew the hatch to the Underground was located. He had watched as three men walked down the alley, opened the hatch, and disappeared below. He gave a short, shrill whistle and two of his team appeared from out of the darkness in the front of the alley. Wiggins motioned wildly for the two to go down the hatch in the dim light as the sun began to rise over the buildings and cast its light in the alley. The two boys complied.

Several minutes had passed and it was getting lighter. A carriage drove up and stopped at the front of the alley. As he watched, a young man in workman's clothing came up from under the hatch, closed it, and walked to the carriage. As soon as he got in, the carriage started off. Wiggins looked on for several minutes and was about to leave his perch when he saw the hatch open again, and the three men who had gone down earlier came up and walked up the alley and then toward Midland Street. Wiggins ducked so that the three men couldn't see him against the lightening sky. As the men disappeared down Midland Street, Wiggins made his way down from the roof and onto the brick pavement of the alley. He walked toward the hatch and as he came to it, the two boys he had sent down opened the hatch and came up.

"We found it, we have."

"What? What'd you find?" asked Wiggins.

"We found two railcars in an alley like off the main line. It's set back like and that's where the men were talking what came out of the ground before us. It's about fifty feet down the main line to the right."

"You're sure then are ya?"

"Yes, we're sure."

"Good, I'll report to Mr. Holmes. Looks like the three of us will have to share the sovereign. Meet me at the safe place at noon and I'll divvy up the pay with you and the others." Wiggins stood tall as the two boys put their knuckles to their brows in salute and wandered off.

Watson awoke and felt refreshed from his night of dreamless sleep. He stood and quickly got himself dressed and ready and went downstairs to greet Holmes, who he expected was already awake. As he entered the sitting room, there was no Holmes. The fire was out, and the room was chilly. Watson started the fire and then checked Holmes's bedroom, but his bed had not been slept in. As he was about to go downstairs and ask Mrs. Hudson for breakfast, she entered the sitting room through the open door.

"Ah, Mrs. Hudson. I need some breakfast this morning. Perhaps two soft-boiled eggs, some toasted bread, and some coffee?"

"Yes, Dr. Watson, I will bring that up shortly. If you are looking for Mr. Holmes, he is gone. Left around half past seven this morning in the company of that street urchin he lets in from time-to-time. Wiggins I think he is called. Wiggins came ringing the bell at just a little after seven this morning and went immediately upstairs to see Mr. Holmes. Thirty minutes later I heard their steps along the stairs and the front door closing. Here is the newspaper. I'll bring your breakfast in just a minute."

Watson sat at the table and began reading the paper. It was half past eight and he had grown accustomed to Holmes's sudden departures and disappearances for hours at a time. He was not the least concerned. His breakfast came and he ate with a voracious appetite. He hadn't anything to do the rest of the morning, or the afternoon, and no plans for the evening. He was completely at Holmes's disposal and with Holmes out, Watson was decidedly bored. He decided to study the plans for the device that Holmes had drawn for delivering the Green Dragon, one more time. He studied it for another two hours and felt that he fully understood the design and how the mechanisms worked. He felt confident that if called upon he could work the mechanisms to any desired effect.

Having finished his study of the device, Watson walked over to the fire and his chair and selecting a cigar, he sat, smoked, and continued reading the book he had started and tried to read over the past week. It was almost noon by the time Watson decided he had enough of reading and as it was another nice day in London, he decided to go for a walk in the park. But as he retrieved his coat from the hook in the hall outside the sitting room, he heard someone come in the front door. He looked down the stairs to see a seedy, old, retired factory worker stumbling and apparently the worse for drink.

"Excuse me? May I help you sir?" asked Watson looking perturbed at the interruption and trespass of the uninvited guest.

The old factory worker looked up at Watson and almost tipped over as he did. "I'm here for Sherlock Holmes. Might you be him, guv'nor?"

"No, I am his friend and colleague. I am afraid that Mr. Holmes isn't in at present. You will need to return later."

"No, I must see him now." The old factory worker began the process of climbing the stairs in a haphazard and jolting fashion.

"I tell you sir that he is not here. You cannot see him at present. Please go away and come back later when he is here."

The man fell flat on his face half-way up the stairs and staggering back to his feet completed his rise to the landing where Watson stood. He smelled of onions and liquor. "I will see Mr. Holmes now, guv'nor, and you will not keep me from it. Is he in there?" he asked pointing in the direction of the sitting room and its open door.

Mrs. Hudson had opened her door on the first floor and stood looking up at the scene. "Listen here mister, you cannot simply barge into my home demanding to see Mr. Holmes. Now you get down here this instant. This instant! I shall call a constable, I shall!"

Watson stepped in front of the man and attempted to block his way into the sitting room, but the man, who was surprisingly strong, shoved him aside and staggered into the sitting room.

"I am going to call a constable!" Mrs. Hudson shouted from below.

Watson leaned over the railing and called down, "No need Mrs. Hudson, I'll take care of the ruffian." With that Watson walked aggressively into the sitting room only to find that the old man had gone into Holmes's bedroom. "You come out here at once!" Watson shouted as he moved toward the fireplace to retrieve the iron poker.

"Watson, I don't think you need to resort to violence, I mean you no harm," came the voice of Sherlock Holmes as the man began to tear off his hair, beard, and false nose. Holmes let out a loud laugh that continued for several seconds, "If you could only see your face, Watson," and he began to laugh again.

Watson replaced the poker and looked at Holmes with a mixture of embarrassment and frustration, "One of these times, Holmes, I am going to cause you serious bodily harm. This penchant for the dramatic you indulge will one day be your undoing!"

"I would never let it come to that, dear Watson." Holmes began to wash and dress in his usual fashion, as Watson walked to the sitting room door and called down to Mrs. Hudson explaining that everything was all right. He walked back to his chair and sat, trying to calm his rapidly beating heart.

Holmes walked to the fire and stretched himself and picking one of his pipes, filled it from the Persian slipper, and sat in his chair for a smoke.

"In addition to scaring the life out of poor Mrs. Hudson, what else have you been doing this morning?" asked Watson.

"A very productive morning indeed dear Watson. As I predicted, Wiggins and the Irregulars have found the location of Moriarty's lab in the very place I had suspected it of being. And Wiggin's flash of inspiration about the maintenance hatch in an alley off Midland Street proved to be prescient. He came around this morning just after seven. I hadn't slept all night and was awake when he came. I couldn't go out the front door as myself, with our rooms being watched, so I sent him out the front door, and in the disguise that you saw me in just now, I went out the back via the alley behind our rooms. I staggered my way down Baker Street with no one the wiser until I was far enough out of sight to hail a hansom. Several passed me by before one fellow stopped, more out of curiosity than anything, but was convinced to take me to Midland Street when I flashed a sovereign.

"Wiggins met me there and led me down the ladder and into the Underground. We stood for several minutes allowing our eyes to adjust to the near total darkness. From under my disguise, I pulled out a dark lantern, lit it, and we proceeded carefully down the tracks about fifty feet to an abandoned tunnel to the right. It was there that we found the lab. It is brilliantly constructed. I dared not go inside in case I left any sign of entrance. We looked in through the windows. I am certain that this is the location of Moriarty's hidden lab.

"I assigned Wiggins and three other boys of his choosing to watch the area around the alley and the area around the lab in the Underground for the next few days. If anything else happens they will notify me immediately. Wiggins and the three are earning extra pay for this dangerous work. In the meantime, I will send a message to the Foreign Office and to Lestrade at Scotland Yard. We have plans to make."

Watson sat rapt by the story that unfolded from Holmes's lips. "You have done it Holmes. You have done it!"

"I have done nothing yet. We must capture the lab books, the lab itself, the chemicals, and anything else that will deprive Moriarty of his prize. If we can capture the chemist and any of Moriarty's men, it will be a very good day indeed."

Holmes went to his desk and wrote several messages, sealed them in separate envelopes, and called for Mrs. Hudson. He gave her instructions to have the messages hand-delivered to Scotland Yard and the Foreign Office immediately. Afterward he sat in his chair by the fire, obviously exhausted from his efforts, lack of sleep, and failure to eat. "We are on the cusp of a great victory here Watson. Perhaps one of my best cases yet."

"Holmes, you are a benefactor to your race. I have said it before, but it bears repeating. You are an incredible man!"

Chapter 24

Saacks sat at the conference table awaiting the arrival of the others for the Friday morning meeting. He was confident. He was excited. He had good news for the Professor and was eager to deliver it. The other generals began to mill around, sitting in their usual places.

The Professor came into the room looking a bit more tired and round-shouldered than usual. As he sat down one of the servants who was allowed in the room before the meeting began, came over to him and asked if he needed anything. The Professor asked for a coffee and the servant brought a coffee to him, hot and black, within seconds. Moriarty took a sip as the room fell silent.

"Reports, please," he said.

"If I may go first, Professor?" asked Saacks.

"Go on then," answered the Professor impatiently.

"I am very pleased to report, Professor, that the Green Dragon affair is proceeding very well. I checked on progress just this morning at the end of the chemist's shift, and he reports that he will have completed a batch of the Green Dragon towards the end of his shift early Saturday morning. He reports also that he has strengthened the formula making it even more lethal and effective for our purposes. He has other ideas about improvements but understands that his priority is to complete this batch. I have provided him with an appropriate test animal, and if all goes as expected, I believe that we will be able to match your device with the two chemicals by early Sunday morning and be prepared to send the same to Spain on Monday." Saacks beamed with pride of accomplishment.

"Yes, good news indeed. What of Holmes?" asked the Professor.

One of the other generals cleared his throat and answered, "For most of the week since his return from Tynemouth he has kept to his rooms. Later in the week, Holmes and the Doctor took a walk in the park after which Holmes was seen making chalk marks on the sides of two buildings on either end of Baker Street. Two hours later he was visited by a gang of street urchins. He has remained in his rooms ever since."

"Nothing to indicate, however slight or apparently unrelated, that Holmes is in any manner aware of our plans?" Moriarty looked him directly in the eyes, his head oscillating from side to side.

"No, Professor. Nothing to indicate."

The Professor sat thinking, staring down at his cup of coffee. The room was silent as he thought. "Very well, we shall proceed on Sunday. Saacks come by my office Saturday afternoon and pick-up the device. I am making one or two small adjustments, but it will be ready for you to take to the chemist early Sunday morning after he has finished the first batch and his test. You are to manage the process of transferring the chemicals to the device yourself. Take two men with you to act as guards and take one of my private carriages. Have a second carriage with four other men follow you to ensure that you are not under surveillance and to provide additional security. Understood?"

"Yes, Professor. I will attend to the details personally. Thank you, Sir." Saacks looked at the others as if to suggest there was going to be a new number one general and it was going to be he.

By three o'clock in the afternoon, Holmes was prepared for the meeting he had requested with the head of Scotland Yard, the Home Secretary, and the Foreign Secretary. He had set-up a chalkboard in the sitting room and had been busy drawing a near scale map of the buildings and area around the maintenance hatch to the Underground. He covered the drawing with a cloth and impatiently waited for his guests to arrive. Watson had dressed for the occasion and had on one of his finest suits. Holmes was dressed as usual, but without his dressing gown, replaced instead by his jacket. Mrs. Hudson had set a nice spread of delights and tea. Watson had busied himself making the sitting room presentable while Holmes had been drawing his map.

Holmes heard the first hansom arrive at Baker Street. He had instructed his guest to come incognito and not use their formal carriages to help disguise with whom Holmes was meeting. He walked over to the window overlooking Baker Street just in time to see one of his guests dart quickly to the open door that Mrs. Hudson was manning like a sentinel. Two other hansoms followed close behind. Soon all three men were in his sitting room and introductions were made all around. Holmes and Watson already knew the Foreign Secretary.

"As I informed you before we left Whitehall, Mr. Holmes has been kind enough to help Her Majesty's government in one or two little puzzles. He helped me in a personal matter as well," His Lordship cleared his throat. "Mr. Holmes informed me recently about the death of one of Germany's spies, whom we had been following, but unfortunately had lost track of. His advice and information have been invaluable to the Crown. Mr. Holmes, if you will, please inform us why we are all here this Friday afternoon." Sir Trelawney Hope finished his monologue and nodded to Holmes who stood from his chair and addressed the group.

"Thank you for being here on such short notice. You are all very busy men, and I will get straight to the point. The Kingdom and the Continent are in the gravest of danger. A danger of a particularly diabolical and sinister kind. A man whom I am sure none of you is aware exists, known only as Professor Moriarty, who has organized almost all that is evil in London and half of what is illegal on the Continent, has developed a mechanical device, no bigger than a solicitor's briefcase, for delivering a lethal gas that is created when certain chemicals are mixed within the device." Holmes paused as the three men looked at each other in astonishment.

"Mr. Holmes, are you trying to convince me that an organized criminal mind exists in Her Majesty's London whom I, as the Home Secretary, have no idea exists? And this man has been involved for some time, I presume, in developing such a deadly weapon right under our very noses?" The Home Secretary scoffed and looked at Holmes with disbelief.

"Yes, that is exactly what I am saying," Holmes sat down on the edge of his chair beside the fire.

"But that is simply preposterous. As Home Secretary I am responsible for law enforcement, and I have Scotland Yard at my disposal. Surely, I would know of the existence of such a man and the creation of such a device. You cannot be serious."

"I am deadly serious."

"I can assure you that we in the Foreign Office have made certain inquiries once Mr. Holmes made us aware, and I have found that his suspicions are collaborated by what our sources in Germany tell us. The Germans are indeed preparing to buy a weapon. The weapon that Mr. Holmes describes fits what we have heard, and the German government has already made certain financial transfers in the hopes of completing the transaction. Though I cannot elaborate on the exact weapon they are planning to purchase, I can tell you that they intend to purchase a weapon that they are particularly eager to obtain." The minister's collaboration seemed to quiet the group for the moment.

"And we in Scotland Yard have heard rumors of an organizing force behind certain criminal activities. Mostly gambling, prostitution, and certain murders. But it is only rumors. Only Mr. Holmes seems capable of deducing his presence and involvement in certain crimes. No witnesses have come forward to collaborate Mr. Holmes's deductions or the rumors we hear. We remain vigilant, but until more concrete evidence is presented, well, there is nothing for us to do." The head of Scotland Yard added as he crossed his arms and looked skeptically at Holmes.

"Yes, well Moriarty's work began in Tynemouth in some underground caves particularly suited for the task. I discovered the scheme when I was retained in a seemingly unrelated murder case, but once I discovered that the victim was one Gustav Oberstein, well, my case went in a different direction." Both the Home Secretary and the head of Scotland Yard nodded their heads in recognition of Oberstein's name. "Oberstein died more directly from a stab wound to the chest, but indirectly from exposure to a highly toxic gas. Before dying the gas had caused physical conditions of a most painful and deadly kind, skin blisters and skin irritation, damage to the lungs and mucosa, and acute paranoia and possibly even insanity.

"Oberstein was stabbed through the chest likely just minutes before he would have succumbed to the effects of the gas. I have determined, and Dr. Watson has collaborated, that the gas is made up of several different elements, including bis(2-chloroethyl) sulfide, nitrous oxide, arsenic, and phenol. The gas is green in color. I can assure you from personal experience that contact with the gas, even if only for a few seconds, causes extreme discomfort and acute paranoia. It is very dangerous and deadly, gentlemen." Holmes walked over to the table and began to pour himself a cup of tea. "Will you help yourselves, gentlemen?" Watson and the other three gathered around the table and began to enjoy the refreshments that Mrs. Hudson had provided.

"Assuming for the moment that you are correct, how do you anticipate that the gas will be delivered?" asked the head of Scotland Yard.

"There you ask for me to speculate. I have done some thinking in that regard and have even drawn some preliminary plans for such a device. I believe that the gas will be delivered by use of a machine little larger than a solicitor's briefcase. It is powered by means of springs and can be set to release the gas by a timing device, allowing the user to set the device to go off after it has been positioned for maximum effect and the bomber has exited the area," Holmes answered as he walked back to his chair with his tea.

The room was silent as the three men drank their tea, ate little cucumber sandwiches, scones, and pate, resumed their seats, and thought about what Holmes had told them. There was much glancing at each other, each calculating whether the other believed Holmes's story and which of them would be first to comment. The head of Scotland Yard, being the one most closely expected to react to the situation, seemed the least eager to speak. While the Home Secretary, being the one who had spoken first seemed perfectly comfortable waiting for one of the others to take the lead. Even the Foreign Secretary seemed to have lost the will to speak. Watson fidgeted in his chair at the silence, and Holmes and Watson exchanged several knowing glances.

Holmes looked at the three men with a bit of frustration and humor. "Come gentlemen, one of you must break the silence and react to what I have told you."

It was the Foreign Secretary who spoke first, "Gentlemen, we must decide here and now whether to believe Mr. Holmes and then decide on a course of action, assuming that Mr. Holmes can give us his best advice about our next steps. This is not a time to play politics, it is a time for decision and action."

"Thank you, Your Lordship. Yes, it is a time for action and with the expectation that I have your full cooperation, I am prepared to suggest a course of action. No, that is not quite right. I am prepared to demand a course of action and within the next forty-eight hours." Holmes sat his tea down on the mantel in front of the fire, turned, and stared at each of the men sitting in front of him with an air of dominance and confident assurance. At length the Home Secretary, having crossed his legs, sat his tea on his lap and began to speak.

"What would you have us do?" he asked Holmes.

It was five o'clock and Poe was awake and dressed for a night in his laboratory in the Underground. He was sitting in front of the fire when Becca came into the room.

"Gigi, how was your day? I feel like I miss all of it because of this schedule. I see you in the morning and then just before I leave for the night. I will be finished this weekend, and hopefully Mr. Saacks will have something for me to do that I can work on during the day."

"Mon amour, I am fine. I had a good day. I sold several pieces and unpacked a new shipment that just arrived. I am still cataloging the new pieces. Are we not to go out to dinner tonight?" Gigi asked as she leaned over Poe and gave him a suggestive kiss.

"Oh, yes. I am sorry my love, I forgot that we had discussed that earlier in the week. Things have progressed to the point that I need to complete the task. As I said, I am confident that I will be finished this weekend and we should be able to go to dinner on Sunday night."

Gigi feigned an exaggerated frown and put her hands on her hips. Poe stood and walked over to her and embraced her. Gigi pressed her body against his, her hair brushing his cheek and neck. *"It will wait till Sunday then. I am so proud of you, Ant. You are working so hard."* Poe beamed at her praise, as he released her and walked to the window looking for the arrival of the carriage and his trip to the Underground.

Poe arrived at his lab in the Underground and began work almost immediately. His job for the evening was to complete his final distillation of the liquid to bring it to full strength, check to ensure that the separate crystals had formed properly and were complete, and to test the gas on the cat that was meowing incessantly in its crate in the corner of the car. Poe knew that the cat was hungry and probably needed to eliminate its bladder and bowls, but there was no sense in feeding the cat if he was about to kill it. That, and he had nothing to feed it. He imagined that if he simply let the cat out in the Underground it would quickly find a rat to eat and plenty of places to eliminate. But he couldn't do that.

He had enough crystals and liquid for one test and to fill whatever mechanical device Mr. Saacks had created to deploy the gas. The crystals had formed nicely and were complete. Distilling the liquid would simply take time, there was no rushing that process. He checked on the distillation and the drip, drip of the clear liquid into a beaker that told him it was proceeding as planned. While the distillation process was proceeding, he set-up the test chamber.

He wasn't looking forward to the test. It was dangerous and he needed to be very careful and take his time. If any of the seals failed or leaked, he could be poisoned and killed from exposure to the gas. He didn't know what his physical reaction would be after exposure, but he knew enough about the chemistry of the gas to presume that it would not be pleasant. It was corrosive to the skin, the eyes, the mouth, and the lungs. He thought it likely that it would burn the skin around his mouth, his tongue, and burn his lungs until each stopped functioning. It would probably be very painful. He would die choking and writhing in pain. He couldn't even guess what the effects might be on his brain and his mind.

He decided to wait a while after the distillation to conduct the test, giving himself time to increase his nerve and boldness. He wished he had some whisky to drink. He decided to go up and get some air. He climbed the ladder and opened the maintenance hatch and climbed out. As he did, he thought he saw a boy up the alley duck into the shadows. He called out, but there was no answer. Poe stood and breathed in the cold air. The night was clear and in the darkness of the alley he could just make out some stars in the night sky.

Poe stood there staring into the sky and breathing deeply. His hands shook, not because of the cold, but because of his fear. He was putting himself in danger for the sake of a job. He took several deep breaths. It was time to stop procrastinating. It was time to conduct the test.

Poe checked the distillation. It was complete. He filled a small dropper with the liquid and sat it down on the lab table. He set the glass base for the test chamber in front of him and the glass globe beside it. He picked up one crystal using a pair of tweezers and placed it carefully inside a small brass tea strainer. Then he took a long wire and wrapping it around the tea strainer, he pushed the wire through the long glass tube and the tube through the hole in the glass globe, making sure that the rubber seal was tight and seated properly.

Poe walked over to the crate that held the cat. He slowly opened the side of the crate and patted the cat gently on the head. The cat purred and pushed its head against Poe's hand. Poe picked up the cat and stroked it and whispered to it as he walked slowly back to the lab table. He sat the cat on the glass base and lifted the glass globe and placed it over the cat, trapping it inside. He could see the cat meow through the glass and lift its paw to touch the sides of the glass globe. He clamped the globe in place and checked the seal between the globe and its glass base. It was secure.

The cat rubbed against the tea strainer hanging from and attached to the glass tube. It continuously meowed, but Poe could no longer hear it through the thick glass. He picked up the dropper and placed the end inside the glass tube. He looked at the cat. He looked at the dropper. He squeezed the rubber plunger, and the clear, distilled liquid went down the tube and directly to the tea strainer. He took the dropper out and sealed the open end of the glass tube with a rubber stopper and waited. It did not take long.

A green gas began to snake its way from the tea strainer, slowly at first and then more and more in quick succession. The green cloud of gas dissipated throughout the glass globe and almost immediately the cat began to react. It pushed against the glass and began to shake uncontrollably. Its muscles spasmed. Blisters appeared on its nose and mouth. Its eyes wide and its pupils fully dilated, it arched its back in pain. It writhed in circles as its eyes began to bleed and its body shook. Its nose and mouth were covered in blisters and its ears and eyes bled freely. The cat turned over on its back, its legs in unnatural angles to its body, and in one violent convulsion, it was dead.

Poe stared at the scene playing out before him in the little world created by the glass globe. A tear ran down his cheek and then more. He covered his mouth in horror at what he had created. He backed away from the globe as the cat's mouth foamed and its dead eyes bled. He turned away and hurried to a trash can and began to vomit. He vomited until he only retched. He was covered in sweat. He made his way out of the lab and toward the ladder. He stopped at the ladder, shaking. He stood and didn't know what to do next. He stood there for what seemed like an hour, but he knew it was only minutes. Recovering, he slowly walked back down the tunnel to the waiting lab and the dead cat.

Chapter 25

Saacks was on his way by hansom to meet the Professor at the warehouse. When he stepped into the Professor's office, he was there, reading a book, smoking a cigar, and having a drink. On the desk in front of him sat a solicitor's briefcase.

"Professor, I am here to retrieve the device, and I have already made all the preparations to meet our chemist in the lab this evening and complete the transfer of the chemicals to the device. Our men are ready, and the precautions have been made. Holmes had three visitors yesterday. Three men in hansoms arrived at Baker Street and met with Holmes for over two hours. They left the same way. We don't know the identities of the three men, but they were well-dressed and had an air of officialness about them. Holmes himself hasn't left his rooms since his walk in the park with the Doctor."

The Professor looked up and nodded. "Right. There is not a great deal that we can do about Holmes at present. He is a bit of a busybody and has people of all types come and go at all hours it appears. Have we any reason to believe that he is aware of our plans? Any unusual goings on at Scotland Yard?"

"No sir. Things are quite normal at Scotland Yard. Nothing to indicate that Holmes is aware of our plans."

"Good. Holmes bears consideration and watching. Ensure that there are sufficient messengers to deliver a message to you and to me immediately should anything change or should Holmes leave the premises. I also want to know if there is anything out of the ordinary happening at Scotland Yard. Until we have information, there is nothing to do but proceed as planned. If there is any sign that we have been found out, you are not to hesitate. Burn the lab books and arm the device and, if you can, get out of the Underground. If you cannot escape, I suggest that you save your last bullet for yourself to avoid exposure and death from the gas. Better to take Holmes and the officials out in the Underground and lose the device than let the chemicals, crystals, and lab books fall into their hands. Are you prepared to take those actions and make the final sacrifice?" The Professor looked into Saacks's eyes with a cold, unfeeling stare.

Saacks thought about it for a few seconds and then responded, "Let's hope it doesn't come to that Professor. But, yes, I am prepared to do what must be done."

"Very good. This is the device here in front of me on this desk. The sides are a simple mock-up to disguise the device inside. All four sides come down to reveal the device by simply releasing four hidden clasps in each top corner. All four sides are hinged at the bottom. You open it as so," the Professor released four hidden clasps designed to look like decorative ornamentation at each of the four top corners of the briefcase, and the four sides lay flat on the desk revealing a rectangular metal frame that contained gears, springs, a brass bowl-like structure with holes drilled in it, reminding Saacks of a kitchen colander, and a glass container above it. There was a fan operated by springs and a timing device. A brass hammer like contraption operated by a strong spring was beside the glass container and appeared, when cocked like the hammer of a gun, to be released by the spring to strike the glass container breaking it and releasing the liquid that would be placed inside it. The sides of the briefcase were drilled with holes as well, apparently to allow the gas to escape.

The Professor explained the device to Saacks and how it operated, including how to arm the hammer and how to set the timer. The timer was calibrated in fifteen-minute intervals up to one hour. "This is the little addition that I have been working on recently. When the hammer has been cocked, if you activate this lever by pushing it downward, as so, if the timer malfunctions or is disabled, or if the springs are tampered with, the lever acts as a kind of hair trigger and when disturbed will cause the hammer to immediately release and break the glass. It is an extra method to ensure that once set and the lever pushed down, there isn't any way to stop the device from activating, if moved or jostled. Before activating the device, you will need to wind the springs by means of this key." The Professor held up a "T" shaped key made of brass. It reminded Saacks of something used in children's wind-up toys. "There are three small round openings along this side of the apparatus. One for the spring that arms the hammer, one for the fan, and the other for the timing device. Each must be wound before the device is ready to be used. The user will place the key in each opening and wind the springs. Mind you, the user must turn the key in a counterclockwise fashion for at least thirty full revolutions to ensure that the springs are wound tight enough that the device works properly. I always prefer to wind it thirty-five full revolutions but no more. Understood?"

"Yes, Professor. An ingenious device, Sir. Amazing construction and a brilliant design." Saacks was truly impressed.

"Yes, Saacks. I agree. This and the air gun that was manufactured to my specifications are indeed ingenious and useful devices. Be very careful with this. It isn't fragile, but no sense in taking the risk of causing any damage. Do not treat it like a piece of luggage. Rather, treat it as a finely tuned machine. A scientific instrument. All clear?"

"Yes, Professor. I understand. May I take the device now?" The Professor nodded, as he closed the four sides, and when each side met its mate there was an audible click of the four clasps.

"Watson, I must confess that I have strong reservations about you accompanying me this evening. This is a desperate and dangerous affair and there will likely be violence. I am sure that Mrs. Watson would be very cross with me if she knew that I were considering including you in this evening's events." Holmes was standing by the fire with his long-stemmed cherrywood pipe in his hand. Watson had just walked into the room having freshened up before dinner. He stopped and looked at Holmes with an air of disappointment.

"I only wish to be useful, Holmes. The danger is no greater for me than it is for you. If I can be of service, I want and plan to join you this evening."

Holmes looked at Watson for several seconds and then said, "As I have said before and will undoubtedly say again, I am lost without my Boswell. You are up for the evening's events? Your leg is up to it?"

"Yes, Holmes. I am prepared both mentally and physically. I have studied your drawings of the anticipated device and I am prepared to put life and limb on the line to protect Her Majesty's government and the peace of our genteel society. As for Mrs. Watson, she knows well the man she has married. And it is quite fortunate that she is on the Continent and many miles away from here. So, as you are fond of saying, 'The game is afoot,' and let us act likewise!"

"Watson, you are a true friend. I hoped and knew that you would not shrink at the last. Excellent. You will of course arm yourself and bring additional ammunition. I too will be armed and with more than my usual weighted stick, I assure you. We must be keen this evening and wary, for our quarry is sharp and deadly."

"I am prepared Holmes." Watson smiled and took his seat at the fire.

"Do not get comfortable, Watson. Inspector MacDonald will be joining us shortly. I have wired for him to come around at five and it is only a few minutes before five now."

"I thought that you didn't trust Scotland Yard and that you were wary of leaks that might go to Moriarty. You told the others as much yesterday when we met."

"We have need of MacDonald and three trusted constables that he selects. He doesn't yet know why I called for him. Once he arrives, I will be circumspect in what I tell him. Rest assured, Watson, the details shall be safely kept secret, and we shall rely on the resources of Her Majesty's army as we have decided. Secrecy there is a way of life."

Holmes heard the hansom pull up in front of Baker Street and walked over to the window. "Ah, he is here." Holmes stood by the window and waited for Inspector MacDonald to walk in.

"Holmes, ye old scoundrel! Ye called me. Need an old hound by ye side on some new adventure?" MacDonald asked as he walked into the sitting room with a smile.

"Something like that, yes," said Holmes.

"Dr. Watson, always the loyal friend. How are ye?" MacDonald took off his coat and threw it over a chair by the table. He walked over to Watson and shook his hand heartily. MacDonald was unusually gregarious and boisterous, a departure from his normally dour and precise nature. Watson was happy to see it. The middle-aged Scottish inspector was one of Holmes's favorites and one of Scotland Yard's finest.

"Please sit, MacDonald. May I offer you a Scotch and soda?" asked Holmes.

"Well, it's after five, so yes. I'll take a wee nip to warm me bones," he said.

Watson did the honors and handed MacDonald a glass of Scotch and soda from the tantalus and gasogene. "Ahh, that's just what I needed, Dr. Watson. Thank ye! So, Mr. Holmes, why have ye called me here this evening and what do ye want me to do?"

Holmes smiled and walking over to his chair by the fire said, "It is a dangerous and secret affair that I will be asking you to help me with tonight. I say secret, because the events of this evening have been finely planned and are known to only a few at the highest levels of Her Majesty's government. You must keep things very close to the vest. Trust no one and tell no one what I am about to reveal to you. Understood?"

"Of course, Mr. Holmes. Mum's the word." MacDonald downed his drink and then transforming from the gregarious Scotsman to the precise and careful inspector, assuming his usual precise and dour nature.

"I want you to select three constables, sturdy, strong and brave men whom you trust implicitly, and you know to be above reproach. These men need to keep things to themselves and not talk around the Yard. Above all, you must be sure that they are not under anyone's influence or on anyone's payroll. They need to be experienced in handling revolvers and comfortable using them if they are called upon to defend themselves. Are you able to do that?"

"Yes, Mr. Holmes, but for what purpose do ye need me and these three men this evening?"

"You recall a few years ago when you and I worked on the Birlstone Manor case?" MacDonald nodded his head. "You came by just as I was getting into the case, and we discussed Professor Moriarty. Do you remember that?"

"Yes, Holmes, I remember that. This Professor is someone that ye have believed for years is behind a great many criminal activities in Her Majesty's Kingdom. If I recall, ye have referred to him as 'the Napoleon of crime.' Do ye mean to tell me that this matter, what ye need me and these constables for this evening, involves the Professor?"

Holmes smiled, "Yes, it does. I doubt that we will find him this evening, but we will deal his organization a terrible blow if what I believe will happen this evening transpires as I have planned. I cannot tell you a great deal, only that we will be going into the Underground to stop a terrible and insidious plot involving national and international interests. Can you help me?"

"Mr. Holmes, all ye had to say was ye need my help to hurt this Professor and his organization. I'm yours to command. Just tell me when and where and I'll come like an old dog sniffing at the fox." MacDonald had a serious and determined look in his eyes. His jaw was set, and his voice was low and menacing.

"Good. I am expecting to receive a messenger who will give us an idea about when, but due to the secrecy involved I will not be able to send for you when I am alerted.

Be at the terminus on the corner of Drummond and Seymour streets at ten o'clock this evening, with the three constables. Make yourselves inconspicuous. Do your best to hide in the shadows and not be seen. I suggest that the constables be in plain clothes. You may spot some street urchins in the area, do not be concerned, they are with me. Watson and I will meet you there likely between ten and midnight. It may be a long cold vigil for you, but there is nothing to be done.

"In the meantime, I suggest you get something to eat and prepare yourself and your men for a late and possibly violent night. Dress warmly, but in a way to fit in with your surroundings. Do not stand together. Separate yourselves and act as if you are not together. Those are my instructions. Be careful and be vigilant. Whatever transpires, do not act until I arrive, and you have further instructions." Holmes stood and MacDonald stood with him. MacDonald shook hands with Holmes and Watson, picked up his coat, and left Baker Street.

"Whom do you expect to hear from this evening?" asked Watson.

"Why, Wiggins of course, or more likely one of his gang of boys sent to alert me. They have the alleyway leading down into the Underground under watch. They will tell me when anyone goes down. That will be our signal to go as well. This is a dirty business, Watson. I am afraid that death follows us this evening and may visit us, we two. Do be careful. I am not a weak man, Watson, but I must confess to being a bit shaken by what will transpire this evening. Very much shaken." As Holmes reached for his pipe on the mantel, his hand shook, and his eyes foretold the horror he expected.

Chapter 26

Poe was riding in a hansom on his way to the lab. It was late and it was dark. The London streets had a strange feel in the darkness, a lonely embrace, filled with mystery as the fog began to fill the streets. The gas lamps diffused their light and gave the streets a surreal gray glow. That glow moved slowly, aimlessly transforming as the fog continuously changed its shape in the darkness. He felt lost inside himself. Detached and floating within his own thoughts. Thoughts that matched the aimless motion of the drifting fog. The effects of both the cocaine and the wine from dinner, he imagined.

He took out his pocket watch and in the dim light as he passed a gas lamp, he saw that he was running late. Saacks had told him to be at the lab by 10:30. It was already ten thirty and he was still several minutes away. He had the driver drop him off two blocks away from the alley and walked the rest of the way in the growing fog. As he approached the alley, he saw the dark shape of two hansoms in the fog. Around one, he could just make out four men standing around and smoking in the cold. As he arrived, they seemed to recognize him and ignored him as he turned into the alley.

He looked back up the alley as he arrived at the maintenance hatch and thought he saw an indistinct figure move along the roof of a building across the street. He laughed to himself, saying, "It's just a trick of the fog." He opened the hatch and descended into the cold and dark of the London Underground.

Baker Street was warm. The fire was lively and bright, and the gas lights lit the room with a warm, comforting glow. Holmes sat in his chair, pipe in mouth, looking into the fire and drumming his fingers rhythmically against the arm of his chair. Watson was starting to doze as his head nodded and his eyes grew heavy. Holmes was too full of nervous energy and anticipation to sleep. He was awaiting word from the Irregulars that Moriarty's men had arrived at the lab. His plans were set. Soldiers from Her Majesty's Army were in place, the Irregulars were keeping watch, and Inspector MacDonald and his men were no doubt at their posts awaiting his arrival. He looked at his watch. It was almost eleven and he was beginning to worry that all his plans were for naught. He stood and began to pace, waking Watson in the process.

"Any word, Holmes?" asked Watson.

"No, Watson. Nothing as yet." Holmes walked over to the window and raising the shade looked down on a foggy Baker Street. "It's a foggy night Watson. That will aid us as we depart our rooms this evening. You remember what to do?"

"Yes, Holmes. I am to hail a hansom and give him my home address. After three blocks I am to ask the driver to stop and wait for you to join me. You will be leaving Baker Street from the alley behind us. Don't worry, old man, everything will go as planned."

Holmes walked back in front of the fire and then turned and went back to the window. He was the picture of anxiety. His barely controlled nervous energy not allowing him to sit or be still. "We should have heard something from Wiggins by now. It is well past eleven and still no word." Holmes walked back in front of the fire.

"Holmes, please sit down." Watson's eyes practically begged Holmes to sit.

Holmes fell into his chair exasperated, dropping his pipe to the floor beside him. "If I am wrong about this evening, Watson..." Holmes left his sentence unfinished, steepling his fingers in front of his face, eyes closed. "Well, my credibility will suffer a great blow, and I will never hear the end of it from Scotland Yard. And more importantly, we may lose our last chance to stop this scheme once and for all." Holmes sat as still as a statue for several minutes. "No, failure is not an option. It must be tonight." He stood and began to pace again.

Watson watched helplessly as Holmes paced back and forth between the window and the fire. He stood and, walking over to the table, began to check his revolver. It was cold and heavy. He checked to ensure that it was fully loaded and checked the box of shells lying next to it. He had fewer than fifty rounds of ammunition and couldn't conceive of a situation where he would ever need that many shells. But Holmes's unusual anxiety about the evening made him wonder whether even this many rounds would be enough to keep Moriarty's men at bay and keep them safe during this struggle between order and chaos. Closing the breach of his revolver he laid it back down on the table and stood, hands in pockets, as Holmes stopped at the window and with a grunt practically threw himself toward the open door of their rooms and down the stairs, just as the bell rang signifying a visitor.

Watson waited by the table and heard as Holmes bounded up the stairs two at a time and reentered their rooms throwing his dressing gown on the back of the settee as he went to his room saying, "That was one of Wiggins' boys. The men are there. Four in the alley and four in the Underground. Get your coat, Watson; we must act with stealth and speed." Watson walked to the hooks just outside their door and retrieved his heavy winter coat and hat. He put the box of cartridges in his left coat pocket and the revolver in the right pocket. He picked up his medical bag and checked its contents to be sure he had what he needed, should anyone be injured or shot. He was ready.

"Go Watson! Hail your hansom and meet me three blocks down Baker Street." Holmes had on his coat, hat, and gloves and was in the process of checking his revolver as he walked swiftly back into the sitting room. Watson nodded and walked out the door and toward the stairs. "Be careful Watson. Take no risks. Do not hesitate to use your revolver against Moriarty's men. For they will not hesitate to use their revolvers on you!"

"Understood, Holmes. And you be careful as well," Watson shouted back as he went quickly down the stairs and through the front door to Baker Street.

Holmes followed Watson down the stairs and made a U-turn behind the stairs and toward the back of the house. He turned the gas off and the short hallway became dark. He stopped at the back door and raised the collars of his coat around his head and face and wrapped a long grey scarf around his neck and the lower half of his face. He opened the door slowly, silently, and carefully peered out into the back alley and the fog. He looked up and down the alley. In the fog he could not see very far. But that also meant that anyone in the alley couldn't see very far either.

He quickly and silently left Baker Street and proceeded down the alley towards the cross street making his way the three blocks before he would turn left and back toward Baker Street. He stopped several times and listened. He could hear no one following him. His own footfalls in the alley were silent, and he crept along quickly moving in and out of heavier patches of fog as he went.

Holmes could hear his own heart beating loudly in his muffled ears. His breaths were short and rapid as he went. His mouth open under the scarf breathing in the cold night air. He arrived at the cross street he wanted and pressed himself against the cold brick wall of the building to his left. He strained to see down the right side of the street but could see only the grey formless movement of the fog in the dampened lights. Keeping close to the building, he turned left and proceeded toward Baker Street.

The hansom had stopped at the corner and Holmes almost walked into the side of it in the fog. He quickly got in and sat next to Watson, knocking on the roof of the hansom to signal the driver to move on. As the hansom lurched forward and moved along Baker Street, Holmes quietly told the driver their true destination. They went along the fogged streets of London in silence. Each man lost in his own thoughts moving toward an uncertain future and the danger and violence that awaited them.

Saacks was in the lab waiting for Poe. He had two men keeping watch in the darkness of the short tunnel. The briefcase-sized device was sitting on a lab table awaiting the chemicals that would make it a deadly weapon. He had been waiting for about ten minutes when he saw Poe outside the door of the car coming in.

"You're late,"

"Yes, I apologize. Dinner went a bit longer than expected, and in this fog, the hansom was slower than usual. Is that the device?" Poe walked in and took off his coat.

"That's correct. Are you ready to transfer the chemicals to the device?"

"Yes. Can you explain the device to me and how it operates so that I understand the risk as I introduce the chemicals to it?" Poe looked focused and kept his eyes on the briefcase sitting on the lab table.

Saacks walked over and opened the four sides by use of the decorative clasps on each corner and began his explanation of how it functioned. Poe listened carefully asking questions as Saacks went through his tutorial. As Saacks finished, Poe understood how ingenious the device was. He examined the glass globe that would hold the liquid. It was held in place by four leather straps that formed an "X" shape across the bottom of the glass. These were held in place by sets of bolts and nuts. The straps held the glass globe in place and a cork stopper with a rubber seal around it covered a round opening in the top center of the globe. He went to a toolbox on another lab table and took out the tools he needed to release the straps.

The work was slow and tedious. Poe had to remove the glass globe to get at the brass bowl that would hold the crystals. Transferring the crystals to the brass bowl wasn't difficult and went quickly. He replaced the glass globe and took out the cork stopper. Transferring the liquid was going to be much more difficult and dangerous. He could not allow even a drop of the liquid to escape and come in contact with the crystals. Doing so would create enough of the gas to at least incapacitate him and Saacks – if not kill them both. He studied the opening in the glass globe carefully.

"This isn't going to be easy, Mr. Saacks. You and your men may want to wait in the alley above while I make the transfer of the liquid."

As Saacks watched Poe, he could see perspiration forming on Poe's forehead and temples. "Do you think that necessary?" he asked.

"Yes. If even one drop of the liquid touches a single crystal, the reaction will take place and release the deadly gas. There is no point in putting you and your men at risk. I can come up and get you once I am finished with the transfer." Poe took out a handkerchief and wiped his brow.

"All right. We will be just outside the maintenance hatch waiting. Don't take too long. As long as we are outside, we are exposed and can be seen. Even in this fog, I don't want to take any chances of being discovered. Good luck." Saacks left the lab car, gathered his men, and lighting a cigarette made his way to the ladder and the surface.

Holmes and Watson arrived at the terminus at the corner of Drummond and Seymour streets and exited the hansom. The terminus was closed at this hour, but Holmes had arranged for one door to be unlocked. He looked around him in the fog and could see nothing but the gray mist. He didn't want to call out as the sound of his voice might alert Moriarty's men. He and Watson waited and soon three figures in old torn clothing appeared from out of the fog. It was MacDonald and two other men. Holmes motioned and the five of them went into the terminus through a side door that was unlocked.

"Are ye sure there are enough of us, Holmes?" asked the inspector.

"There are more, I assure you. Let's go down to the Underground where there should be several soldiers from Her Majesty's Army waiting for us with two Underground railcars." Holmes spoke in whispers even though they were safely inside the terminus.

"Sounds like ye've done it up nicely, Mr. Holmes. These are two constables who I know and trust. Between the three of us, we've got ye and the Doctor covered." MacDonald was deliberate and focused. His stern face revealing the seriousness of the situation.

Holmes led the way, and the five men took a long hallway to some stairs and down to the Underground and the boarding platform. As they arrived, they immediately saw two railcars almost full of armed soldiers. An officer was waiting for them on the platform.

"Mr. Sherlock Holmes, I presume?" he asked.

"Yes. This is my friend and colleague, Doctor Watson, and Inspector MacDonald from Scotland Yard and his two constables. Are your men ready?" Holmes shook the officer's hand.

"Yes, sir. Just waiting on your arrival."

"Good. Inspector, I want you and your men to go back outside and position yourselves just ahead of the alleyway. I suspect that there may be a few of Moriarty's men at the entrance to the alley. My lads tell me there are four men hanging about smoking, and two empty hansoms. It will be your responsibility to arrest these four men and then secure the maintenance hatch so that no one escapes that way. Understood?" Holmes had his face close to MacDonald's ear and spoke just above a whisper.

"Yes, understood. What is this all about Holmes?" asked the inspector.

"Down the maintenance hatch, turning right, and about five hundred feet down the track there is a maintenance and turnaround tunnel that is about ninety feet deep. Moriarty has staged a lab in an Underground railcar there. His men have manufactured a horrible chemical weapon, and I have reason to believe that they are there tonight preparing the weapon for operation. The weapon releases a deadly gas. We must stop the weapon from leaving the lab and do so without causing the release of the gas." MacDonald let out a low whistle and looked at the men around him.

Holmes continued, "Yes, it is quite dangerous. If you feel the need to fire your revolvers, be very careful what you shoot at in those tunnels. A stray round hitting the device could set it off and kill us all. Understood?" The officer, the inspector, the two constables, and Watson all nodded their heads showing they understood. Their eyes were wide and their faces pale with tension and fear. "Watson and I will accompany the officer and his men in the railcar and block the tracks just past the maintenance tunnel. We will approach from that direction."

"I suggest that after we arrest the men in the alley, that me men and I go down the ladder and block the tracks from the other side," suggested MacDonald and Holmes agreed.

"We need to be very careful that we don't get ourselves in a crossfire, Mr. Holmes," one of the officers warned.

"Yes, I agree. We cannot avoid that in these tunnels. Be sure to shoot only into the maintenance tunnel and not down either end of the main track." Holmes took out his revolver from his coat pocket and gave it one more check. "Are we ready, gentlemen?" Everyone nodded.

Poe studied the device further, especially the glass globe. It would be better to take the glass globe out of the device and fill it away from the crystals, but he had nothing that would hold the globe upright and steady while he poured, and he didn't want to take the chance of throwing something together last minute and spill the liquid. He would have to take the risk.

The liquid was in a cylindrical brass distillation tank with a faucet like spout on its lower end. He decided he would fill a breaker with the liquid and slowly pour the liquid into the opening of the glass globe. It would mean several trips back and forth between the tank and the globe and take more time than he wanted to take, but it was the safest means to fill the globe. He stopped and took several deep breaths, closing his eyes and calming himself as much as possible. He was ready.

Poe took a half-liter beaker and opening the spout of the distillation cylinder, he carefully poured the liquid into the beaker, leaving about two inches empty at the top. That would give him room to pour the liquid without risking spillage. He brought the beaker over to the device and sat it down beside it on the lab table. His hands were sweating, and he dried them on a towel that lay by an adjacent piece of lab equipment. He picked up the beaker with two hands, ensuring that the lip of the beaker faced away from him, and he slowly lifted it above the globe. Very slowly he began to pour the liquid into the globe. His hands began to shake, and he had to stop and calm himself. He continued until the contents of the beaker were in the globe. He estimated that he would need to repeat this process three more times. He was covered in sweat despite the coldness in the tunnel.

By the time he was on the last beaker of liquid, his arms ached and intermittently shook. He took a break and stretched his back and arms, rubbing his biceps and shoulders. He took several deep breaths and steadied his nerves. He carried the last beaker of liquid over to the lab table and set it down as before. His eyes stung from the salt of his sweat and his hair was wet along the edges. He dried his hands again and picked up the beaker and began to slowly pour the liquid into the globe. The beaker slipped and he just managed to catch it and right it before it fell, and any liquid escaped. He sat the beaker down again and rested. Almost done. He was very close. But the last drop had to be as carefully poured as the first. He looked at his watch. He had been at this for forty-five minutes.

Just as he was about to resume, he heard footsteps outside the car and saw Saacks and his two men appear in the light of the lab. Saacks motioned for the men to wait away from the lab and stepped inside.

"We couldn't chance waiting outside any longer. Almost finished?" he asked.

"Yes, just what's left in that beaker to pour." Poe looked exhausted.

"It's taken its toll on you, that's for sure. Go ahead and finish, unless you want me to take over."

"No! I'll finish it. Just give me a minute to gather myself." Poe looked away from Saacks and closed his eyes, trying to calm his nerves and still his aching arms. He turned back to the table and picking up the beaker as before finished his last pour, filling the glass globe. He sat the beaker down and with trembling fingers replaced the cork stopper and then leaned back with a sigh. "Just the leather straps now," he said. Poe placed the leather straps in their positions and began to tighten the bolts and nuts. As he tightened the last bolt, he thought he heard something outside the car. "What was that?" he asked.

"I heard it too." Saacks opened the door and instructed his men to investigate the sound. "Are you finished?" he asked.

"Yes, all done. The device is secure and ready for use." Poe sat down on a crate and tried to let the tension leave his aching muscles. As he did one of the men came rushing back to the lab car.

"It's an Underground train, Sir. It's just stopped about ten yards short of this tunnel. Its light is too bright to notice anything in the cars themselves. What do you want us to do?" The man seemed both nervous and at a loss for what to do.

"I'll come and take a look myself," said Saacks. "You stay here and watch over the device, Poe. Understand?"

"Yes, understood." Poe looked tired and glad to stay sitting.

Saacks left the lab and walked with his man to the front of the curved tunnel. As he came close to the beginning of the tunnel, he leaned against its brick walls and slowly made his way to the main line. He glanced around the corner and saw the bright light of the Underground railcar and almost nothing else. From the other end of the tunnel, toward the ladder he thought her heard shots being fired, but they were muffled. He looked that way and could just make out a bright light shining into the tunnel from the maintenance hatch above. His heart sank in his chest.

Chapter 27

Inspector MacDonald and his men walked quietly but quickly in the fog toward the alley. Soon they could just make out the shape of a hansom and four men smoking. He could see the red tips of their cigarettes as they inhaled. The inspector signaled for one of his men to go across the street and approach the four men from that angle. He sent the other constable around the block to approach from the opposite direction. He lowered himself to a crouch and waited the five minutes he thought it would take the constable to make the trip around the block and position himself opposite of his position.

He could hear the four men's muffled voices as they spoke with one another. He recognized the danger, but he was steady and calm as he took out his revolver and stood. He took three steps forward and then in a loud voice said, "This is Inspector MacDonald from Scotland Yard. Ye are surrounded. Raise ye hands. In the name of Her Majesty, ye are all under arrest."

Things moved very quickly after that. But from MacDonald's perspective it seemed to happen in slow motion. All four men dropped their cigarettes and immediately drew their guns and looked wildly around them, but they could not clearly see anyone in the fog. "We're doing nothing of the kind! Defend ya selves, gents!" yelled one of the men as all four took positions around the hansom.

"I repeat, ye are all under arrest. Drop ye weapons!" yelled MacDonald taking two more steps.

One of the men saw his movement in the fog and raised his revolver in MacDonald's direction. The inspector immediately aimed and fired. His shot hit its mark and the man crumpled to the ground as the other three turned in his direction, moved forward, and raised their weapons to fire. From across the street and behind the men the two constables opened fire and two of the three men fell to the ground. The remaining man picked up a dark lantern from off the ground and firing his weapon twice ran into the alley. MacDonald rushed forward and checked on the three men laying on the cold pavement. Two were alive but unconscious. The other was dead, having been hit directly in the heart. MacDonald kicked their weapons under the hansom as the two constables joined him.

"The other one went into the alley. We need to be careful. No more warnings. Ye each take a side and keep ye-selves glued to the walls as ye make ye way forward. I will come up the middle. Do not wait for the man to fire. If ye see him, take him down. Let's go." MacDonald, having finished his instructions turned and began to make his way into the alley as the two constables each went to one side of the alley and began to make their way down the alley as well.

MacDonald could not see anything but fog. The alley was dark and that didn't help. He walked slowly, crouching from time to time, and tried to control his breathing. He had gotten ten steps into the alley, and he could just make out the glow of a light in front of him. He had lost sight of the two constables in the fog and was concerned about each shooting the other in the confusion. He took another two steps, and the glow began to take on a more definite shape. Suddenly a shot rang out in the alley and a bullet whizzed by his left shoulder, just inches away. He dropped to a crouch and aimed his revolver at the glow and fired at the same time he saw a shadow in front of the light. He heard the metallic twang of his shot hitting metal. Immediately afterward, he heard two shots almost simultaneously fired from both sides of him and slightly in front. The shots were followed by a guttural exclamation, two dragged steps, and the sound of something heavy hitting metal. Then silence.

MacDonald waited in the fog for what seemed like an eternity. Finally, he called out and was answered by the two constables. One said, "Don't shoot. We are at the maintenance hatch and the last man has fallen through to the tunnel below. One or both of us hit him with our shot. I don't think he poses much of a threat anymore. Walk toward the sound of our voices and the light, Inspector."

Inspector MacDonald walked forward quickly and arrived at the open maintenance hatch. The last of Moriarty's men had placed the dark lantern so that its light flooded the ladder and the ground below. "Ye lads all right?" MacDonald asked. Both answered that they were fine. "Let's go. Be very careful, we can't be sure whether he's dead or injured. The last one down bring that dark lantern with ye."

MacDonald went down the ladder first. When he arrived in the Underground, he saw the body of the man shot by the constables and walked out of the shaft of light created by the dark lantern above and over to the man in the dark. His neck was broken, and he had been shot as MacDonald could feel that his chest was wet with blood. He wiped his hand on the dead man's pants. The two constables were beside him now, one shining his light on the dead man's body, his head twisted in an unnatural angle.

Saacks could see that the shaft of light down the tunnel was now moving. He leaned back against the cold walls of the tunnel and tried to think. He had definitely heard gun shots. There was only one conclusion to draw, they had been discovered. He looked over his left shoulder at the two men awaiting his instructions.

"Do not let anyone get past you. You stay here and you go to the other side of the tunnel. Fire at anything that moves. Understood?" Both men grunted and one ran to the other side of the tunnel. Saacks started to walk back to the lab when a voice was heard coming from the railcar.

"This is Captain Forrester of Her Majesty's army. I order you to give up your weapons and come out of the tunnel. You may consider yourselves under arrest. Comply immediately."

Saacks stopped and turned toward the entrance to the tunnel. "A captain no less. Welcome to the Underground. You will find that we aren't so easily persuaded. We have the advantage. Anyone coming in the direction of this tunnel will be shot."

"I am afraid that the advantage is all ours," Holmes yelled. "We have at least two dozen or more of Her Majesty's finest and both exits from your position are blocked. It is hopeless to resist. You will lose your lives. Is the Professor worth dying for?"

"I'd be careful saying that name. Is it Mr. Holmes I hear?"

"Yes, the same. Your plans have been quite undone. I know about the poisonous gas and the Professor's plans to sell it to Germany. I know about your secret lab in this tunnel. It is finished. There is no reason to die in the process. To whom am I speaking?"

"My name doesn't matter, Holmes. Your rooms have been watched. By now he will have been alerted. You will not get to him. Our lives are forfeit to the greater plan. If you know about the gas, then you know all I have to do is release it and you will all be dead. So, ask yourself, Mr. Holmes, am I and the gas worth your life and the lives of your men?"

There was no answer from Holmes. Saacks stood in the middle of the tunnel away from the walls and listened. Because the tunnel he was in was at a right angle to the main railway line, he could not clearly hear what was happening on the other side. Only a shouted voice helped by a voice trumpet made its way into his part of the tunnel. He stood trying to decide what to do when a deafening bang filled the tunnel with sound. It was the combined sound of several military rifles being fired at the same instant. His ears rang and he felt a searing stab in his left leg and left shoulder. The impact caused him to spin to his left and fall to the ground. He had been shot, twice. Neither shot was deadly. The bullets had passed through the muscle in his thigh and the soft tissue of his left shoulder. He yelled out to the other two men to fire but heard nothing. He climbed to his feet and made his way to the lab.

As he arrived inside the lab, Poe was lying face down on the floor of the railcar. "What the devil is going on?" the scientist shouted. There were several broken windows in the railcar and the pock marks of bullets at the far end of the car.

"Shut up! Where's the device?" shouted Saacks.

"I moved it under that lab table behind several chemical barrels for protection." Poe motioned behind and to his right.

Saacks limped over to the location of the device and as he did, he heard the voice of the captain again. "We have your two men in custody. We are placed at the entrance to this tunnel and are making our way in. It is futile to resist any further. You cannot escape."

Saacks lifted the device with his good arm and placed it on the lab table in front of him. "Take this key and begin winding the three springs in a counterclockwise direction," he ordered.

Poe looked at Saacks like he was mad. "I will do no such thing!"

"I have very little time. I am in pain and bleeding. I will only ask one more time. Stand up and using this key, wind each of these springs in a counterclockwise direction thirty full revolutions. Do it! Do it now! Or so help me I will shoot you where you lie."

Poe stood and taking the key from Saacks inserted it into the first slot and began to wind the spring as ordered. Saacks left the car and made his way to the front car. He had a difficult time climbing up the side and almost passed out. Once inside, he shut the power off, putting the two railcars in total darkness. He breathed heavily and his body was covered in sweat. He was bleeding from his leg and shoulder. He made his way out of the front car and back into the lab. He could hear the slow steps of the soldiers grinding against the gravel floor of the tunnel.

Poe had finished winding the one spring, but in the darkness could not see to wind the other two. Saacks lit a match long enough for Poe to insert the key into the second slot. "There is a lab flame on that table behind me, please find it and light it," Poe said, out of breath and scared. Saacks complied and there was a small amount of light from the blue flame. Enough for Poe to see what he was doing.

"We cannot set off this device! I saw what this gas did to that cat. I will not die like that, Mr. Saacks. I will not wind the last spring. You will have to shoot me." Poe, having wound the second spring, stood with the key in his hand and stared at Saacks in the near darkness of the lab. Only the blue flame provided any light. Saacks took a step forward and looked in Poe's eyes.

"No, I don't suppose you will wind the last spring." With that Saacks lifted his right arm and fired his revolver into Poe's forehead, shattering his skull and littering the side of the railcar with Poe's brains. He was dead, his body falling to the floor of the railcar. Saacks knelt in pain and took the key from Poe's dead hand. Standing and wincing in pain struggling to remain conscious, he inserted the key into the last slot and began to wind it. He counted as he turned the key. "Five, six, seven..." He was fading quickly, and he knew he had only minutes of consciousness left, his leg and shoulder throbbing to the beat of his heart. His breaths quick and shallow. "Twelve, thirteen, fourteen..." His mind was empty except for the counting. He thought of nothing else. He realized that as he counted the revolutions of the key, he was counting down the seconds that remained of his life. "Twenty-one, twenty-two, twenty-three..." He could see the blue flame to the side of him and it danced strangely in the dark. It seemed to call him to it. Inviting him to join it in its flickering dance. Promising him relief and escape from his pain. "Twenty-eight, twenty-nine, thirty."

Saacks took the key out and set it down beside the device. His body moved back and forth, and he struggled to keep himself upright. He reached into the device and set the timer for a quarter of an hour. He took his arm out and with fading vision he reached into the device to push the lever of the hair trigger. He then closed the sides of the case and took a deep breath. He heard a deafening shot ring out, close by, and then there was nothing but darkness. The blue flame welcomed him.

Holmes stood in the door of the railcar. His revolver smoking as he had fired a shot directly into the back of Saacks head. From behind Holmes, several dark lanterns were immediately trained on the inside of the car, as Watson ran up and pushed his way through the several soldiers behind Holmes carrying his revolver in one hand and his medical bag in the other.

"Are you all right, Holmes?" Watson asked out of breath and wide eyed.

"I am afraid he may have armed the device, Watson." Holmes pushed Saacks's dead body off the lab table, took one of the dark lanterns from a soldier, fully opened its shutters, and looked closely at the device. Holmes carefully examined it and discovered it opened at the corners. He cautiously pushed each of the corner clasps until the four sides of the device were free from the top. He then slowly took the top off and lowered the four sides. Looking inside, Holmes said, "The crystals are in place, the glass globe is filled, there is a ticking, and a movement of gears."

Chapter 28

Watson stood staring in disbelief at the ticking chemical bomb in front of him. Holmes was crouched over the device shining his light into it and studying its design. The soldiers had been ordered to remain outside the lab and Inspector MacDonald was standing beside Holmes.

"Can you shut the bloody thing off?" he asked Holmes.

"I am afraid it may be a bit more complicated than that, Inspector. Watson look at this lever. There is a third spring that is activated by the lever. The lever and those additional springs appear to be connected to the hammer. I did not foresee this addition when I made my own drawings. I cannot be sure, but I believe it is a hair trigger. With that potential hair trigger engaged it may immediately trip that lever and send the hammer into the glass globe releasing the liquid into the crystals in the brass bowl. If I could only be sure." Holmes raised himself to his full height, with his right hand on his chin in full concentration. "It is hard to tell Watson, especially with only the light of this lantern. It is hard to decide what to do next."

"It's been several minutes, Holmes. How long do we have?" asked Watson.

"Again, I cannot be sure, but it appears that the timer is divided into quarter of an hour increments. A total of four notches are etched into the round switch. By the pace of these gears and the movement of the timer I would say we have only a few minutes before the device goes off." Holmes turned to his left and spoke rapidly to the inspector. "Get yourself and these men out of here immediately. Go back to the railcars and drive them as fast as you can away from this area of the Underground. Send a man up the ladder to sound the alarm and evacuate anyone that may be on the streets above. Be sure to get Wiggins and my Irregulars to safety. Leave! Leave now!"

MacDonald went immediately out of the railcar and began to bark orders. The captain echoed his orders, and the tunnel was soon empty. Holmes stood looking at the device. "You should leave too Watson. You are a married man and Mrs. Watson does not deserve to be made a widow."

"No, Holmes. I have been with you all these years through many a case and I shall not abandon you at the end." Watson stood with his legs apart and his hands on his hips.

"Very well, Watson. But my death is for nothing. Yours, old man, your death is not something that I have foreseen all these years. I have always thought that I would go first. I am sorry."

Both men stared down at the device. Holmes looked suddenly to his right as Inspector MacDonald entered the railcar. "I'm not leaving ye and the Doctor to die alone. It's as much my case now as it is yours. I'll see it to its end, just the same as ye."

Watson suddenly let out a little cry of realization and dove out the railcar. "Where the bloody hell is he going?" asked the Inspector.

It was only a minute later when Watson came back into the carriage carrying his medical bag. "I am not sure there be anything in that bag that's going to help us now, Doctor," said MacDonald with a wry smile.

Watson sat his bag down on the lab table and opened it. He took out three wood tongue depressors and began to wrap the three in gauze. After making thick layers of gauze around the three depressors he said, "Holmes, shine that light between the glass globe and the hammer. Quickly man!"

"I see what you are doing, Watson. Excellent!" Holmes shined the light where Watson had indicated, and Watson carefully placed the tongue depressors wrapped in gauze between the hammer and the glass globe. As he did so, he tapped the metal skeleton of the device with his elbow and the whole device moved. Holmes, the Inspector, and Watson held their breaths. The lever clicked and the hammer came down, but not on the glass, instead it came down on the tongue depressors wrapped in gauze with a dull thump and a barely audible clink of the glass. All three men stood like statues, not daring to breath, and then Holmes slapped Watson on the back saying, "Good man! Watson, you are a genius!" Watson took a step back and almost passed out, grabbing the wall of the railcar to steady himself.

"I'll be damned. Tongue depressors and gauze. Quick thinking Doctor. I believe I owe ye my life. As does Mr.

Holmes. Good man!" MacDonald walked over and shook Watson's hand heartily.

The sun had risen as Holmes, Watson and Inspector MacDonald arrived back at Baker Street. It was a brilliant, but cold Sunday morning. The streets were quiet, and the fog had lifted, revealing blue skies with just a touch of wispy clouds. The three men had arrived in an official Scotland Yard carriage and Holmes alighted first, stretching as he did. He looked down Baker Street in the direction of where he had seen Blind Bart and could not see anyone at present. As he walked to the front door and took out his keys, the door opened, and Mrs. Hudson stood in her house coat and scarf and welcomed the men home.

"You have been out all night, Mr. Holmes. I awoke early and have been making you a good breakfast. I'll have it up to you shortly."

"Mrs. Hudson, thank you. You never cease to amaze me with your perspicacity." Holmes smiled as he, Watson and the inspector came through the door and made their way up the seventeen steps to the sitting room.

"Well, I'm not sure I know what that means, Mr. Holmes. But by the smile on your face, I am sure it's a compliment. Go on, I'll be up shortly." Mrs. Hudson shut the door and turned to go through her door and her apartment mumbling to herself something about "catch your death of cold."

After preventing the chemical weapon from effectively activating, Holmes and Watson had carefully taken the device apart and separated the crystals from the liquid. Watson moved the crystals to one side of the railcar and the liquid to the other side. MacDonald had gone up to the terminus and brought the captain and one of his constables back down to the Underground. He had sent one constable off to Scotland Yard to bring in more help as they cleaned up the crime scene and removed the bodies to the morgue. Holmes sent a message through the captain to the minister and invited him to Baker Street later that morning.

As help arrived from Scotland Yard, the tunnel was secured with guards at all possible exits and entrances. Holmes secured the lab books, and the device was placed inside one of the empty crates lying on the floor of the railcar. After all was secured, the men left the crime scene in the hands of the constables and Her Majesty's Army and departed for Baker Street.

Watson had lit the fire and Holmes was in his dressing gown and sitting in his chair beside the fire. MacDonald, despite the earliness of the hour, was helping himself to the tantalus and a stiff drink of whisky. "So, ye have to tell me how it is that you stumbled upon this little mystery and were able to solve it so completely, Mr. Holmes," MacDonald said as he took a seat on the settee.

"It's a bit of a long story, Inspector. Perhaps for another time over drinks. Suffice it to say that I was engaged by two charwomen to help one's husband out of a bit of a sticky wicket and one thing led to another. Our old accomplice, Porlock, did his part as well. The rest, I am afraid, remains a bit of a state secret." Holmes was choosing a pipe and filling it with tobacco from the Persian slipper.

"What do ye suppose the Professor is going to do now?" asked MacDonald.

Holmes let out a cloud of smoke and shrugged his shoulders. "I suspect that the little chess match between the Professor and me will get a bit more dangerous. I am working on some evidence that I will be happy to share with you in a few months that will likely mean the end of both the Professor and his organization. Until then, I expect my life will be more challenging and my own personal safety less secure."

MacDonald looked over at Watson who had just sat in his own chair. Both men gave each other knowing looks and then turned to Holmes with looks of concern and worry. "I think a bit of time off, Holmes, is just the thing you need. Why don't we join Mrs. Watson in the south of Spain?" Watson knew what Holmes's reply would be.

"I cannot go now, Watson. The case I am working on for the French government will begin to take up my attention and efforts again shortly. No, I will stay here in London and keep to my routine." All three men remained silent, each lost in his own thoughts and emotions for several minutes.

"Well, gentlemen, I am off to Scotland Yard and the paperwork that awaits me. There are reports to write. Thank ye for the drink." MacDonald stood and shook Watson's hand and then Holmes's hand. "It has been a pleasure as always, Mr. Holmes."

"Inspector, thank you for coming when I called and for performing so excellently. I appreciate it." Holmes smiled at MacDonald who beamed at the praise from Holmes. With that, MacDonald left.

Just then Mrs. Hudson brought up breakfast. "I have eggs, ham, toast, coffee, and what's left of a nice beef roast," she said as she lay everything at the table.

Watson was first to sit at the table and began to help himself as Holmes stood and walked over to the window overlooking Baker Street. "Thank you, Mrs. Hudson," he said.

"Do eat, Mr. Holmes. You need your strength."

"Presently, Mrs. Hudson. Presently." Holmes looked out on Baker Street and thought to himself. Watson began to eat his breakfast with gusto. Mrs. Hudson turned and walked down the stairs mumbling to herself. It was a normal morning at 221B Baker Street.

Epilogue

It had been little more than twenty-four hours since Moriarty had received news that the Green Dragon affair had failed miserably because of Holmes and his meddling. Moriarty had gone into a rage and closed himself in his apartment refusing any visitors and arranging, through Lilith, for one of his working girls to serve as his victim. The cost of his genius, of his madness, was the pain he inflicted on others. He would inflict more pain before he was finished. Not in his pleasure room, but outside on the streets of London, within his own organization, and eventually to Holmes himself.

Saacks was dead. The chemist was dead. The secret lab dismantled. The lab books confiscated. The chemicals taken. And his device secreted away and likely being studied by the government he despised. His work. His genius. For naught. His reputation on the Continent ruined. His power weakened. His influence, thwarted. And all because of one man...Sherlock Holmes. His only adversary. His only equal. He would have to be dealt with, but first, to deal with those who had failed him.

Roger Stapleton had been working quietly at his desk managing the communications of the Professor's far-flung organization. He had of course heard about the Professor's failure and how Holmes had managed to outwit him once again. He had kept a low profile these past two weeks, keeping to himself, and doing his work. He was as efficient as always. He saw no signs that the Professor or anyone else in the syndicate knew that he had assisted Holmes in his campaign against the Green Dragon and he was beginning to feel that things had returned to normal. He began to ease his anxiety and his heightened scrutiny of the expressions and tone of his co-workers. He was again able to sleep at night. He had finished for the day and was about to leave when one of the generals stopped by to see him.

"I am sorry, Stapleton. About to leave, are you?" he asked.

"Yes, sir. I am finished for the day. Is there something that I can do for you?"

"The Professor has asked that you hand deliver this very important message to an address in the East End. Can you manage that his evening? The Professor would like it delivered within the hour. It's urgent and important, that's why he is asking that you handle it personally."

"Of course, Sir. I will take it straight away." Stapleton smiled and took the envelope he was handed.

Having put on his coat, Stapleton left the warehouse and hailed a hansom. He gave the driver a cross street, but not the address. He would walk to his destination without the driver knowing the address. A precaution that he had learned to adopt after years of working in the employ of the Professor.

The ride in the hansom was not long. He got out, paid the driver, and began to walk down a street of row houses in a bad side of town. There were dirty children in the street and dingy laundry hanging on rope above his head. The streets were narrow and crisscrossed with even narrower alley ways. The whole area smelled of human filth.

Stapleton was only three blocks away from the address where he would deliver the envelope he carried in his left hand. He walked with a comfortable gait. He wasn't in a hurry. As he was passing an alley to his left, he heard a woman cry out, but didn't investigate. He kept walking as if he had heard nothing. His eyes staring at the pavement in front of him. He felt himself suddenly grabbed from behind and dragged into the alley he had just passed. Two men held him against the brick wall of one of the dilapidated buildings forming the alley way. A large hand covered his mouth and the other three hands of the two men held him in place with a vice like grip.

A third man appeared in front of his face. Dirty and missing teeth. "The Professor sends his salutations and this gift," he said.

Stapleton felt the searing pain of a sharp knife in his stomach. The man with the knife stared into his eyes with hatred and satisfaction. He twisted the knife blade and pulled it full across the width of Stapleton's stomach. He pulled the knife out and showed the blood-stained blade to Stapleton as the men released him. Stapleton couldn't even scream. His hands went to his stomach. His waistcoat and shirt were ripped, and his bowels were exposed. One of the men who had been holding him against the side of the building reached into his gut with a gloved hand and pulled at his intestines. Stapleton felt himself falling and felt his bowels fall from his stomach as he did. He lay in the alley gasping, bleeding, and trying to hold in his guts. The lights faded. His breath stopped. He was dead.

Blind Bart was at his usual corner plying his trade as a professional beggar. It had been a good week and he was making good money. People felt sorry for a blind man in the cold and were being particularly generous. His dark square glasses hid his eyes and thus allowed him to work his con on the unsuspecting Londoners. He wasn't blind. He dressed the part. Worn bowler hat, old ill-fitting clothes, torn coat, worn gloves, and most importantly a long white cane that announced to the world that he was blind. His dented tin cup finished his costume and this evening, it was heavier than usual.

It was almost dark and time for him to leave his post for the day and make his way to the rooms he called home. But before he went home, he would stop by his usual pub and have a drink and some dinner. More than likely, more than one drink – a lot more. He licked his lips at the thought of it. A growing desire to drink his fill of cheap gin and beer.

He made his way to the street corner and raised his left hand calling for a hansom. Several passed him by. He shouted for a hansom while acting as if he could not see. A local man stopped to help him and soon he was in a hansom on his way to *The Prize Cock*, his favorite pub. Upon arriving, he took off his dark glasses and worn bowler and assumed his normal persona. No one in the pub cared how he made his money, and no one would ever think of betraying him to the authorities and taking away his living. He was safe and amongst his people.

He ate greasy fish and chips and lost count of how many cups of gin and beer he drank during his three hours at the pub. He was feeling happy and drunk and decided it was time to walk the five blocks to his rooms. He left the pub staggering a bit as he passed the threshold. This part of London was not well lit. He walked in the street to avoid the occasional man or woman lying in the gutter, too drunk to make it home. As he walked, he failed to notice the three men following him from a discreet distance. He sang to himself as he staggered down the street.

Blind Bart stopped and decided he needed to piss. He staggered into a dark alley to accomplish this, nearly tripping over an old homeless beggar sleeping against the wall. He made his way into the alley and undoing his trousers, he began to urinate against the side of a brick building, his left hand supporting himself against the wall, while his right guided the stream. As he leaned urinating strong arms simultaneously grabbed and pushed him against the wall.

"Turn the bastard around so I can see him," said a man. The two holding him turned him around and held him fast. "Damn it, he's pissing on me leg!" Blind Bart was too drunk and too startled to control his urine stream and just kept urinating until he was done.

"Hold him steady!" The two men lifted Blind Bart so that his feet barely touched the ground under him. "The Professor sends his greetings." With that the man took out a knife, grabbed Blind Bart's hair and forced his head upward, exposing his neck. With one swift motion he slashed the long sharp knife across Blind Bart's neck, nearly severing his head from his body. Blood spurted like a fountain as his heart pumped his life-giving blood onto the ground below. The two men holding him backed off to avoid the blood. Blind Bart simply sank to the ground holding his neck and letting out gurgling sounds as the air from his lungs mixed with the blood pouring from his open wound. Within seconds, Blind Bart was dead.

Becca was busy in her shop assisting customers as they viewed works of art. Her beauty and her feminine poise made her an excellent salesperson. She knew how to convince indecisive buyers and easily lead customers to more expensive pieces of art. Customers liked her and enjoyed discussing the works with her before making their purchases. She was knowledgeable and had a sophisticated and stately way about her.

It had been three weeks since she had last seen Poe. She had concluded that the Professor's men had likely killed him since they were finished with him, and he had completed his task. Becca knew that she would never see him again and was glad of it. She had taken his things and piled them in the alley behind her shop, knowing that by the next day the items would be gone. Clothes and personal effects would be taken by passersby at night, those in search of such treasures in the back alleys of London.

She was helping a customer decide between a Grecian vase and a bust of Napoleon when she heard the bell above her shop door ring. Still speaking with the customer, she turned toward the door and noticed three men walk into her shop, all were well-dressed. The man who stood in front of the other two was a tall, thin man. Clean shaven, pale, and ascetic looking. He had a prominent doomed forehead and deeply sunken eyes. His shoulders were rounded as if from much study. As he looked around the shop his head oscillated from side-to-side in a peculiar reptilian manner.

Becca instinctively knew that the man was powerful and dangerous. She felt a chill go through her as he looked at her and their eyes met. She was immediately on guard. Nothing about this man was normal or ordinary. She would use her feminine charm and her usual control over men to determine whether he was a threat. She left the customer she was with, excusing herself, and walked toward the three men.

"Gentlemen, welcome," she cooed with a smile and a feminine tilt of her head. "How may I help you?"

"I am very pleased to meet you, Miss Saint John," the man said holding out his hand in introduction. Becca took his hand and as she did the man leaned into her and said, "You wanted to meet me, so here I am. My friends refer to me as the Professor."

The End

CPSIA information can be obtained
at www.ICGtesting.com
Printed in the USA
BVHW051154060223
657963BV00013B/820

9 781804 241125